I0660304

Priscillia M. Manjoh

Miraclaire Publishing
Kansas City (MO)

MIRACLAIRE PUBLISHING LLC
Kansas City, (MO) USA

Kansas City, MO 64138, USA
Email: info@miraclairepublishing.com
Website: www.miraclairepublishing.com

ISBN-13: 978-0615828121

ISBN-10: 0615828124

Copyright © 2013 Miraclaire Publishing LLC
Priscillia M. Manjoh

All rights reserved. No part of this publication may be reproduced by any means, graphic, electronic, or mechanical, including photocopying, recording, taping or by any information storage retrieval system without the prior written permission of the copyright holders.

Printed in the United States of America

Miraclaire Publishing makes every effort to ensure the accuracy of all the information ("Content") in its publications. However, Miraclaire and its agents and licensors make no representations or warranties whatsoever as to the accuracy, completeness, or suitability for any purpose of the Content and disclaim all such representations and warranties, whether expressed or implied to the maximum extent permitted by law. Any views expressed in this publication are the views of the author and are not necessarily the views of Miraclaire.

This is a work of fiction. Names, characters, places, and incidents are either the author's invention or they are used fictitiously. Any resemblance to actual places and persons, living or dead, events, or locales is coincidental.

For my husband

Epah K. Elad

One
Flughafen Tempelhof

It was a very cold winter morning, barely three months after Gerhard Fritz Kurt Schröder became the *Bundeskanzler*. Everywhere was covered with snow at the *Flughafen* Tempelhof. Cars were orderly packed in rows ranging from taxis to yellow public transport buses which came and went with people boarding and alighting. The air was filled with the hum of aircrafts landing and taking off. At about 9:30am, three young Africans, Nji, Ogochuku and Fonjock, were pacing inside the reception hall anxiously. They walked past travel agencies, airline companies, and some shops without paying attention to anything on the display windows. They were even oblivious to the policemen moving up and down in a calculated aimless gait. The confidence that the trio inspired dissuaded these cops from stopping them and controlling their passports. It was evident from their manner of quick long steps and attire that these three were not illegal immigrants trying to sneak into the country. It was clear to all that they were awaiting the arrival of someone as they constantly glanced at the arrival board.

The trio walked closer to the arrival board and stared at it. They looked at their watches almost simultaneously and looked up at each other. They looked around disappointedly and Fonjock gave a sigh.

"So the flight is delayed and will not arrive until 11."

He looked thoughtfully at the other two who remained silent.

"I hope the guy is dressed to suit this weather. It's minus five degrees," added Fonjock as he yawned.

"Maybe we should have asked him to practice living under this condition before coming," Nji suggested. The other two forced a heartless laughter. This of course was not possible because there are hardly such temperatures in Africa. Ogochuku suddenly stopped laughing, "I have an idea; he could do this by practising to sit in a deep freezer for some time."

The three now burst out laughing more heartily. Then, they stopped abruptly as they heard the announcement of the arrival of *SABENA*. They rushed forward, strained their eyes trying to see through to the runway.

"Ogochuku, call for your mother, tell her the flight has arrived," Fonjock requested.

Then, Ogochuku called out to a white lady who was sipping coffee and smoking a cigarette in a nearby kiosk, "Steffi?"

And then, the forty-nine year old Steffi answered "*I Kom*," as she walked over to join them.

Women like Steffi were popularly known as *Afrikanische Frauen*. This was because they were extremely fat. Most often, German men wondered why African men preferred very fat women. The reason for such preference and the truth of such famous assumption is yet to be proven.

"I am scared of such a sizeable woman lying on me during lovemaking," a German once complained to his African friend. But the African reminded him of the variety of positions. "In that case, it will be *Missionarsstellung* all the time." The two of them had laughed and shook hands happily. But, between Ogochuku and Steffi, anything thought to be impossible was possible.

Steffi walked up to the boys and gave Ogochuku a kiss. Looking at Steffi, she resembled the proverbial cat that had swallowed the canary. Yet it was difficult for one to decipher this cause of total satisfaction. It was clear that the feeling of contentment arose from some underlying agenda since nothing on the surface could point to it. Everyone could see that her husband's display of affection was fake, though she seemed completely oblivious of this fact. Was it as a result of their different cultural backgrounds or was it because of the fact that the boy had used *ngambé* on her? Yes, witchcraft, *juju.* One would wonder. Clearly Ogochuku did not love Steffi, in fact he detested her. But to Steffi, they were happily married. To Ogochuku, it was a matter of time. Three years to wait for his permanent residence visa was not much of a time. When asked by his friends how he managed to summon an erection to make love to such an old woman like Steffi, he told them that, all he did was picture his passport with a German resident permit in it, and then he would get all the erections he needed and whatever ability it took to make love to Steffi in whatever position she chose.

A few minutes later, Jerry checked out and walked towards his friends and Steffi. Jerry, a Paysan and a close friend to Nji and the other two boys was about twenty-five like them. He was strikingly handsome and the look on his baby-like broad face mirrored his faith in the world. He was well built, and all his features from high cheekbones to brown eyes came together perfectly. Carrying his bag in one hand and pulling his valise with the other, Jerry's piercing eyes lingered briefly around him and shot searchingly ahead trying to make out a familiar face. He finally glimpsed his friends as he approached the exit. He broke into a broad smile that lit the distance, revealing a set of well-formed white teeth. His teeth were so white that they contrasted his very shiny dark complexion. On seeing a set of white teeth from a distance his friends smiled and waved him over. Jerry was overdressed even for winter. He was wearing a thick wool hat that covered even his ears, several thick pullovers and a pair of black jeans trousers. He complemented the attire with an overcoat and a pair of faded high-heeled cowboys' boots which added inches to his height. Since he had used the identification papers of a village uncle to process his visa and since the uncle was taller than Jerry, he had taken his boots to the shoe mender to add the extra inches he lacked. His friends laughed at this when they saw him and could not help pointing out that he looked almost like Prince Nico in those days of Ahidjo. Jerry's friends hugged him again and again in their warm embraces as they shouted excitedly.

"Look here! Oh my man Jerry, welcome to Germany. Welcome, welcome big man. Jerry, welcome to the land of stress!" said Fonjock, shaking Jerry's hand once more.

They quickly took him out of the airport premises and left. On their way home, Nji looked at Jerry and smiled as he noticed that Jerry was watching them with admiration.

"Big man, welcome oh! *Na de land dis.* This is the place! You are heartily welcome. *A no say if you no bi cam, you for kill some man.* You would have killed somebody, wouldn't you? Thank God you succeeded. How about everybody back home? Welcome to the land of stress," Nji shook Jerry again and again, still smiling.

"Whoa! Guys, you people are looking good m-e-n!" said Jerry excitedly.

He was excited to have finally made it to Germany. Looking at how his friends were dressed, he knew that he had indeed made it to paradise. His friends tried to make him see that "not all that glitters is gold," but Jerry did not even listen to them. "What else could one hope for?" he thought to himself. So, they just smiled and let him be for the moment.

Meanwhile, Jerry's friends broke into an argument over what means of public transport was best for them to travel with. The best and most effective means would be to take the subway U6 from the station Platz der Luftbrücke which was closest to the airport and then change after two stations onto another train – the *S-Bahn* S4 going to Westhafen. This train would take them straight to where they lived - Storkowerstrasse within a very short space of time. But the boys wouldn't do this because they did not have train tickets nor planned to buy any. It was very risky to go by *S-Bahn* if you didn't have a ticket. It was held that the *S-Bahn* was the most highly controlled train, more than the other trains and buses; especially the S4 line which connected almost the whole city of Berlin. Every African who had lived in Berlin for at least six months knew that the *S-Bahn* connected people easily to wherever they wanted to go, and that it was efficient and the fastest means of public transport, sometimes faster than even a taxi. The BVG Company was very strict on matters relating to ticket control, most of their controllers concealed their identities to make the process more effective. Any defaulter was required to pay a fine of 60 Deutsche Mark. Delaying to pay this amount was dangerous as the company kept sending reminders which led to an increase of the amount in the long run, or even a court order in the end. Most Africans dreaded this procedure since there were rumours that some Paysans had been locked up on account of defaulting. In this case the individual's friends would contribute the money and pay on his behalf or he was obliged to do community service to cover the bill. It was rumoured that this was what had happened to a Paysan called Andrew at one time when he was locked up, but in fact, this was not true. Andrew had been caught by the police, driving into an *Einbahnstrasse* from the closed end with no valid driver's licence. Once, he was idling around a *Schrottplatz* and a man wanted to dispose of his old Toyota Corolla, Andrew opted to have it. He bought it for one Deutsche Mark and planned to ship it to Pays whenever he would have the money to do so. Meantime, he thought of enjoying it first. Caught driving wrongly in this one-way street, he was fined and locked up when he failed to pay several months after. His friends paid part of the bill for him while he did some community work to cover the remainder. Africans dreaded such proceedings because it could lead to deportation in cases where one's papers were invalid. The issue of fines and being locked up was for those who at least had student visas and would not face deportation. Those who were not students were mostly illegal or asylum seekers; for at that time, marriage between blacks and whites was not so common except for a few hard cores like Ogochuku who dared.

Ogochuku was one of the few guys from Naija who when asked to sing the national anthem of their country, will start off with "O Pays, thou cradle of our fathers - - - " before realising themselves. Born, bred and educated in Pays, he would pass very well for a Paysan. But then, he was not a Paysan but an Awala man. Ogochuku was famous for having experienced hell in Russia before finally succeeding to cross over to Germany by swimming through a river for weeks. There was a story of a girl and two boys who also trekked from Denmark to Germany. But that was later on. But at this point in time, people like Ogochuku still had the most powerful stories. This girl and the two boys arrived Hamburg from where they later on found their way to Wuppertal. The story reached the others in Berlin through several telephone calls and the news went around that the Danish borders were opened and so several telephone calls were made to the people back home. Getting a visa to Denmark was easier than getting one to Germany. You needed to trek just for a few weeks and nights. What was this compared to living all your life in a third world country? It was nothing compared to this paradise of a place called Germany. Germany, Germany, a united country; no more just West Germany; *Bundes*! Apart from this record, none could beat Ogochuku's. These were the tough guys who had gone through thick and thin and so knew how to get and keep a German woman in spite of all odds and gross differences in emancipation between these women and those they were used to and saw their fathers being used to. When his friends complained that they found it difficult to date such an old woman because it brought to mind the memory of their mothers, Ogochuku would outline a good number of differences between these women and those mothers back home. He wondered why his friends should feel that way.

"For example, look at that woman driving a train. Can your mother drive a train?" he would ask.

When a black person was caught without a ticket, the first thing was that the controllers asked for the person's passport in order to issue a fine. If the person was not carrying a passport, a police officer was called immediately. The police would accompany the person to his residence to see if he had a passport and a valid visa. Situations such as these had led to many Africans being repatriated. With all this knowledge, it would have been foolhardy for the boys to travel with the S4. So they decided on the option of travelling with the underground train right up to Seestrasse where they would change onto a *Tram* which moved only in the Eastern parts of Berlin; going to very significant places such as Hohenschönehausen. This tram was to take them right up to Möllerndorfstrasse/Storkowerstrasse and they would be home. Although this was a very long way for them, they preferred it because the controllers at least could be identified from the uniforms they put on and so they could easily escape early enough. Fonjock was still a *dago man* in the country. Being an illegal who had not yet sought for asylum was dangerous. Although, there was no big difference between being a *dago man* or an *adoro*.

"Ah! Ticket Controllers... *„Schön guten Tag, Fahrschein zur Kontrolle bitte."* I don't want to go back to Pays, at least not yet," Fonjock said.

"What is *far shine, uban*?" Jerry asked. "You will know, don't worry," answered Nji.

Steffi and the boys finally boarded the U6. While the others were looking out for controllers, Jerry was trying to take in the sights. Everything was interesting, from the two teenagers kissing openly in public, the older couple who were madly in love; holding hands, the arrival boards at the train stations, the trains that by-passed theirs and even the buildings. It was all so new and exciting and more than what he had ever dreamt Germany to be. To Jerry it was sleeping and waking up in paradise and he could understand why most people did not bother returning home once they arrived. He nodded most of the time and at times, shook his head in wonder. His friends asked him about Pays and the people back home. They asked after life in general and Jerry told them that living conditions had become more deplorable than ever, following a second salary cut.

At length, Jerry tried to give Ogochucku news of his old girlfriend but was quickly hushed. He was warned never to discuss other women in front of Ogochuku's German wife.

"Na kwale be dis –o!" This was Paper! This was Ogochuku's Papers, his future, this white woman! He explained to Jerry in Pidgin English that his German woman was his resident permit, his house rent and sometimes his daily bread as well, "until further notice", he said sternly. Jerry was surprised because according to what he heard in Pays before he travelled to Germany, Ogochuku was supposed to have regularised his stay by now. When he asked the boys why they had not yet regularised their stay, they all laughed and then Ogochuku said, "Okay this is the stay I am regularising, just you have a look."   He turned and kissed Steffi passionately and explained to her in broken German that he was telling their friend who just arrived how much he loved his wife. This brought a smile to Steffi's face. Steffi was already visibly angry that the boys had been conversing for a long time in Pidgin English.

Jerry, like many young men planning to make it big in Europe, had been sold a lie by some *doki men* in Pays. They insisted that it sufficed for one to successfully set foot on German soil or any other European country or the United States, they could regularise their stay within a few weeks with the help of friends. Jerry was such a believer as he was very anxious to travel abroad. He thought his chances were really great as he had so many friends in Europe. His ambition, as he told his friends during the train ride was to regularise his stay for just two years, work really hard, earn huge sums and return home.

"You people should just give me the connections m-e-n! Even if it is to wash corpses, I will do it. I know the white people will not like doing such a nasty job and will certainly pay well for it. Even to sweep the streets, I will do it. After all, what am I ashamed of? Nobody knows me around here. I don't plan to date any girl. After those two years, I will go back with a diamond ring for my queen's finger. Pamela, Pamela."

"Who is Pamela?" asked Fonjock as the boys who had been laughing, all stopped laughing. "This man, you are mad.

Secondly, who will allow you near a white corpse?" Fonjock continued.

"You guys should take it easy with him, he just came in," Nji said. "But on a serious note, see Jerry, just forget about whatsoever stupid idea you have been fed with back home on regularising your stay and listen to us whenever you can. As for the Pamela you are talking of, don't even say anything. We already know where you are heading. It is the same old story we have been listening to when a new person arrives. Just focus on life here. Think of the money your parents have raised through the sale of their piece of land, which was their only investment. Think of how you can make some money for them. As for girls, there are a few black girls around here; Paysans too for that matter. You can make a life with any of them."

"No, no, no!" retorted Fonjock; "*Lie, lie, darkie girls dem na stress for dis land.* They are a burden. Nji, don't you advise this guy wrongly simply because you are lucky to be hooked up with a hardworking and submissive girl like Akwi. See Jerry, if you can muster the courage to, just copy what Ogochuku is doing, that's the best for you." By this time Ogochuku who had taken his woman a short distance away from the other boys to sit elsewhere, threw a brief ugly look at them on hearing his name being mentioned.

"What?" Exclaimed Jerry. "You guys are sick, all sick."

"No. I said if you could muster the courage to," Fonjock replied. "Don't go near any black girl. You trust our girls, don't you...? Give me money for this, I don't have *rubbing oil*, I can't visit you because I don't have a ticket so you have to give me money for a ticket first. Coupled with all the stress of this land, you will die before long."

Jerry merely stared at him and then at Nji who looked at him for some time and said, "I accept, Akwi is the only good girl. Let us leave Jerry to see things for himself; after all, he is not a kid. Anyone who can travel from Pays to Deutschland is no longer a kid."

"Now you are talking," smiled Jerry as he started to pull out a packet containing some pictures from his bag. The other boys stood up hastily and made for the door. *"Umsteigen, umsteigen,"* they called out to a bewildered Jerry who had no option but to grab his luggage and pictures and rush after them.

They all alighted from the train, went onto the street and crossed the road to board the *Tram*. Watching from a distance, one could see a tall Ogochuku holding the hand of a short plump Steffi under his armpit, taking long strides while Steffi's old-fashioned handbag swung from his left hand side and Steffi toddled at his side almost after him. Nji and Fonjock followed, carrying Jerry's luggage with Jerry hurrying behind them, handbag in one hand, Pamela's pictures in the other.

The *Straßenbahn* – Tram 23, to the direction of Warschauerstrasse was boarded. After they were seated on this train, Jerry showed them Pamela's pictures. "You see, this is Pam whom I met on one fine afternoon returning from school."

As his friends looked at the pictures, Nji asked, "Which school does she attend?"

"UB, UB," replied Jerry. "University of Bart - UNIBA you know, is the newly created Anglophone University in the country," Jerry added. "Their girls are the talk of all the Anglophone men, both young and old," he told them.

"UB girls!" exclaimed Fonjock. "I hear those girls are bad, more dangerous than those of UNISAM in Moussadi."

"No, no, no" Jerry protested. "Not all of them, some are very nice; the nicest things a man can ever hope for."

"Just like your baby," Fonjock put in with a laugh.

"Yes, just like my baby Pamela. Pam, Pam!"

Two

Pamela

When Jerry saw her that afternoon, with her friend Beri, the young and beautiful Pamela was dressed impeccably as always. Jerry hurried after them shouting, "Excuse me, Miss. Please, excuse me, one minute." When the girls heard this, they stopped, turned around and looked at Jerry. Pamela quickly assessed Jerry who had on very new but low quality white T-Shirt over grey trousers. He also wore a pair of well-polished second-hand shoes. Pamela could not believe that Jerry was referring to her and so while Beri stood to wait for Jerry, she simply sighed and moved on; but Jerry instead walked past Beri and struggled to get Pamela's attention. "No! Not you. It is Pamela I want to talk to."

Pamela turned around abruptly with a hand on her waist. "Who is it you want to what?!" She snapped. Jerry caught up with Pamela, smiling sheepishly. He offered to shake her hand. She merely stared angrily at Jerry's hand. Jerry was very shy but he managed to say "Good afternoon, *cheri*. You see I would like to see you."

Lifting her glasses gently, Pamela gazed down at Jerry from toe to hair. "Did I hear you well, Mister? Aren't you seeing me like this? How else would you want to see me?"

Jerry became shyer and more scared. He avoided meeting Pamela's eyes as he said, "I mean, I would like us to form a company."

"And why not a corporation?" retorted Pamela. Pamela gave a long sigh and continued walking off. But Jerry hastened his pace after her. "I mean, you being my partner. You and I being together," he managed.

Pamela was very annoyed and shouted from a short distance, "Partner in what? In this so-called company you want to form? I am sorry; I don't want to be a shareholder in this company of yours. Good day!" She walked fast ahead, and then took a few steps back and pulled Beri, who had been lagging behind, by the hand, and off they went.

Jerry was disappointed, but he merely smiled as he watched them leave. Then, he turned into a nearby street. By this time, Pamela and Beri had resumed their normal stroll of swinging hips and steady strides. But, Pamela was still burning with annoyance as she complained and insulted Jerry all through their way home. "Can you imagine that idiot? Does he think I belong to his class of girls? Did he examine me well before approaching me? Just you have a look at me, Beri. Nonsense!" Beri merely smiled admirably at Pamela as usual. Her eyes caught Pamela's huge breast, and then moved to her well-formed protruding buttocks. Pamela's friends had always envied her beauty. They always referred to her as "Pamela - ed; the figure eight girl." With a height of about one meter seventy, and a slightly sharp chin on a face with high cheek bones, Pamela's hair flowed in waves to adorn her dark complexion which always shone,especially in the cold breeze of the morning sun of Lower Custains Bart. Pamela had a perfect skin and a warm beautiful smile that could light up a room. Although Beri was not an ugly girl and came from a wealthy family, she always respected Pamela because of her beauty.

"She is pretty," Nji commented. "Yes, she is really beautiful; *darkie* girls, they are simply the best."

"*But how man go do for dis land?* Stress, stress, stress. *Ehe!*" said Fonjock.

Jerry smiled and held a chain on his neck with a love symbol on which was engraved Pamela.

The *Tram* finally reached Möllerndorfstrasse/

Storkowerstrasse and the boys alighted with Steffi and Ogochuku keeping a distance from the group as usual. The entourage set off for the Student Hostel. Then, Jerry suddenly saw a man running with all his might towards the *Tram.* And then he saw a woman coming from another direction and running in the same manner. "What is happening?" he asked. "Why is that man and lady running?"

Nji looked at him and laughed.

"What do you mean by happening?" asked Fonjock. "Do you also want to run? Those people are simply running to catch the train," Fonjock told Jerry who was very perplexed that the people were running just to catch the train.

"But, I thought you said these trains pass by every five minutes," he said.

"These people don't want to be late for work even for five minutes. Instead, they prefer to go fifteen minutes earlier. Or do you think this is Pays? In Pays, every other person is pregnant. They are like Lord Tenny's drowsy lotus eaters. They sleepwalk even to work. Tell me. Why will the economy not sleep?"

"Maybe it is because of too much sun that gives the people this somnambulistic attitude," Jerry said.

"It is at least well that the young people of this time can travel abroad and so can learn something from the Whiteman. They can learn to be hard-working, sun or no sun. The Whiteman's country is the way it is because of hard work and Patriotism. Patriotism is the watch word and through this love for one's country, hard work grows. But what is puzzling is that even the few people who came before now to study abroad, saw all these things, practiced them in the West but on going back home, they did what the Romans do when one is in Rome," Nji simply laughed.

Three

Nji's Residence

The party finally arrived at Nji's residence in the *Studentenwohnheim Ferdinand Thomas* on Storkowerstraße. Nji lived in a room in an apartment; a *Wohngemeinschaft* he shared with two other students. Akwi had just come back from work looking very tired and worn out. Apart from the hard work, she had to go to Western Union after work to send some money to Pays instead of heading straight home.

Akwi was Nji's girlfriend; she was about Pamela's age and very pretty too. She was cooking in the kitchen whilst Fonjock's fat oversized German girlfriend and Andrew were sitting on the sofa, watching a talk show on television. Andrew's friends referred to him as *Mustering* and *Ohne Stress*. He had been nicknamed *Mustering* because one day he saw a girl at a party and planned to talk the girl into loving him. He couldn't muster the courage to do so and so he drank a lot of alcohol in order to get bolder. Due to too much alcohol, he ended up embarrassing himself by shouting his intentions at the top of his voice when he finally faced the lady in question. Everyone thought the two were quarrelling which annoyed the girl. The incident was made known to the host who threw Andrew out of the party. Andrew's friends were even more surprised that he could even declare his interest in any girl even under the influence of alcohol. He was the one that fed and housed the girls while others dated them.

When he came to his senses, Andrew was so ashamed of himself that he could not even muster the courage to need a woman in his life. For the three years that his friends knew him, they had never seen him with any woman of his own. He had a lot of female friends whom he was always ready to help; either with their shopping, transportation or in building up their wardrobes or their beds. Each time a new girl arrived and did not have somewhere to live, he kept the girl in his place, fed her, clothed her and took care of her every need until she was ready to leave his place and look for her own place, no matter how long it took.

His friends always made fun of him and sometimes called him Rip Van Winkgirls or Prufrock. When asked by his friends when he intended to get a woman of his own, he would tell them that he was still mustering. His friends once advised him to visit a brothel for some sexual release but he scorned them saying that it was very immoral to do such a filthy thing. Rumours started circulating that he was impotent and this alarmed Andrew. To prove the contrary to his friends, he devised a method by setting his alarm to ring, and pretending that a lady was calling, he would say for instance, "I am fine, and you?" Then, he would take a pause and continue, "See, Flora, I have told you, I can't put up with you anymore. I prefer older girls who are a little more mature. I just feel that you are too young for me. I am sorry; I didn't mean to hurt you. You will find another guy." At such moments, everyone around would be listening keenly to Andrew, although pretending otherwise. Thereafter, they would meet in small groups to discuss what they overheard, trying to figure out who Flora might be. And Andrew whistled through life, *ohne* stress. One very peculiar thing about him was that he never sent money back home. He had nothing to do with Western Union. Andrew knocked down every system and so happiness was his portion.

Akwi welcomed Steffi, Ogochuku, and Fonjock. She gave Nji a kiss and hugged Jerry. Jerry glanced quickly around and did not fail to notice the smallness and somewhat awkward components of Nji's one bedroom apartment. The room comprised one small sized bed with an old mattress under it; one big old plank box with an old tablecloth and an old TV set on it, an old large broken sofa; an old cupboard with some tea cups and plates in it; a second-hand musical set on it, an old modelled wardrobe, some boxes and an unnecessarily large dining table with no stools around it but for a single toilet stool standing nonchalantly by its side. The size of the table did not fit the size of the room and there was also a large wall clock. An uneasy feeling gripped Jerry, but he told himself that this could not be. This contrasted the sophistication he saw on the photographs, which Nji used to send to him back home. Maybe they were just stopping over for some reason before going to Nji's real home. The ill feeling he had was too strong for him to have the courage to ask if this was really where his friend lived.

"Hey Jerry," Akwi interrupted his thoughts. "Make yourself comfortable on the sofa. You are welcome once more. I've heard so much about you from Nji. So how is Pays?"

"Pays is nice but for the hardship."

"It's a nice thing that you finally picked up a visa. At least you can see what you can do this way. Sit down; let me get you something to eat. You must be hungry."

"Yes, I got a visa after a long struggle. There was a long queue at the embassy, all wanting a visa. It's so difficult to get a German visa these days, it's like everyone wants to come over here to Germany."

Akwi returned home from work a little earlier on this day. This was because there were not many used rooms in the hotel to be cleaned. She worked as *Zimmermädchen* in Hotel Berlin. It was winter and there were not many customers lodging at the hotels and so there was limited work. She did just three hours on this day and succeeded to clean 10 rooms. That's 40 D-Mark because it was 4 D-Mark per room. Although weekend was approaching and Saturday was one of the busiest days for hotel workers, unfortunately for Akwi, she did not have to go to work on the forthcoming Saturday.

16

She had to work on the following day, which was a Friday, and then wait until when she would be called up next; that is, when next she would be needed. She was not made permanent because this would be unprofitable to her *Arbeitgeber*. Besides, Akwi was supposed to be studying in Germany and not working.

While Akwi set up the meal, Nji and Andrew took Jerry to the next house in their building, to Andrew's apartment to enable Jerry call his family to inform them of his safe arrival. The only privacy that the tiny apartment suggested was in the toilet. So Jerry took a seat on the toilet and called his parents and then Pamela. Jerry was told that to call from Andrew's line was very cheap so he took advantage of the offer; he finished and they joined the others at Nji's apartment who were all waiting for the guest of honour to start the meal.

Nji served Jerry the rice and tomato sauce with chunks and chunks of chicken. When Jerry received his plate, he could not believe his eyes.

"All of this for me alone? Just for one person. You people are really enjoying in this place." Nji took a can of BECK'S beer from a six-pack at the edge of the table, opened and placed it beside Jerry. "Or, would you prefer a Berliner Kindl; what we Berliners drink? Enjoy your meal J.J." Then, he joined the others and served himself.

Jerry's welcome party had just begun. When any new person arrived, the Paysans always came together and welcomed him/her with a little celebration. Since it was a small apartment everyone found a spot wherever they could to sit down, with Ogochuku and Steffi taking up ample space on the bed.

"Schatz, können wir gehen?" she said.

Ogochuku felt some disappointment as he answered, half stammering, *"Aber ich möchte noch mit meinem Freund Jerry reden. Ich habe noch nicht mit ihm geredet."* Ogochuku was disappointed that Steffi wanted to leave so soon, but it was her normal way of behavior whenever they met with Ogochuku's *contri* people. It was difficult for her to tolerate such company.

"*Aber Schatz, ich brauche dich jetzt, wir können Jerry zu uns einladen.*" After deciding that they would invite Jerry to their place, she told Akwi and Nji goodbye, moved towards the kitchen, on the corridor to light another cigarette. "*Na ja, ich komme gleich. Ich trinke mein Getränk aus, ich mache fertig Schatz,*" Ogochuku said. Ogochuku moved around shaking hands with his friends as he grumbled painfully, "*Massa Jerry, we go see nah? Nah so dis Oyibo ngah dem dey. Make a just di go. We go see. Na docki man di finam.* One is simply looking for paper." Ogochuku said this and then joined Steffi in the kitchen, "*Schatz, wir können gehen.*"

Steffi, who had been *genervt* as her mind had wandered inadvertently to the pots and pans of many sizes and colours displayed on the electric cooker while she was smoking, joined Ogochuku. Looking at these pots and pans which stood as if each and every one of them had decided on its position and posture, Steffi did not have much trouble of wondering where they came from. Being an expert, Steffi knew they were from a *Flohmarkt*. A non-expert would think they were from an antique shop, especially a gigantic saucepan with a lid. The colour and the angry look posed by this saucepan made its weight twice visible than it actually was.

As they left, they bypassed some Paysans who were returning from work and on their way to Nji's residence. There was more drinking after the meal and this gave them the opportunity to recount more woes about the dreaded train controllers and other setbacks faced by Paysans. A boy recounted to the others how he was almost caught by ticket controllers. On his way from Western Union after finishing work, he was controlled but he did not have any ticket for the train. He had to accompany the controllers out of the train. As soon as he got out, he looked left and right and then ran away. They tried to follow him but to no avail. He ran until he was breathless. Then, he saw a bus coming. He did not even care to check where the bus was heading to but just got onto it and then got off at the very next station and started trekking home. It was also interesting that a Paysan who had an accident at a construction site melted into thin air before the ambulance arrived because he did not have papers. All these stories intrigued Jerry and from the questions he kept asking, it was obvious that he was naive about the immigrant status and their brushes with the law.

"So, he wasn't rushed to the hospital. Suppose there was something seriously wrong with him? Maybe internally, how would you people know?" Jerry was perplexed.

The boy smiled, "God will take care. My man, considering the type of jobs one does in this country, isn't there something already wrong internally with us without a fall on debris? It's only God who takes care of us. When one finally goes back to Pays, if one doesn't take care, one would live only a few years and die."

Jerry's welcome party went on as the drinking continued. Those who felt hungry took Akwi to the side and she gave them something to eat. Finally the big table was taken to the corner of the room and there was enough dancing space for everyone as the music got louder and louder. It was only after midnight that the friends took their leave, one after the other. This was because Nji's neighbour had threatened to call the police for noise pollution.

After the visitors had left, Jerry looked around feeling uncomfortable. He wondered why Nji would not take him home. But when he saw Akwi unpacking his bag, it suddenly dawned on him that he was home.

Akwi unpacked Jerry's bag which contained mainly foodstuff. She took out some smoked fish, which was getting bad, shook off the maggots from it, cut a little piece and ate. "This tastes good," she said. Jerry looked around and took in a deep breath. Everyone was now gone except Nji, Fonjock, Andrew, Akwi, Fonjock's girlfriend and Jerry. Fonjock had to see off his girlfriend as she was only seventeen years of age and therefore a minor. Jerry was dumbfounded that a young girl of that age could be so bold and wanton in front of people, kissing Fonjock publicly all the time.

"*Man go see tin dem for dis place.*" Jerry marvelled at the seventeen year old.

"You will see more. Don't worry. Please, Jerry, go to sleep. You must be very tired." said Fonjock.

Andrew, who lived next door got up sluggishly and moved out with Fonjock and his girlfriend. By this time, Nji and Akwi were already sleeping on the bed; Jerry went to sleep on the sofa. When Fonjock came back later on, he pulled out the mattress from under the bed and slept on it.

Jerry got up at 8am and found the whole place deserted. His hosts had been up by 5am and were already on their way to work by 6am. He was confused. He stared out the window for some time looking at the snow outside. He sat down on the sofa and switched on the television - each time stopping at CNN, BBC or TV5. He watched television for some time and then he started feeling bored and hungry. He went to the general kitchen and prepared some toast, omelette and a warm chocolate drink for himself. He ate while he watched CNN. Then he became bored with CNN and then with BBC and even with TV5 and so he changed to the German channel PRO 7 where a film was going on. He concentrated on the film for some time, and then felt thirsty. He went to the kitchen to look for water; he opened the fridge and took up a bottle, he read what was written on it–*Wasser.* Then he took up another bottle and read *Orangensaft.* He took up several containers from the fridge; he opened some, sniffed the contents and replaced them. Then he became fed up. He took a glass and fetched some water from the tap to drink but then he thought, "I was told that this is recycled water; I doubt if it is fit for drinking."

Back in the room, Jerry watched more television while thinking hard. Then, he opened a cupboard and saw an English/German dictionary. He looked up the word water from the dictionary. Water-*Wasser.* Jerry repeated the word to himself happily, *wasir,* No! *Wassa.* He went to the fridge once more and looked for the bottle of *Wasser,* took it out happily and poured some of its content into a glass. He gulped it down rapidly but spat it out almost immediately. He was frightened, "My goodness! Is this water or soda?" He could remember his class five primary school teacher very well, "Pure drinkable water should have no taste, no smell, and no colour." He poured away the remaining water from the glass, and went back to continue watching television. Then it was time for adverts as the word *Werbung* appeared on the screen. Jerry was so bored that he fell asleep and was woken up only by the sound of the doorbell ringing. He went and opened the door for Andrew. He was relieved and could converse with Andrew until the others came back.

Four

Afrikanische Frauen

A few weeks later, Steffi finally allowed Ogochuku to invite Jerry and his friends. She also told him, he could cook an African meal. It was Saturday morning and Ogochuku was very happy as he cleaned and set the first set of pots on fire. One contained chopped cow legs and the other the intestines of the cow popularly known as *towel* or *Pansen*. Both pots were boiling. Steffi went to the kitchen, looked disgustedly at the pots on the fire and held her breath from puking. She was very angry. She got out of the kitchen very fast slamming the door behind her. Ogochuku sensed her discomfort and enquired if she was well.

"Just a slight headache, *Schatz*." She told him, she had been tending the pots on fire when a terrible headache struck her.

"Oh, no, you just lie down, darling, I will take care of that," said Ogochuku. Steffi went to the bedroom feeling frustrated. From time to time, she looked at the clock, wondering how much more time it would take to prepare the meal. She imagined the amount of gas it was consuming and she grew more and more angry. This was one of the reasons why she hated things that had to do with Ogochuku's culture. She wondered why a meal should take that long to cook. She got up, went to the kitchen and switched off the cooker. When Ogochuku noticed what she had done and questioned her, she said, she thought that the food was ready. Ogochuku knew his wife very well and knew she was lying. He too pretended and said, "Yes, yes, it is ready; you are right." Meanwhile as he added the pepper soup spices he had prepared to the *foot for cow and the towel* now in one pot, he grumbled, *"Foolish oyigbo, to go eat for restaurant and to just boil this cow leg and cow belly, which one com dey expensive?* Which is more expensive *ehe? No fit dey cook for house sef.* If it were about going on *Urlaub* to Ostsee, or to buy that big teddy bear which is expensive for nothing, just to put it in the sitting room, it wouldn't be expensive. Even *sef,* this cat, the money spent on its food can feed all the people in Omeneki village. Don't use too much gas, don't use much hot water, *Omofia, tofia qua!"* Ogochuku exclaimed and sighed at the same time as he continued to prepare the meal.

Two hours later, Nji, Fonjock, Jerry and Akwi came in. This was an hour after Schweinsteiger, Lautenschlager, Busenbinder and Schweinsteiger's girlfriend Svenja had arrived. But Steffi's friends were used to Ogochuku's country people´s own time, "black man time." The table was set. When all were seated, Steffi ordered for some silence. Jerry immediately closed his eyes and then quickly opened them again when instead of hearing something like or related to "Bless us oh Lord and bless this Thy gift . . . ," he instead heard Steffi who was brandishing a glass explaining the use of the cutleries to them. Holding each up, she would say for instance, this is a fork and it is to be held in the left hand while this knife is meant for the right hand. She went on and on, explaining to them the various uses of different glasses with different shapes and sizes. The one for water, juice, wine and so on and so forth. Ogochuku did not like all these explanations but he pretended as if everything was alright as his friends stared blankly at Steffi. Jerry almost said something as Ogochuku had expected and so he cut in on time saying jokingly to Jerry, *"Ina, na kwale bi dis o,* no word, no word."*

As all of them ate, Steffi's friends wondered how the *foot cow* and *towel* pepper soup with which Ogochuku's friends ate their own *Kartoffeln* tasted. As they ate their *sauerkraut* and boiled pork, they stole looks from time to time at how these special friends of theirs tore at the *cow legs*. Steffi felt some pride as she explained to them how much her in-laws valued such delicacies. Svenja was the first to serve herself some of this, immediately after she heard Steffi's explanation. For some reason, she finally abandoned her own meal and ate *foot cow* and *towel* pepper soup, not minding the pepper. Ogochuku and his friends were surprised as well as impressed that she could cope with the pepper. They praised her. As Svenja ate, she stole lustful looks at Fonjock. Fonjock noticed this and alerted his friends in high Pidgin English, commonly known as *Nbohko,* which even Akwi did not understand. Meanwhile, Steffi was busy making sure that the Africans didn't destroy her things or misuse them for she believed strongly that they were not used to such things.

While they were still eating, Steffi went to the toilet, immediately after Jerry came out from using it. When she returned, she called Ogochuku and took him there. As they entered the toilet, she closed the door and started to scold Ogochuku. Pointing at a tiny drop of liquid on the toilet seat, she said in bad English, "I told you about your people, but you would not listen. Look at my toilet seat. See how soiled it is. Even you, when you come to take your bath, you stay too long under the shower. This costs money. In fact, I don't think, I can take all this."

"So, what would you have me do? Do you want to divorce me or what?" Ogochuku asked.

"I didn't say so. It is just that your people, they are…, they are…oh forget it."

"What is wrong with my people? I told you that, according to the African tradition, you get married to the whole family and sometimes to the whole village or clan and not just to a man. I told you this and you said no problem but now you are complaining. If you don't want my friends coming here again, just tell me."

"We are not in Africa here, not in your village!" Steffi was bitter.

Ogochuku was not surprised; Steffi had always been like that. Because of things like this, during the last African Experts meeting, Ogochuku did not walk to the front when it was announced that all those who were henpecked by their wives should go to the front.

The African Experts' meeting was a monthly meeting between the *Afrikanische Frauen*, also known as Experts on Africa and their exotic men.

These women were experts for real; for amongst so many other things, they had the ability to distinguish a black man from Africa from those of other countries like Britain, France or America or even Jamaica. When Ogochuku had not met Steffi, he and Fonjock went to a Singles' nightclub and returned home with two white ladies. On their way home, Fonjock lied to his own lady that he was from Jamaica. The lady was excited by this and asked his hometown. He was taken aback, but fortunately he knew the name Kingston in Jamaica. Meanwhile, Ogochuku also lied to his own lady that he was from Texas.

On arrival at the boys' apartment, one of the ladies opened a kitchen cupboard in search for a glass and saw lots and lots of packets of *Grieß*; she immediately knew the guys were from Africa. The lady was disappointed and so signaled her friend and they took their leave.

On their way they commented on their knowledge of Africans. "All we want is the truth. No doubt, Ogochuku; instead of saying, "The teacher who taught me in primary school," he said, "The teacher who teach me in primary school." The other time he said, *"Ina, I say, make you di com let's go."* He also said something like, *"Even sef, I have a car, it's just that a friend of mine borrowed it."* I almost thought I am the one who doesn't know the English language well, not an American graduate," the lady said to her friend.

"Und was bedeutet even sef?" the other asked.

"Ich weiss nicht," said the friend. It is hard to know everything in so short a time. This is why it is often said that, "Rome was not built in one day." Even experts need time to establish facts.

"What puzzles me and what I hate is the fact that these guys lie all the time," she continued.

To Ogochuku and his friends, this was the only way to gain a little respect from these ladies. It was better for them to realize who they actually were later on when they were already in a relationship, and then it would be hard for them to withdraw.

On this particular day, the African Experts meeting started as usual with "Quiz of the Month." The President of the union, Anke, started off: "Place and Continent: Where did civilization begin?"

One of the experts stood up and said, "In Egypt, Africa." Everyone clapped and the men smiled.

Anke continued: "Where was the first University in the world founded?"

Another expert stood up and said, "In Timbuktu, somewhere in Africa."

"Cor--rect!" Anke said and everyone clapped again.

Then she said, "Race and Continent: What race had in the past inhabited the land which maltreated God's chosen people and was cursed?"

"Black Race, Africa," an expert said and received applause. The men were uneasy; they tried to force smiles in vain. Then, they started murmuring.

"Order!" shouted Anke, and they all kept quiet.

But one of them Mbasi, stood up and asked, "What is the name of the city where a most remarkable conference was held in 1884 to decide the fate of a most remarkable race?"

"Sit down, sit down!" all the experts shouted.

"I am not yet through!" Anke added.

The ladies whispered amongst themselves, "What did he mean by that?" they asked each other.

But no one seemed to know the answer to the question.

Then, the President continued: "A complaint was brought up by one of you on the fact that your wives were terrorizing you; so all those whom this happens to should come to the forefront." All his pals but Ogochuku went to the front.

Because one of them did not go to the front, the President and the other experts declared the point invalid and unfounded.

"Nullified!" Anke shouted.

The meeting went on and on and then *Grieß fufu* and vegetable okro soup was served during the refreshment break. They all enjoyed the meal as they licked their fingers. At the close of it, the *Afrikanische Frauen* experts said, the monthly meetings should end because the question which Mbasi asked was too difficult for them.

On their way home, his friends asked Ogochuku with admiration what strategy he used with his wife. He told them carefully that he did not want to stand out in front because he was afraid of the unimaginable consequence from his wife. He was too scared of his wife to stand out front with them.

Ogochuku looked at the toilet seat again and tried to plead with Steffi, saying that it might be water from the tap when his friend was washing his hands after using the toilet and not necessarily urine. Steffi was still angry. *"You make always problems,"* she said. *"Why send you always money either to Awala or to Pays? And sometimes I don't bekom anything from you."* Ogochuku merely scratched his head. It was only after a rehearsal of the consummation of marriage that Ogochuku could get her smile back and they joined the others.

Steffi brought in an *Erdbeertorte* for desert with some *Erdnüsse- geröstet und gesalzen, which* she had bought from Meyer Beck, where she most often did her shopping for it was just two blocks away. She served the peanuts with some *kavrulmus Misir,* she bought from *Gazi* for Ogochuku's friends. As Steffi's friends rushed for the cake, Ogochuku's friends dexterously emptied handfuls of the roasted peanuts and maize into their mouths. They crunched *gru, gru, gru* as they all played cards and emptied cans of BECK'S beer. Akwi did not play cards; she simply watched the others as she sipped her juice. Lautenschlager told a story of how he won over a hundred D-Mark from his friends the last time they played darts in the *Kneipe.* The whole of that week, Busenbinder and Schweinsteiger had to rely on him for

27

sustenance until their social benefits for the next month came in.

It was late at night and Steffi´s friends prepared to leave. Shockingly to Schweinsteiger, Svenja did not want to go. He looked around him and sensed it at once. "Is it because of these long penises which you see around here that you don't want to go?" He insulted Svenja and insisted that Svenja must leave with him. Svenja hid behind Nji and Schweinsteiger tried to pull her away resulting in a tug of war when Fonjock joined in. Steffi broke the fight and insisted that Schweinsteiger wait for Svenja downstairs. She went to the kitchen to deposit some glasses which she had on a tray and when she came back, her friend Svenja was nowhere in sight. She was satisfied when the boys informed her that Svenja had followed Schweinsteiger home. Steffi warned Fonjock to stay off Svenja for she was in love with her man.

But the boys had lied; they knew Svenja was hiding up the staircase on the last floor; the one next to the roof. The boys took their leave after they were sure Schweinsteiger had given up. They fetched Svenja from the *Dachgeschoss* and she took Fonjock to her apartment where they spent the night together.

Five
Weekend

It was a snowy Saturday and Jerry was about a month old in Germany. Jerry, Nji and Akwi went out to shop groceries from ALDI. Jerry watched his friends with interest as they picked up items from the shelves and dropped them in the shopping cart ranging from tomatoes, toilet tissue, and water to wine and rice. Jerry picked up a packet of rice and Akwi explained to him that the packet was 1000g and costs 89Pfennig. That's about three hundred Francs CFA. Jerry was surprised at the vast difference in standards.

After shopping at ALDI, they stopped at another supermarket – EXTRA to get _Grieß_, _Suppenhuhn_, beer, _Maggi_ and red beans. They shopped from ALDI because it was relatively cheap, but it did not have all the foodstuffs which these Africans needed for cooking. By now they had learnt to adapt some of these foodstuffs to suit their taste. _Grieß_ for example was a good supplement for _fufu_. And so it was hard to go to an African's house without seeing so many packets of _Grieß_, _fufu_ being what they were very much used to back at home in spite of the fact that they had potatoes, rice and many other foodstuffs as well. Back home they ate a different variety of _fufu_ almost every day. Also, they realised that _Spinat_ could be used in place of waterleaf especially for the preparation of _eru_, and a mixture of _Grieß_ and _Kartoffelmehl_ would give you something like _kumkum_ or *water fufu* if the dough was harder.

On her way home from work on the previous day, a friend had taken Akwi to the lone Afro shop in town and she bought some fresh *okro*. As they got home, Akwi prepared a pot of *okro* soup using some fresh meat and many of the things that Jerry brought which included dried smoked fish, *egusi,* crayfish and some *ogwono*. The soup was very delicious and everyone ate it with a sumptuous portion of *Grieß* made in the manner of *fufu*, not with sugar or milk as the *Deutschen* would consume it. After eating, they rested a bit and prepared to attend a friend's birthday party.

They did not leave for the party until it was 10pm although on the invitation it said 8pm. This was because they knew that people would start coming at the earliest two hours after the actual time. 8pm was just a formality. They finally arrived at the party at 10:30pm since the place was not very far away from them. The party was taking place in a hall at another student hostel, which the Africans referred to as *Coppi* because it was on Coppistrasse. They were on time. When they arrived there were a handful of people there, mainly Paysans and German women. It was so interesting how adventurous and inspiring the German women were. Not very often would you find a German male at such gatherings as you would find their women interacting so freely with the unknown.

Bobby, the host, was a typical Paysan who always looked good. Like the President of his noble nation, every average citizen from this nation aspires to look presentable. Bobby was clothed in a *Super Cent* suit and a pair of *Morrishi* shoes. It was rumoured that, on passing through Germany, their President had stopped at the renowned KADEWE shop on a Sunday to buy a pair of shoes of the *Morrishi* brand. He had paid an extra fee for this outstanding department store to open specially for him on a Sunday. Thus, his picture was displayed by the side of a pair of *Morrishi* for a month. This was a very good example for the citizens of his nation, for every male from this country residing in Berlin struggled amidst all odds to get himself a pair of the same shoes in spite of its cut throat price as this was a mark of *finesse*, which is what really matters in life. The cut throat price of these shoes coupled with the fact that it was a Sunday and the President could not go without the shoes but preferred to pay an extra price, showed that it was a commodity worth sacrificing for.

Jerry, Nji, Akwi, Andrew, Ogochuku, Steffi, Fonjock's girlfriend and Fonjock arrived when the host was at his welcome speech. They occupied a whole table. Other items on the agenda included the cutting of the cake. A Paysan lady working at a brothel was called up to "unveil the cake", which she did with the sum of 500 D-Mark, and a slice of the cake was taken on a plate to her table, which of course was the "High Table"

Only those with special invitations, the VIPs, sat at this table. The names of all these people were called up to cut the cake. Being important personalities, their table was reserved on the stage in this hall. Some of them walked up to cut the cake with 100 D-Mark, some with 50D-Mark, 20 D-Mark or whatever they had to offer to the celebrant, and then were rewarded with a little slice of the cake on paper napkins which they took back to their seats. Nji's name was on the list although he didn't sit at the High Table but preferred to sit in the crowd with his friends. When his name was called, Akwi was the one who went forward with 50 D-Mark and it was whispered around that they were not just dating but lived together. "Partially married!" her friends shouted. Each time someone went up to cut the cake, the amount she/he donated was announced, but more often than not, not the real sum was announced. They inflated it a bit in order to encourage the others who were still to come up to give a high sum. Sometimes the people negotiated with the announcer to state a specific higher amount than what they have offered and all these would be announced over the microphone. For instance it was announced that the lady had unveiled the cake with 1000 D-Mark.

"Cutting of the cake" took close to two hours and at about 1am, the dishes were opened and dinner was served. There was quite a lot to eat, *Grieß* (*fufu*) and *eru*, *ndole* and plantains, rice and stew, boiled potatoes and pepper soup, fried potatoes and fried ripe plantains with red beans, fried chicken as well as fried fish. The eating lasted about an hour or two. Thereafter, there was drinking and dancing. People paced up and down. Amongst the German ladies who were there, a particular one was always looking and smiling at Jerry. Steffi and Fonjock's girlfriend were enjoying themselves, drinking and nodding to the music and puffing smoke from their cigarettes and also trying to hum the African tunes playing. They moved to the floor and started to dance to a *makossa* tune. From the way they danced, it was clear that they had a different music playing in their heads, not the one in the hall.Their steps were either before or after the rhythm.

Then, Andrew looked at Jerry and asked, "Why is that girl staring at you, Jerry?"

"Maybe the girl wants to move him," Nji chuckled.

"Move whom? She will certainly move but herself," said Jerry. "I have told you people to keep all the insinuations to yourselves. I told you several times, only one girl moves me and that is Pamela."

"What do you mean?" Fonjock asked. "Ha! Ha! Ha! Where is Her Royal Highness, Princess Pamela? Thousands of kilometres away. And here you are in all this cold preaching Pamela, Pamela!"

"I don't believe in long distance love," Ogochuku said.

This annoyed Akwi. "You people should leave him alone; he is being faithful which is of course good. Is it a bad thing to love someone so dearly? You people embarrass me."

Then Fonjock said, "Don't take it too hard Akwi. I mean, what this guy is trying to do is illogical. Does he know what Pamela herself is doing right now in Pays?"

"What are you insinuating? How can somebody be talking about his woman and you talk of infidelity?" Akwi asked.

"What woman? They didn't get married before Jerry left," retorted Fonjock.

"Even if they didn't get married officially, at least he knows the girl very well before laying his trust on her. Not so Jerry?"

"Why do you suffer to explain all that to them? It seems Europe has done so much harm to their brains. Someone like Ogochuku, I don't understand him anymore. The girl he loved so dearly some years back before leaving Pays is now past tense. All he talks about is colonial debt. I love Pamela and that is final," said Jerry categorically.

As the boys left for the dance floor, Jerry turned once more to Akwi; "That reminds me, I have not even told you about Pam. In fact, it is a long story how we fell in love. Sitting here right now, it's all coming back to me. The second time I met her..." Jerry's thoughts fled.

Six

An Unplanned Encounter

One Friday evening, a week after Jerry had met with Pamela and her friend Beri, he stumbled on Pamela, Beri, and their other friend Immaculate in front of a nightclub. He was excited as he approached the girls. "What are you girls doing? Why are you just standing about? Will you mind sitting down somewhere? Or why don't you let me take you people into the club?" Jerry had asked. Pamela told him that they were supposed to meet a friend of theirs and her husband at the bar of the nightclub and that they could not find them and so they were on their way home. Jerry encouraged them to stay though they seemed bent on going to do their homework. After Pamela finally accepted the invitation with feigned reluctance, he bought drinks and food for them. Paying for these did not bother Jerry, who was interested only in pleasing. Pamela saw this as a plus, he was beginning to pay "encouragement fee".

They sat down in the bar, ate and drank their UCB Pamplemousse drinks and Pamela decided to retain Jerry's name. This was how Pamela came to retain the name Jerry Asongbang who lived in Bart town with his parents. A graduate from the Faculty of English Modern Letters of the Samedi University. This university was in the capital city. The city was initially called Saturday, but later on, during the early nineties, the President signed a decree abolishing the name Saturday and replacing it with Samedi in a decentralisation policy to enhance development. Jerry ran a small provision store. Thinking that Pamela had taken an interest in him, Jerry was happy to give more and more information about himself as he crunched the leftover vertebrates from the girls' roasted fish. "Why are you people not eating this thing?" he had asked. "It is nice, it contains calcium." He went on to explain to Pamela that, his father was a court registrar and his mother a schoolteacher, until Pamela rudely interrupted him, "We would like to take our leave!" Jerry did not notice the rudeness as he said,

"*Eh...* Pamela. Please, I would like you to come and know my place. Here is some money for your transport fare." Jerry gave Pamela a thousand Francs CFA and directed her to his residence somewhere in Bart town. Pamela accepted the money and barely nodded her head slowly. The girls stood up, stretched their bodies while their eyes accurately surveyed their vicinity. "Okay, I will be waiting for you tomorrow at 2 pm," Jerry said as he moved to the roadside and boarded a taxi home.

As Jerry was relating all these things to Akwi, Nji came over to them and said they should get ready to leave for the party was slowly getting to an end. "It is a very long story," said Jerry to Akwi. "I will continue some other time, let's get going."

It was indeed a long story, for as soon as Jerry left the nightclub premises, the three girls burst out laughing and instead of going home, they lingered around the nightclub premises making themselves as conspicuous as possible. Then they noticed Mr E, a 56 year-old-potbellied man walking to his car. They ran and hid themselves behind some trees. Mr E was a nickname given to him by the girls. He was Pamela's *Mboma* and as generous as sugar daddies come.

The idea of *Mboma* came all the way from the girls of the Samedi University; it was taken up by the Bart University girls and later on spread to the high school and secondary school girls as well. Once, some Samedi University boys were very disappointed that the girls were flirting with aged married men who were rich enough to care for their daily needs, so they came up with the *Mboma* story. One of the boys worked for a local newspaper, and so, one day he put up a story in this paper that a rich aged man had turned into an anaconda, locally known as *Mboma,* and swallowed up a very pretty girl after having sex with her. This made the girls tremble. For some time, they were scared. In order to be on their guard, they tried to find out more information about the story; where precisely it had happened, how and why? They were told it happened in Tudig. They went to Tudig in order to get more information about the identity of this girl. This would help them know the man behind this act so that they could avoid his advances and those of the people he kept as friends as well.

"I was at Tudig yesterday but my cousin told me that the incident took place at Nyen," said one girl to her friends. "No! It can't be Nyen!" shouted another girl from the group. I live in Nyen, in Njinedeh Nyen. There is no way this could have happened there without my knowledge. Instead, I was told that it was at Guneku. Another girl said it was around Njidom, and some others said it was at Njinibi, some said Mbomi, and to some it was Ngyen Mbo, and yet others insisted it was at Mbemi. The girls were getting confused and started doubting the validity of this story. They finally concluded that it was a lie when two days later, another rumour came out that it was at Moussadi. They all laughed. "Then, I am certainly the one that the *Mboma* swallowed," each girl went about saying. "Yet, I'm still alive. Isn't that awesome?" They laughed. They turned the whole thing into a joke, made fun of it and started referring to their Sugar daddies as *Mbomas.* It was common to hear a girl telling her friend, "*Massa*, I have to be swallowed up today. I have a *rendez-vous* with this wonderful *Mboma*. He is so rich and such a gentleman. He is a real anaconda; too gallant for his age. Even his performance in bed is so artistic. I can't wait to have him swallow me up tonight." The boys were disappointed, for this meant they had failed and would still have no access to these girls whose bills they could not contain.

When Mr E drove off, the girls came out from their hiding and continued to linger around, looking keenly at the parked cars and trying hard to guess the type of people who had come to the nightclub that night. Finally, a very famous money doubler who was their friend came by and took them into the nightclub without paying gate fee for himself or the girls. The nightclub was full of people drinking, dancing and smoking. Pamela and her friends moved about in the club for a brief moment trying to take stock of the worth of the people in the club that night. Then, they went to the dance floor and started dancing. A few admirers came to dance with them. They snobbed at them, but finally, they settled on some who looked prosperous and promising. They danced with them and they bought drinks for the girls.

The following day at 2pm, Jerry waited for Pamela in vain. It was barely two hours after she and her friends had gotten up from sleep. They had overslept and only got up at mid-day. Sitting on the veranda in front of Pamela's room, the girls ate a late brunch of some overnight roast fish and *miondo* and recounted the high points of the previous evening. As they washed down their meal with soft drinks, they discussed a party that was coming up that evening. After the updates they returned to catch some sleep in preparation for the evening party as it began to rain.

Seven

No Jobs? No Jobs!

Jerry felt much more disappointed as he went back into the building and into the apartment as it began to drizzle. This happened on a Monday morning during Jerry's third month in Germany. Every other person had gone out to work or to hustle as usual. Jerry was alone at home. He stared out the window, and saw a bright sunlight. There was no snow. It was the dawn of spring. Although the vegetation had started to turn green, Jerry was stressed up with the confinement. He took the elevator and went downstairs. As he came out of the elevator, he saw an elderly man waiting out to board the lift.

"*Good Morging,*" he said to the man.

The man looked at him strangely and asked, "*Kennst du mich?*"

"These people with their *Kennst du mich?* Must I know you before greeting you?" Jerry thought to himself as he bypassed the man.

Jerry went out and stood in front of the building, looking up and down. He noticed a German boy unlocking his bicycle and went over to talk to him. The young man was surprised yet nodded his head. "I am Jerry, I come from Pays. Your bike looks good. Are you going out?" Jerry asked. The boy stood up, looked at Jerry and said; "Pays, *Fussball,* Roger Milla." Jerry smiled, looked at him briefly and then said to him, "Do you know what? It's getting to three months since I came to this country. I have had no job. I have not earned even one Franc. Even the little money I brought with

38

me is finished. I now live from my friends' pockets. I do not even have money anymore to make telephone calls to my girl or my parents. They will think I have completely forgotten about them. When I ask my friends about a job, they say I do not have papers and that jobs are scarce. They also tell me I cannot even speak the German language. Some even ask me to go and seek asylum. Oh! I miss everything about Pays but my business is no longer there. Then, there is Pamela. What will I tell her after having promised I will bring her to Europe in order that we will get married? I must struggle. I must be a man! Yes, I must struggle. After all, others have made something out of the place. Pamela you know, is my girl and …" The boy merely looked at Jerry shook his head and said, *"Es tut mir leid ich verstehe kein Englisch,"* and rode off. Jerry stared blankly after him, sighed and quickly went back into the building as the first light showers of rain touched him.

Watching from the window of the apartment, Jerry seemed to enjoy the little showers of rain. It reminded him of a similar day when he had waited for Pamela's visit all in vain. He smiled to himself as the thought came back to him. Jerry was happy in his ignorance because while he had been busy putting some finishing touches to his room, Pamela and her friends were trying to catch up some sleep in preparation for a party.

Some moments later, he had heard a knock on the door and was elated; he jumped up, quickly re-arranged his bed once again and went to the door with a huge smile on his face. But it was a goat hitting its horn against the door as it struggled to eat some unripe plantains. Jerry was annoyed with the goat and so had chased it as far away as he could, making the poor animal to forgo its meal for its life. This attracted his two sisters from the main building who looked out the window and scolded Jerry for tormenting the poor goat.

It was close to 8pm and the rain, which had ceased, started all over again. Jerry took an umbrella and a spare one and went to the roadside. He stood there looking into every taxi that went by. After an hour, he sighed and decided to go back home. On his way, he fell into a muddy ditch; he got up grumbling and limped home with one slipper in his hand.

When Jerry got home, after sighing for some time, he switched on his radio to FM 105 and listened to some music. While he listened to the music and the animation from the radio, he became less restless and then a thought came to his mind. There was a party going on. The Bart University branch of the MECUDA cultural group was hosting a big party on campus. He was very certain Pamela would be there. So he quickly dressed up and left for the party.

Immediately Jerry got to the party hall, he strained his eyes and looked for Pamela everywhere but to no avail. Then he saw a friend of his and they sat at a table in a corner drinking and conversing.

Pamela was still on the bed; leaning against the wall in the dimly lit hotel room with the sheets around her chest. Mr E was sitting beside her in boxer shorts. When they were finally dressed Mr E enquired, "So, when are you and your friends leaving for the party?"

"In about an hour's time," Pamela replied. Mr E handed Pamela 50,000 Francs, "Here, this is the money I promised you. Take good care of yourself. Let me give you a lift. I will call you tomorrow."

"Thank you very much daddy," Pamela was delighted. Mr E wasn't doing very badly, this was her type of man. He always did the right thing at the right time. He always gave Pamela money whenever she needed it. This was pure love, for how else could love be expressed. They left the hotel room to Mr E's 4- wheel -drive car.

Pamela entered her room, locked the door behind her and started to dress up hurriedly when she heard a knock on the door. "Who is there?"

"It's me, Beri. Pam, your heart is outside." Pamela opened the door revealing a nice-looking young gentleman, Didier, her fiancé. Didier took Pamela and her friends in his car to the party where Beri joined a boyfriend of hers and Immaculate her man friend.

Eight
ICE

It was now one week after the party; Jerry was at an Inter City Express bus station in Commercial trying to board a bus to the South West Province. This town was the commercial capital of Pays and so it was named after this fact. Jerry planned to board a bus to Tengern and then another one to Bart. Amidst the busy atmosphere, Jerry figured out Pamela at the canteen sipping a drink. He walked up and took a seat next to her. "Hello Pam! How is it?" he asked.

"Oh! Fine," said Pamela. She continued to sip her drink and looked at Jerry with a sneer. "Are you travelling or something?" Jerry asked.

"Oh yes, I am travelling, as you can see, to Samedi," Pamela retorted.

"I see. Pam, I don't know when next I can see you. The other day you kept me waiting and when we met at the party you even refused to dance with me."

Pamela was very bitter, "So? What about that? Was I obliged to dance with you? Did I invite you to the party?"

Jerry tried to calm Pamela down, "Not like that, Pam. Not like that. Do not take it too hard. I mean, I love and care about you very much, so I do not feel very happy when you treat me like this you know. Moreover, now that I am about to travel, I would really like us to know each other very well. So in future we can even spend our lives together."

41

Pamela burst out laughing. "What has your travelling to Samedi got to do with me? See, I will strongly advise you to go elsewhere and look for your class of…"

Jerry also cut in laughing as he took out his passport from the pocket of his jacket. "Who is talking about Samedi here? See, I am travelling to Germany. See, Pam I have gotten a visa, a German visa." Jerry opened his passport and showed Pamela the page carrying the visa.

Pamela was speechless and without thinking twice, she jumped up and embraced Jerry. "Ha! German visa! Let me see. Let me see. Wao!" She took the passport from Jerry and opened it to the first page carrying the picture. "Oh! How great! Fine boy."

"Just have a look at this photograph on your passport; it is so cute. Ah! A German visa. How wonderful. Have a sip," Pamela offered Jerry her drink and stared at him with love and respect. Then, Jerry ordered for some more drinks.

"Look at me o! I was running my mouth, talking about you travelling to Samedi." Then, Pamela thought hard and pretending to be angry, said, "Why didn't you tell me you were making arrangements to travel abroad? I mean to travel to Germany, you know. I feel you don't love me, you don't care about me."

"No, no, Pam, don't be annoyed," Jerry pleaded, "I wanted to be very sure before letting the cat out of the bag. I didn't want to count my chickens before they are hatched."

Just then, a classmate of Pamela, Patty, walked up to them to greet Pamela. Patty had come to the bus station to see off her aunt who was travelling to Samedi and to board a bus to Vick Town herself. She had spent the weekend at her aunt's place and it was already Monday. After explaining all this to Pamela, she added that her aunt travelled with the bus that had just left and she had to reach Vick Town before 5pm. "Now, it's already getting to 4pm. O.k.! Good-bye, see you later in Bart, Pam," Patty said.

"Hey, you have not greeted my fiancé," Pamela said and hugged Jerry. "And do you know what? He just got a visa to go to *Bundes*. His name is Jerry, Jerry Asongbang."

Jerry smiled and Patty looked at Pamela admirably as she shook hands with Jerry. "Congrats. Such a fine boy! I hope you remember us when you get there," she said sitting down without invitation. She looked at Jerry and then at the passport admirably and seductively. Pamela noticed the look and immediately collected the passport from Jerry and fanned herself with it proudly. She leaned closer to Jerry and said, "Honey, so where are we going to from here?"

"I have to go now straight to Bart. My mother will be so happy," Jerry said. "Were you about travelling to Samedi?" he asked.

"Yes. I mean, no," answered Pamela. "I suppose we take a taxi from here to *Rund Point*, from where we can easily catch a bus to Bart. See you later Patty." Pamela said and took Jerry by the arm and they walked away to board a taxi leaving Patty in suspense.

Pamela and Jerry travelled to Bart and went straight to Pamela's apartment in Lower Custains Bart where they spent the rest of the evening and the night together. Jerry got up early in the morning and started to dress up. "Where is my darling going to this very early morning?" asked Pamela as she held and kissed Jerry.

"Home, of course. My family hasn't seen me ever since I picked up my visa," Jerry answered. "Oh! No J.J., there is still time. I will feel very lonely if you should leave me now."

Jerry explained to Pamela that he needed at least a change of clothes. Pamela offered Jerry her toothbrush to use, gave him a T-Shirt of hers and then she went out, locked the door behind her and went to a nearby store and returned with some beverages, bread, some other breakfast items and some new clothes for Jerry. Then she went out again, locked the door and went to a telephone kiosk. Jerry walked to the door, tried it and found it locked. He moved to the window and looked out, and then he saw Pamela in the telephone kiosk. He watched from the window as she spoke on the telephone admiringly.

Pamela was on the phone with Didier, her fiancé. She

lied to him that her younger sister had had an accident and was in a coma and so they couldn't meet again as planned. Pamela continued to phone, unaware that Jerry was watching her. She opened her phone book and dialled another number and sold the same story to Mr E. Jerry walked up to the cooker and started preparing breakfast from the items Pamela had brought in.

By the time Pamela returned, Jerry had served omelette on two plates and was slicing bread while a kettle of water was boiling on the cooker.

"Ha! Whom do I have here? A husband or a cook? Oh! Darling, why didn't you allow me to come and do that?" Pamela moved over and held Jerry from behind about his shoulders.

"Oh! Never mind, I can cook. I am a man with a difference. You see, I need to assist my woman. Just sit down and relax, I will serve you. I am almost through. By the way, whom were you talking to on the phone?" Pamela was half-surprised and she giggled mischievously, "Ah! You saw me. *Em*... It is our course head. I was asking after my test paper. The fool doesn't seem to know where he kept it."

"I see. Those course heads. That's how they are, always wanting to reassert themselves," Jerry said.

Then, Pamela, being overtly nice, said promptly, "See, darling I must help you with this cooking." Pamela brought out two teacups, placed them on the table and poured out some hot water for an *Ovaltine* drink.

Pamela acted as though she had known Jerry all her life. She fed him and they kissed between mouthfuls. They could not be disturbed by anyone though Pamela's friends knocked at the door several times. Later on when they were satiated with each other they decided to go to a famous beach in Vick Town. After swimming, they played on the sand like the two love birds they had decided to turn themselves into. They ran after each other on the beach and played on the sand, teasing one another. And when they got tired, they sat somewhere, ate and drank and then moved about on the beach, hand in hand, conversing *tête-à-tête*. They kissed like two pigeons and then Jerry picked up Pamela and threatened to throw her into the sea waves. Pamela resisted. He dropped her on the sand and Pamela ran after him, both of them choking with laughter. After all these re-enactments, they were of course spent. They got their bag and made for the road where they boarded a cab back to Lower Custains Bart.

Jerry sighed as all these thoughts kept coming back to him. He paced up and down, got something to eat and watched more television. Jerry was stuck up in this little room, he couldn't go out. The city was too big for a newcomer like him to comprehend, secondly, he did not speak the language and thirdly, he had no valid visa; he might encounter the police and get repatriated. He was still a *dago* man; he had not yet sought asylum. He was unknown yet, unregistered. This was a very risky status.

Nine

Business Was Good

Andrew always visited Jerry to keep him company when the others were out. He fed him with some gossip and rumours mainly on the lives of other Paysans; who they were dating, the problems they were having. Jerry anticipated his visit and went to check on him when he did not come around. Andrew was not home. "He must be visiting some other person or running errands and making deliveries," thought Jerry as he returned to the apartment dejected.

It was rumoured that Andrew visited everyone, knew where they lived, knew their time table and everyone's telephone number. If one needed any Paysan's telephone number in Berlin, Andrew was the one to call, not the *Auskunft*. Andrew also knew all what was happening in Pays, especially in connection to Germany; the people who would be travelling to Germany, especially to Berlin from Pays and especially girls whom he always volunteered to pick up and assist. His telephone line got frozen by the *Deutsche Telekom* several times. Seeing that he could not pay the bills to get it reinstalled, he proceeded to order a new telephone line using a name which only existed somewhere in his remote village in Pays. After all, to install a telephone was just to call *Deutsche Telekom* and tell them you were the new occupant of an apartment, tell them any fake name and date of birth of your choice.

Andrew always had a way out for almost everything, he didn't have the stress genes that plagued other people. No doubt, he was the *Ohne Stress* man. He explained to his friends that he found this society too democratic for stress. Although, in Pays one could reduce one's age if one was willing, the leniency in this land was something else. Whenever he came up with any new ideas, Andrew explained to his pals that the system was lenient. Moreover, he was gifted in many things. He knew how to make his friends have internet services for almost free. He moved from one friend's apartment to another to provide them with a life-time internet facility for just 30 D-Mark. Because he had a free telephone line connection, his pals could telephone home very cheaply from his place; he was the one who also invented a telephone card, which could be used on any *Deutsche Telekom* telephone booth to call any number in the world for as long as one wanted. This made small, small businesspersons spring up here and there who indulged in leasing as a source of financing their living. It had never been the best thing to do odd jobs all the time. With this new innovation by Andrew, a month's full time student job was all that was needed to get into business. Since student jobs were tax free, the monthly income a student received as a part time worker could be up to at least 2,000 D-Mark. Averagely, students needed at most 1,000D-Mark to live on and the remaining 1,000 D-Mark could be invested in the business of buying the card.

Business was good; it involved simply lying down all day long and leasing out this card to the other pals to call home. There was no risk involved for the supplier but for the consumer. Once a Paysan boy who was using this card got caught by the security officers, he told them that he had picked it up on the streets. He knew the supplier would deny knowing him, let alone accepting the fact that he gave him such a card. Luckily for this boy, he was a student; he could only be fined and not repatriated. A fine in a democratic society like this one was not so bad because you could choose to carry out *Raten zahlung. Germany fine o o o!* These folks could not believe their luck to be able to find themselves within the realms of such democracy. In their fatherland, things would not be the same. Nevertheless, this made business to slow down and finally it died out.

But that notwithstanding, before long, Andrew started selling designer clothing and shoes at give-away prices. Where Andrew got them from, no one could tell. Not until it became rumoured that one could order items from catalogues using a fake name and address, or the name of someone you know and the person's address. Then, on the day of delivery, linger in front of the building of that address and watch out for the delivery van to receive your package by simply giving specifications concerning this package.

Andrew did his door to door delivery and everyone was excited to purchase, most especially, so as to have something to send back home. It was on one of these delivery missions that Andrew had gone, when Jerry missed him so badly.

Ten

Baptism

As usual, Jerry was sleeping after watching TV. Then, some moments later, the bell rang and he jumped up to open the door for Nji.

"I have good news for you! Tomorrow, you are going to be baptised!" Nji said.

"What! Baptised?" Jerry asked.

"You heard me right, Jerry. However, not with water this time around. Anyway, you already had that. But with dust *art thou* going to be baptised, Jerry, so get ready. Our *Chef* says the company needs somebody to join us at the work place, and so I told him I would bring someone, meaning you. So, tomorrow at 5am, we are off, for the place is far; besides, it is advisable to come earlier than the time work actually starts. This impresses the *Chef* and he might let you stay in the job a little bit longer than he intended to."

Nji and Jerry got up very early the next day and at about 5.30am they were already on their way to work. It was still a little bit dark. Nji peered at the bus arrival schedule on the shield briefly and decided that they should walk to the train station for it would take a little bit longer for the bus to come.

"See, like I was telling you. Good morning is *Guten Morgen,*" Nji said.

"*Good Morging?*" Jerry asked.

"Yes, then *danke* means thank you," Nji continued.

"Tanken?"

"No! Jerry, not *T* but *D*. D-a –n-k-e."

"O.k. *Dan—ke.*"

"Yes that's much better. Something like that. If you are asked, *Wie heißt du?* or *Wie heißen Sie?* You just have to say your name. But not your real name, I hope you don't forget that. Then see, anything you are told which you don't understand, just say *ja.*"

"What does *Ya* mean?" Jerry asked.

"It means yes."

Jerry nodded his head, "Okay, I see. *Danke, ya, good morning, no I mean morging, highz do, highz zi.* "

"Good," Nji applauded.

Then they started running as they saw the train coming from a distance. They finally caught the train and arrived at the building construction site early enough although the *Chef* was already there. *"Good   Morging,"* Jerry said to the *Chef.*

"Morgen. Wie heißt du?"

"Andrew Tembeng."

" *Deinen Pass und Schein.*"

Then, Nji whispered to Jerry, *"docki."*

Jerry hurriedly presented the borrowed documents. *"Jetzt können Sie gehen, ,, s*aid the *Chef.* Then he said to Nji , " *Nimm Andrew dorthin mit, wo du gestern mit den anderen gearbeitet hast.*"

They joined one other boy and the three of them started work immediately, *stemming* and breaking down walls. Then, one of the permanent workers called out to Jerry as he was coming from throwing debris in a container.*" Du! Bring mir einen Besen,"* he ordered. But Jerry stared at him blankly. *"Einen Besen!"* shouted the man harshly.

"Okay! Basin, basin!" Jerry exclaimed. Jerry looked around the *Baustelle* and found an old abandoned basin and brought it to the man.

The man stared at him and said, *"Ich meine einen Besen!"* Nji heard the shout, stopped working, and from a short distance indicated the art of sweeping to Jerry. Then Jerry hurried off and fetched a broom for the man. At the close of the day, the man reported this incident to the *Chef,* *"Der versteht kein Deutsch. Ich habe ihn gebeten, mir einen Besen zu bringen, stattdessen hat er mir ein Becken gebracht."*

„Aber der hat mir die richtigen Papiere gezeigt. Der ist Student schon seit vier Jahren. So steht es in seinem Pass," said the *Chef.* The *Chef* simply waved the complaint off for he could not understand why the man said Jerry did not understand simple German. On Jerry's passport it was indicated that he had been a student for four years. There is no way someone could be a student in the country for four years with no basic knowledge of the language. But what he didn't know was the fact that the passport belonged to someone else.

So, the boys continued their work, day after day with Nji helping out Jerry from time to time when he didn't understand the language, until the eventful day. This was a week later, Nji was taken to another *Baustelle* in the *Chef's* car. Then, the *Chef* returned some moments later, "Andrew, *wo bist du?"*

"Ya!" Jerry answered as he ran to meet the *Chef.*
"Bist du schon fertige oder hast du noch etwas zu tun?"

"Ya, "Jerry answered again.
The *Chef* stared at him surprisingly. *"Was? Bin ich doof oder was?"* he asked.

"Ya!" Jerry answered.

The *Chef* smiled wryly and shook his head in disapproval. *"Komm her, Dummkopfe!"* he said to Jerry and then pointed at a wall, *"Siehst du diese Wand? Du musst sie nicht stemmen,"* still indicating the same wall with emphasis, *"Diese muss bleiben, nicht stemmen! Verstehst du?" "Ya!"* Said Jerry.

"Du musst aber diese stemmen," the *Chef* said, indicating another wall. *"Aber die andere bitte nicht. Ich komme später wieder. Ich gehe auf die andere Baustelle."*

After the *Chef* had left, Jerry thought over what he

was supposed to do. Then, he went to the wall, which he was not supposed to break and broke it down with all devotedness. The *Chef* returned after a while, he saw what Jerry had done and he was very angry and so he dismissed Jerry from work for breaking down the wrong wall. Jerry was dejected and lamented the job loss. He particularly regretted the fact that he could not send money home, especially to Pamela and his parents who were eager for him to succeed.

Eleven
Our Wife

One morning, as Jerry was looking at his photo album, the bell rang and Andrew came in. He had brought some videos so that they could watch together. He sat down and Jerry quickly prepared omelette and some toast. While Andrew ate, Jerry showed him pictures in his photo album: his parents, his two sisters, some old friends and then Pamela. "You see this dress Pam is putting on in this picture? It is the same dress she had on the day she saw me off at the airport. You know, after I picked up my visa, I spent some days with Pam. It was on the morning of the third day that I got home. We had been at the beach the previous day and early the following morning as we were lying down in bed, I just got up and started putting on my clothes. "Where are you hurrying to?" Pam asked.

"For three days now, I've not been home. And I am due to travel in two days' time. I think I should go home. My parents were expecting me three days ago," I told her.

"Yes, it's true. I will come with you. I am sure mami must have missed you so much," said Pamela. Pamela and Jerry had lingered, ate breakfast and played a game called *dodging*, just the two of them, although this game actually requires three people. It was not until afternoon that they boarded a taxi to Jerry's family house in Bart town. By the time they got there, Jerry's parents, Mr and Mrs Asongbang, were sitting on the veranda of their house, eating fresh groundnuts and roasted fresh corn on the cob as they conversed. Theirs was an average home of educated parents according to Pays standards.

"Good afternoon, Mum," Jerry greeted.

"Mami, good afternoon, good afternoon, papa," Pamela followed suit.

"Jerry! Where have you been for the past three days? How could you just disappear like that into thin air?" Jerry's mother queried him.

"Won't you allow the young man to sit down first? Besides, don't you see he is with a guest?" said Dad to Mum as he shook hands with Pamela. "Welcome, my dear."

"Thank you, papa," Pamela said.

"Good afternoon, my girl," said Jerry's mother as she shook Pamela's hand. Then, Jerry moved closer to his mother.

"Mum, relax, Dad, see I have some good news for you people. First, before I forget, this is Pamela, my friend. Pamela, meet my Mum and Dad."

"Welcome my child," Jerry's parents said once more to Pamela.

"Thank you," Pamela answered back.

"So what good news do you have, Jerry?" Jerry's mother asked impatiently.

Jerry showed them his passport with the visa in it. His mother danced around happily while his father smiled happily. Jerry's two sisters, Maureen and Isabelle were attracted by the noise outside and so they rushed to the veranda from within. "Mum, what is it? Why are you so happy?" asked Maureen, Jerry's elder sister. On looking around, they saw Pamela, and both girls said welcome to her.

"Your brother has gotten a visa to go to Germany. Look at it in his passport," their mother, told them.

"Wao! Daddy, *arousé, arousé!*" Isabelle cried out.

Their father stood up with his face beaming with a smile and said, "O.k., o.k. let me look for *A-ROU-SE-MENT*. Come in, everybody. Come in, let's do a little celebration."

They all went into the living room and took their seats. Jerry sat in-between his parents. The two sisters sat together, with Pamela next to them. Dad got up and brought out some wine from the cupboard while Mum brought out some cake and some side-plates.

Pamela turning to Maureen and Isabelle said, "*Em...* Jerry told me a lot about you people. We were in a hurry, so I could not bring anything for you. Next time, for sure."

"No problem. It is okay, are you in U. B.?" Asked Maureen.

"Yes, and I live in Lower Custains Bart. You both can visit me whenever you have time," said Pamela. Isabelle merely stole a glance at Pamela without saying anything. Then, Mum served everyone some cake while Dad offered everyone a pint of wine. After a while, Pamela decided to take her leave and she and Jerry went to the roadside.

"*Sssip!*" Jerry called out. A taxi slowed down. "Lower Custains." The taxi man nodded and came to a halt. Closing the door on Pamela, Jerry paid her fare to the driver and waved as the car sped off.

The following day, Pamela got up very early in the morning and took a taxi to Jerry's place. She got there when only Jerry's mother had gotten up from bed; the others were still sleeping. She was behind the house as Pamela greeted her, shaking hands with her, and as usual offering the right hand and holding it with the left one. It is a great sign of respect to greet an elderly person in this fashion with both hands. Jerry's mother did not miss this as she thought to herself that her son had made a good choice. This act of respectfulness showed that Pamela was not only well brought up, but was also a good girl.

"What got you up so early from your bed, my dear?" Jerry's mother asked with a broad smile. Pamela, in a manner that could be interpreted as coy or shy depending on the interpreter, said, "Oh Mummy, I could not just continue to sleep when I thought of the whole bulk of work that you have in trying to prepare Jerry's things for travelling. I just thought I should come early and help."

"Thank you, my dear, that is so thoughtful of you," said Jerry's mother. "Come, put your bag in Jerry's room, I am sure he is already up. Let me see if your sisters are up also. Maureen-ne, I-sa-bel-la," she called out as she moved into the building and Pamela moved to the Boys' Quarters where Jerry's room was.

Pamela changed into casual attire, and when she came out, she helped Jerry's mother first with the preparation of the breakfast which consisted of omelette, bread and a warm *Bournvita* drink. She took Jerry's father's breakfast to the dining table in the sitting room and then hers and Jerry's to Jerry's room. Maureen and Isabelle had theirs on a table behind the house while Mum paced about munching a piece of bread as she tried to set the things ready for preparing what Jerry had to travel with.

After breakfast, Pamela helped Mum and Jerry's sisters in preparing items Jerry would travel with to Europe, which included *bitter leaf,* smoked fish, smoked meat, *eru, egusi,* crayfish, *ogwono, kwacoco bible* and even kola nuts. Pamela worked hard, washing the bitter leaf in the sink and spreading it under the sun, she ground the egusi and before Jerry's mother could notice it, she also spread the *eru* under the sun for conservation. It was noon when she asked Jerry's mother what they would have for lunch.

"I think we should be having *achu.* Jerry likes it a lot and he is going to miss it while abroad." As Jerry's mother and the two sisters fixed the *achu* cocoyams and put them in the pot, Pamela took the *achu* spices and grounded them on the pepper stone and thereafter she grounded the fresh pepper which Mum had kept by the side.

"Pamela, take care, that pepper is too hot. Let me do it myself. Don't strain yourself too much, take a rest," Jerry's mother cried out.

But Pamela barely smiled, saying, "Never mind mum, it is okay. I am good at doing kitchen work."

Jerry's mother was very impressed. She scolded her two daughters, "Do you see how a woman should be hard working? If it were you, you would complain about using a pepper stone. You would want to grind *achu* spices in a machine, forgetting to know that it spoils the taste. You children of nowadays, I wonder who would get married to you!"

Pamela stayed with Jerry and his family until Jerry's day of departure. On the last day, she helped in packing Jerry's box and bag and prepared the meal for the guests who came to wish Jerry farewell. While this went on, Jerry was in his room most of the time. Pamela went to keep him company from time to time and they lay down on the bed and conversed briefly.

Jerry had refused a very big send-off party to which he would invite all his friends, acquaintances and so many relatives. He feared that someone envious of him could set him up or make a direct report to the airport authorities that his tourist visa was a fake. Someone could even go to a *medicine-man* and tie him up with *boloh* or witchery in order for him not to travel. It was believed that when someone did this, something mysterious, uncalled for could happen all of a sudden that would hinder the journey. For instance, he might become seriously sick, maybe to the point of dying for as long as it took for the visa to be expired, say two weeks in some cases such as that of tourist visa.

At one time, a girl's mother wanted to visit her daughter in the United States when she had just given birth; the mother of this girl's husband was very envious. Although the baby was named after her and she too was invited to travel to America with the girl's mother, she was still very jealous of the fact that the girl's mother would be part of the spree. She rejected the invitation and it was later on rumoured that she went to a witch doctor and bewitched her son to become very poor in order not to have money for the mother-in-law's air ticket, nor money to feed the new born baby and its mother. The girl's mother, being a born again Christian, prayed and prayed and when one month of her visa was gone, the son-in-law finally got some money and she travelled to spend two months with the young family instead of three. These two months were months of hardship because the boy was afflicted again and again by hardship as his mother back home relentlessly worked hand in hand with several witch doctors to impede his progress. After working with witch doctors for a long time, this woman herself became a fortified witch. She started using these evil charms against other people, people whom she did not like. She manifested her evil at night when people were sleeping; she would appear as a ghost and sniff life out of them. Many people were said to have died overnight in their sleep, and even the doctors could not decipher the cause. One night, this woman tried to sniff life out of a neighbour whom she did not know was a stronger witch than her and this neighbour held the ghost hostage and tormented it. This delayed the ghost from returning, in order for her spirit to go back into her body. By the time the ghost returned at dawn, the body was dead and the spirit which was caught in the form of the ghost simply lingered around the corpse and the mourners.

Also, there was another story of a girl who envied her best friend who was about to travel and through witchcraft caused an accident which almost took her friend's life. She had confessed when she realised that the ploy to detain her friend backfired. The friend recovered partially and still succeeded to travel on time.

Jerry thought of all these stories and decided to keep the send-off party low. He invited just two of his friends, a paternal and maternal aunt with their families. Late in the evening, the party was over and the guests dispersed while Jerry and his family started for the airport in Commercial with an aunt, her husband and one of their sons.

Jerry and his entourage arrived at the airport in two cars and on time. As usual, the airport was busy. Cars drove in and out while travellers and other people moved in and out. Some moved about looking for something to steal while others were looking for clients whose luggage weighed above the required weight for travelling, yet some were there to see off or receive loved ones. Jerry's father and his cousin helped him with his luggage. After checking in his luggage, Jerry gave everyone a good-bye hug. While he hugged Pamela, she sobbed bitterly, removed her chain from around her neck, and put it on Jerry's neck, handing him a packet containing her pictures. Jerry finally checked into *SABENA*. His party waited for the plane to take off. After midnight, the plane finally took off and they all waved at the flying plane until it disappeared. Then they also left, driving out of the airport premises back to Bart.

After telling Andrew about how he finally took leave of his family and Pamela at the airport, Jerry held out the chain and kissed it. Andrew laughed, "Jerry you have not yet come out of Pays. Never mind, with time you will adjust." Jerry just laughed, shook his head and switched on one of the videos.

Later that day, when Nji returned, he brought home 500D-Mark from the *Chef* as Jerry's payment for the one week of work. Jerry was overjoyed as he took the money.

"One hundred and seventy thousand Francs CFA for just a week's work? This is unbelievable!" He handed out 150 D-Mark of the money to Andrew immediately as percentage for using his papers to work with and then gave Nji 100 D-Mark as settlement for a debt he owed him and finally put the rest of the money into his wallet and went with Andrew to his apartment where he made a telephone call to Pamela.

Twelve

Esisi

Pamela was in an old Land Rover toddling down the hills from Njase to Esisi. She struggled to make the mud on her shoes less visible with an old handkerchief. She and the other passengers had just finished trekking over a short distance to allow some stronger passengers to push the vehicle out of a gutter into which it got stuck on this muddy road. Sitting in front with two other passengers, she managed to make herself seem comfortable with one leg crossed over close to the driver's, so that the gear box was in-between her legs, and so the driver's right elbow brushed on her left breast each time he changed the gear or pretended to. The driver had personally chosen Pamela to sit there because it would be more comfortable for her than sitting behind with five other people or on the two benches facing each other at the rear of the vehicle with nine others. This was a special preference Mambo gave to beautiful girls who travelled in from the township, and moreover it was also better since Pamela was slim; for this would ease the driving a little bit.

Mambo was a very renown and popular driver who was loved, especially by his *motorboys* because, while they were loading the vehicle, he would just sit in a bar drinking beer, so they could collect tips for themselves from passengers with luggages even without his consent. All he needed was for them to call him when they had the right amount of passengers and the car fully loaded; then he would gulp down his last bottle of beer and set off for the road. He was a most excellent driver.

Sitting seemingly comfortable besides Mambo now, Pamela heard her mobile phone ringing. Everyone in the vehicle turned and looked at Pamela with admiration. Some looked at her intently just to see what a mobile phone looked like and tried to conjecture how this wireless machine worked. Others kept smiling at her as she answered the call, and as she said, "*Eh* J.J, how is Germany?," everyone was spellbound until one woman who was a primary school teacher broke the silence by telling the others in Pidgin English, "*a know yi, na ma friend ei man ei pikin,* Mr. Tah." By telling the people that she knew Pamela and that she was the daughter of her friend's husband, one would think Pamela was not the daughter of Mrs. Tah as well.

"Oh…oh, is she the one studying at the Bart University?" asked a male passenger.

"Yes," answered the school teacher.

"I didn't know she had grown this big. Children of nowadays, they grow so fast."

"Pamela is a big girl," said the teacher proudly in a way that one might mistake her for Mrs. Tah. By this time, Pamela had finished talking with Jerry. She asked Jerry to call her the following day in the evening.

The school teacher turned to her and asked in good English this time, "Are you through, my dear?"

"Yes, Miss," answered Pamela shyly. Mrs. Mandy, who was married with five kids, had always been referred to as "Miss" by the entire village as a sign of respect for the lettered school teacher.

By this time, the landrover had reached the market square where there was a signpost nailed to a big mango tree which read ESISI VILLAGE. The landrover drove round this tree and down into the village, and then it went one last time *vroom, vroom, crik, crik* and pulled to a halt at the centre of the village known as Three Corners. All the passengers alighted. Some carried their luggage and went upward in the direction from where the vehicle came from for they lived in Up Dey which meant up there, and some others trodded with their luggage to Down Dey or down there. From Three Corners one could see the street on which Pamela's family lived. This street was in-between Up Dey and Down Dey. It was called Brukaka. This was because a plantain stem once produced the fattest and longest bunch of plantain there in the days of Ahidjo. After alighting from the vehicle, Pamela also struggled with her luggage towards Brukaka.

Pamela's mother had gone to fetch water from the public tap, which, fortunately for them, was situated just in front of their house. The taps had dried up. The people could not understand why each time, after a heavy downpour of rain, the taps would suddenly dry up, and it would become very difficult to get even a drop of water. Pamela's mother watched as a little girl sucked and pulled at the mouth of the tap for water to come out in vain. Instead, the child spat out parts of a dead frog which included the limbs and a part of the head. "This is because it had rained heavily the previous day," Pamela's mother explained. The little animals and birds died as a result of this heavy rain and were swept by the rain water commonly referred to by the people as *water rain,* into the water cistern and then into the pipe of the taps.

"At least one can understand why all the taps often go dry in the dry season, but not in the rainy season," Pamela's mother said with a sigh. She sighed one more time and turned her head as she remembered that she had heard the sound of the landrover. Then, she saw Pamela from a distance. She immediately moved towards her house and shouted out for Pamela's junior sisters and brother who all came running to welcome her. Some of the neighbours also joined in welcoming her while others stood and stared with admiration. She walked with her siblings down to their compound. Her father was very pleased to see her. She unpacked her bag and gave her junior ones a parcel each and then she gave them some bread and sardine, which they took to their mother to be locked up for breakfast in a big wooden cupboard. No one left the towns to the village without at least some bread for those she or he loved.

The following day, Pamela went to the cocoa oven to visit Sone, her village lover. Sone was a handsome farmer whose handsomeness was already blemished by a lot of farm work. He used to be very intelligent in school, but due to poverty that resulted from an economic crisis shortly after a new President came to power, he could not continue his education but worked on his father's farm to make ends meet. He had "A" grades in eight subjects and "B" grades in two at the Ordinary Levels Examination. Looking at him, one could not tell if he was a man or a boy. In short, Sone was a Man-Boy - a man who never went through boyhood. Pamela handed Sone his own loaf of bread in a plastic bag and started conversing with this young but old farmer. The farmer tended his cocoa on the oven with a long wooden spatula.

After some flirtatious remarks about his muscles, Pamela teased him, "I hear there are a lot of new girls visiting the village this holiday."

"Besem stop it, you know I don't have an eye for any other woman but you," Sone said. Pamela started to laugh.

"Did you receive the money I sent?" he asked.

"Oh yes. In fact, that money helped me a lot. Thanks a million."

"How is school?"

"School is fine," Pamela answered.

"How is your mother?"

"She is doing fine, she went to the farm, I am sure she is back now."

After conversing with Sone at length, Pamela said she was leaving. She told Sone that she would need some money for her upkeep. She needed it for her body lotion and for her hairdo as well. This, Sone promised to give her as soon as he sold his cocoa to the vendors.

"So, where would you like me to take you to on Sunday?" Sone asked.

"I don't want us to go to Central Bar, but to Mr Michè's Bar in Down Dey. Central Bar is too close to our house; my father can storm in at any time. You know him, don't you?"

Sone laughed. "He sometimes behaves as if he will be the one to marry you."

Pamela and Sone concluded to meet at Mr. Michè's bar in two days time after church service to share a drink. Mr. Michè was actually a Francophone from the Western Province who migrated to Esisi like many others. He owned a petty shop and a bar. Actually, he was Monsieur Jean-Marie. The villagers did not know that *Monsieur* is a title; they thought it was his first name and decided to call him by it. They ended up twisting it to Michè because they found it too difficult to pronounce the word *Monsieur*.

Pamela strolled slowly back home. On reaching their compound, her father was sitting in front of their house as usual in a wooden armchair. Pamela greeted him in the vernacular, *"Papa afor zie?* Papa, did you stay?" This was a way of saying good afternoon or good evening in Papa's language.

The father responded angrily in Pidgin English saying to Pamela. *"Wusai you comot?"*

"A comot for see ma friend way ei di dry ei kaka for oven." Pamela told the father exactly where she was coming from.

Papa was angrier and said, *"Which friend? Which kaka? Na ya kaka?* Is it your cocoa, *eh*? I have told you, I don't want you mingling with these village boys, you will not listen. You said you were going to Swimming and now you say you are coming from the oven. Come on, go behind there and help your mother with the cooking. B.A. holder, my foot!"

Actually Pamela forgot that she had told her junior sister to lie to their father that she had gone to fetch water from a nearby stream called Swimming. When the taps failed, this was where the villagers went to fetch water. It was called Swimming because in real life people swim in streams and rivers.

Pamela's father charged after her, insulting her with every day common insults in his vernacular, "May you be struck down by thunder! May your intestines be plagued by wounds! You idiot, stupid, nonsense!"

Pamela ran to the back of the house as her father returned to take his usual position in front of the house. Pamela grumbled,"I am a graduate. I know what to do and what not to do. I am a big girl; you keep on wanting to control my life. I don't like it, I don't li…"

As she was standing between the main building and the kitchen building, her mobile phone started to ring. "Hello! Hello! Oh Jerry darling, how are you? How is *Bundes*? I know you people are enjoying yourselves over there," Pamela said.

"Everything is fine. Everything is o.k. So how are you doing? I miss you so much Pam," Jerry said.

"Oh darling, I miss you too. How much I long to be there with you. Darling, when am I coming over?"

"Don't worry, you will come soon. Everything is fine. Just take good care of yourself."

"Oh yes I will do. The things you sent me were very beautiful. I saw the money too. Everyone is so impressed by you. I even talked to my father about you," Pamela lied. "Please speak with my mother. Mami, Mami, come and take, it's Jerry," Pamela cried out.

Her mother jumped out of the kitchen shouting at one of Pamela's junior sisters who was standing in her way, "Get out of my way, lest your vagina sting!" The sister stepped to the side and then hurried after the mother. The mother took the phone from Pamela anxiously and started talking "Hello my son, how are you? Pam has been telling me about you. How about your place? You people call it *Bundes*?"

"Yes, Mum. This place, it's a paradise. It is so different from our place there. Totally different," Jerry answered.

Then, the mother went on saying, "You are a big *man-o-o. Ehe-* next time when you are sending Pam things, try to send me something *too-o-o.*"

"Oh yes, Mum, I will do. That is no problem. Pam told me about your back ache, I will send some money for the treatment," Jerry was pleased to say.

Then, Pamela's mother said, "O.k. my son, stay well, let me hand you over to Pam." She handed the phone back to Pamela and returned to the kitchen. The sister pleaded to speak to Jerry on the phone. Just then Pamela saw her father coming from the main house to meet them; she seized the phone from her sister who was struggling to talk to Jerry and ran to the back of the kitchen.

"Come back here, Besem! I say come here, lest you drown in blood!" Pamela disappeared to the back of the kitchen. Then Papa turned to Mami, "And you, this woman! I have warned you to talk to your daughter. How can somebody be in Europe, hundreds of miles away and have a woman in Pays? Are there no girls in Germany? How can you separate from a woman for a long time and still call her your own? These young men of nowadays, I don't understand how they do their own things. This is what happened when Mr Nyanga's daughter who had a fiancé abroad suddenly brought shame to the family when the boy came back and found her pregnant for another man.

"Who is this boy?" Mami asked.

"Don't you know the one who brought Mr. Nyanga that bicycle he is using from overseas? I have told you woman, if you and your daughter want to bring disgrace onto me, it will not work. Not to me, Tah. It will not work!" He moved away saying, "It will not work! To disgrace me, Tah? No way!"

66

Thirteen

DJ Wanted

Ever since Jerry missed his parents on the phone and planned to call some other time, he had not done so. Weeks had passed when he decided to visit Andrew to talk to his family. He called the house phone and got his sister Maureen on the phone. "Hello Mau."

"Hello, J.J.," Maureen was excited. "How are you doing?"

"I am fine, I am fine. Where is Dad?"

"He is right here. Let me hand you over to him."

"Hello, Dad, I just want to greet you people. In fact, things are hard."

"Is that so my son?" asked the father.

"It's really hard to regularise one's stay here. And it's even harder finding a job. I just get thrown out of jobs because I can't even speak the language. If I succeed to get a job, I will save some money to come down in December to fix my student papers."

"Take it easy, God will bless you. Your mother is not home. She has gone for a meeting in church. Just like I said, don't kill yourself, if there is nothing to send to us, no problem."

"Greet Mum when she comes. My regards to Isabelle."

"Yes, I will greet them and just like I said, don't kill

yourself. If there is nothing to send to us, we are fine.Okay good bye."

"Bye Dad," Jerry hung up.

Maureen, who had been eavesdropping, grumbled as she went to join Isabelle in their room. "Nothing to send to us. Meanwhile, I saw that girl Pamela and she showed me a lot of things from you."

After the phone call, Andrew blamed Jerry for calling Pays to say that things were hard. "That's not the way we operate here, Jerry. What happens here remains here. By the way, would you like to work in an Indian restaurant for 10 D-Mark per hour?"

"What kind of job is that?" Jerry asked, less interested in Andrew's previous statement.

"What else can it be? If you hear of an Indian restaurant, just know it is to work on the Turn Table, especially if you are a new employee. Anyway, some people are lucky and get promoted even right up to the position of a cook," Andrew told Jerry.

"Is that so? Then, I like the job. I don't even need to be a cook. What for? Playing music is more fun to me. I mean I can do the DJ work," Jerry said.

Andrew barely looked at Jerry and smiled pensively. "Get ready, and let me take you to the place."

Jerry hurriedly dressed up and within an hour's time they were at the Indian restaurant. Andrew introduced him to the owner of the restaurant who was a young Indian man.

"*Versteht der Deutsch?*" the man asked.

"*Nur ein bißchen,*" Andrew replied.

"*Dann zeige ihm seine Arbeit in der Küche.*"

Andrew took Jerry behind a counter to a brief, stuffed and not too tidy kitchen. On one side of the sink, was a pile of big white plates, which almost touched the roof. Jerry was perplexed as Andrew pointed to the pile with a big grin on his face.

"See! You have to take a plate from the pile, put it in the soapy water in this first sink, wash it very fast and then drop it in this other sink filled with clean water where you will rinse off the soap and put it out here to dry. In addition, you have to be fast and very swift; if you are not you will have the plates touching the roof, because many customers are still to come. So enjoy the music and see you. I have to go."

Andrew left; Jerry watched him leave, took a deep breath and started washing the plates. At first slowly, but then more and more plates kept coming in and so he unconsciously increased his speed.

Jerry worked for two months in this restaurant. He worked ten hours a day and almost every day, he took some food back home such as rice and curry sauce. He had become so fond of the place that he smelled of Indian spices and curry sauce. Jerry was therefore sad when he was told that his job will end by the end of the week. Although the money was not enough to take him to Pays to prepare a student visa for himself and bring Pamela over, it could tide him along for some time. Jerry's phone rang as he was pondering on these events and he picked it up absently.

"Hello! Big man. What's up?" he asked Nji on phone.

"Man, there is a job opportunity somewhere."

"O.k. Thank you. This Teller *waschen* job is soon getting to an end," Jerry told Nji.

"Yes, Ford is recruiting workers to meet up with the order they have for this year. So just call on Andrew for his *Ersatz lohnsteuerkarte* and you will give him just 30% in the end as usual," Nji told Jerry.

"How much is Ford paying?" Jerry asked, not believing his luck.

"25 D-mark per hour," said Nji.

"Wao! That's great. I will collect the number from you on my way home and meet Andrew to make the call," Jerry was very excited.

Jerry, Nji, Akwi, and many other African students, students from Japan, Bulgaria, Russia, Mongolia, Vietnam, China and several other parts of the world as well as German students were working for Ford because it was summer holidays. Their job was to assist in every stage of car assembling such as fitting in the doors and electrifying the cars. They worked in shifts and went on break in shifts as well.

"I hear the wages for this month have been sent to our accounts." Jerry asked Nji one day over lunch.

"Yes. I have already taken out the statement of account."

"How much is it?" Jerry asked. "About 5.000 D-Mark.You know, with all the night-shifts and over-time," Nji replied.

Jerry lifted up his two feet excitedly. "And this is just the first month. We still have two months to go. *Massa, money dey dis land - o!* There is money in this country!"

"No. No. No. No. No! You have to be careful the way you look at some of these things," Nji warned Jerry. "This is something that happens just once in a very great while. So the better use you make of the money, the better for you," Nji cautioned him.

"You are very right; I will go to Pays after this, fix my papers and bring over my queen, my Chantal. At least that's something substantial. Thank God I also saved some money from the restaurant job."

"Suit yourself, suit yourself, it's your *dough*," Nji replied. "After all, you were big enough to board a flight to Deutschland all alone."

Fourteen
Jarmann Wander

Jerry was about five weeks old in Pays when he drove in a fairly used MERCEDES BENZ with Pamela sitting on the co-driver's seat into the premises of the famous *Mboma* and Girls Snack Bar/ Restaurant/ Night Club in Bart. There were many people sitting on the premise of the snack bar drinking, smoking and conversing. There were women roasting fish as usual. Jerry parked his car right at the entrance to the snack bar to ensure that everyone saw him alight. There was loud Techno music coming out from his car. He stepped out of the car, leaving the driver's door conspicuously open, went round and opened the door for Pamela. He took her out and kissed her passionately. Two friends who lived in Pays approached and greeted him admirably. He opened the trunk of his car and took out a bottle of wine, opened it and started drinking. Cigarette in one hand, bottle in the other, he struggled to kiss Pamela at the same time. Some more friends joined them and they all took their seats by a large table. Then, Jerry looked at one of the friends and said, "Hey you! Jack, when are you also going to buy drinks for us? You only know how to move about drinking from others. "

Jack who was not as well dressed as Jerry in a suit looked at the latter sheepishly, looked to the ground and then looked away trying uncomfortably to force a smile. Jerry ordered drinks for everyone as he continued talking to his friends. This time he complained about the weather. "Ah! This country is very hot."

He took out some Deutschmark notes from his pocket, stood up and waved them at the boys proudly. "Can someone go and buy me a fan right now? I need a fan right here where I am standing. There seems to be no sky in this part of the world. My country is not this hot, no, not at this time of the year; December, every place is covered with snow," he laughed.

Suddenly, a boy called Metuge who was also from Germany saw Jerry from a short distance and shouted out "Berlin *und* Brandenburg!" as he moved to shake hands with Jerry. Another old acquaintance of Metuge who used to live in the same *quartier* as him before he travelled to Europe saw him and rushed to him with a big smile on his face.

"Long time, *amueh, chan?*" the guy greeted.

Metuge simply gave him a cold look and turned to Jerry, "*Wie geht es dir?*"

"*Danke, gut. Und to du auch?*" Jerry answered.

"*Na ja, es geht,*" Metuge responded

Metuge's girlfriend recognised Pamela as a member of the Bundes Girls group to which she belonged. She went to Pamela and gave her a peck on the cheek. The Bundes Girls were a certain group of female students from the Bart University who had connections in *Die Bundesrepublik Deutschland*, especially boyfriends and fiancés and a few others who had connections elsewhere abroad. They met each week to discuss about their connections abroad. During such meetings, these girls drank only wine and nothing less. They talked about when they last received a call or a letter from their darlings. They worked on a continuous assessment of what life was like in Germany, based on what they were told over the phone or read in the letters they received.

"My own told me that, there, everyone is so busy. Everyone has his apartment furnished with a TV set, a radio set, furniture etc. All of which can just be picked up from the streets if you are not interested in buying. Early in the morning, everyone is gone to work and comes back late in the evening," one girl had explained to the others.

"Mine told me that the pay packages are very high and during weekends they used to gather in one person's apartment to have fun, drinking wine, champagne and very expensive beer such as BECK'S beer," another tipped in.

"When I get there, the car I would love to have is VW Golf, I hear it is the latest design from the Volkswagen Company," said another.

The girls would talk and talk at length; they could not stop imagining when their lovers would take them over to Germany. They planned on an improved dressing pattern, hairdo and expensive make-ups they would love to have. These girls, the Bundes Girls, were very popular on campus.

"I didn't see you at the last Bundes Girls Meeting," Metuge's girlfriend said to Pamela while their two boyfriends were busy with their own conversation.

"I travelled to Samedi to see my parents," Pamela lied, as always trying not to identify with Esisi village.

After conversing with Jerry and Pamela, Metuge and his girlfriend took their leave while Jerry continued talking to his admiring friends. "I hear the party tonight has been annulled, *das ist es tut mir leid; ist schuldigung sie bitte. Nah? Nicht wahr? Mann---oh!*" he exclaimed and laughed loud as he took his seat and kissed Pamela.

Just then, all of them were distracted by a brawl at one corner of the bar. A boy in high temper was talking bitterly and wanting to fight. His two friends held him back.

"Look at me these *Bush-Fallers!*" What do they think they are? You think because you have been to Europe or America, you can snatch my girlfriend just like that? Can you imagine this, simply because he is a *Jarmann Wander*?" the boy complained.

"Calm down, man. I think we should be blaming our greedy girls and not the *Bush-Fallers,*" his friend told him.

"I support your idea, you are right," said another friend."

The friend's girlfriend said, "I like my fellow sisters. I mean, I trust them; for as soon as the *Bush-Fallers'* money is finished, they will give them a kick in the ass. Although, there are some silly ones who will allow themselves to be deceived by the *Bush-Fallers* with fake promises of marrying and taking them abroad."

"Shut up your mouth," her boyfriend shouted at her. "Since when did you become an expert on *Bush Fallers'* affairs? I see, you want to look for your own *Bush-Faller* too, not so? Go ahead, go ahead and get yourself one."

"Is that what I said?" the girl asked angrily.

"Look here, let me tell you this today, if I hear or notice any foul play between you and any *Faller*, know it's over between us. Don't think I will go about fighting like Samba is doing!"

After a few rounds of drinks with his friends, Jerry took Pamela in his car and they drove home to meet Jerry's family. Jerry and Pamela came in, greeted everyone warmly and sat down. Then Jerry stood up.

"Dad, Mum, this is Pamela whom you all know already and I want to say that I would be taking her to Germany."

"So, you want to take Pamela to Germany?" asked his father.

"Yes, Daddy." Jerry explained to his father that Pamela and himself would work hard in Germany, gather some money and come back in a few years time to get married.

"Ours will be the wedding of the year. Is that not so, Pam?"

"Yes, really," answered Pamela.

"You are welcome, my girl," said Jerry's father.

"Thank you, Daddy," Pamela said

"But why have you never paid us a visit ever since Jerry travelled?" asked Jerry's father.

"She used to come sometimes. It's just that she has never met you at home," Jerry's mother cut in before Pamela could say a word.

"Is that so? Ah!"

"Yes, Daddy," Pamela acknowledged.

"Who did you say your parents are? Where do they live, what tribe are you?" asked Jerry's mother impatiently.

"We live in.... My uncle lives here in Bart, in Prisso. He is a journalist at radio Bart," Pamela stammered.

"A journalist? What's his name?" the father asked.

"Mr. Peter Agbor, he is my mother's younger brother."

"I know him. And your real father?" The mother cut in sharply.

"Pam's parents live in Esisi," Jerry put in defensively. "Ah, you won't know the place. Esisi village, it is a nice place. The people there are very nice as you will come to know them." There was dead silence and then Jerry's mother, still looking unsatisfied, got up and went to the kitchen while Maureen followed her. Mum and Maureen returned with drinks and food on a tray. Jerry invited Pamela to the dining table and they ate quietly. While they ate, Maureen and Isabelle were in their room.

Isabelle had eavesdropped to Pamela's conversation with her parents from the corridor. "That girl looks so unreal to me," she told her sister.

"What do you mean by unreal?" the sister asked.

"She looks like a schemer."

"What do you mean?"

"Didn't you take note she was hiding the fact that her parents are some poor wretched people in a bush village?" Isabelle said.

"Isabelle! Watch your tongue," the sister cautioned. "How dare you insult someone's parents?"

"Okay! I am sorry. But if my opinion is sought after, Jerry shouldn't marry that gold digger."
"Where did you see a mine? Ain't no mines around here, no gold mine. And, fair enough, no one seeks a kid's opinion when marriage matters are sorted out."

"A kid? Is that your opinion of me?"

"See, Isabelle, Jerry has made his choice and that's it. He is the one who is going to be spending the rest of his life with the girl and not any of us. So just leave him alone. You are a woman, one day you will meet your man and if someone becomes prejudicial, will that be fair? Think about it."

When they finished eating, Pamela took the used plates to the kitchen. When she returned, Jerry was sitting with his parents in their bedroom. So, Pamela waited on the veranda for him. Dad sat on a stool opposite Jerry and his mother who were sitting on the bed. He cleared his throat and began.

"So, my son, have you thought carefully before spending all the money you are giving out on this girl? Are you sure this girl really loves you? Because these young girls of nowadays are not to be trusted."

"Dad, I am sure she loves me. In fact I love her very much. And I'll very much love to do anything to keep her to myself," Jerry said.

"The question is not whether you love her and you are ready to do anything. The point is whether she loves and will always love you, no matter the condition. In my own opinion, you should look for a nice girl there in Germany, struggle together with her and make a good life and future with her. But if you insist that you want just this Pamela girl, then no problem. I just want you to think carefully and be very careful. Remember, you are coming from Europe. No woman will deny you. They will think you have money and will accept you even if they don't love you."

Jerry thought hard, cleared his throat and said, "Yes Dad, I have heard. She is a very good girl. In fact, you need to see the letters she wrote to me while I was abroad; they were so full of emotion and concern."

It was clear to Jerry that his family had misgivings about Pamela but he was intent on fighting for his love. He thought it his duty to encourage his family to like his wife to be.

Jerry moved out of his parents' bedroom and called out for Maureen and Isabelle as he went to join Pamela while Maureen and Isabelle joined them out front. Jerry, Pamela, Maureen and Isabelle were about to get into the car. Maureen opened the door to the back seat. But Pamela cried out, "No! *Grandsoeur* let me get behind. You have to ride in front." Pamela and Isabelle sat behind while Maureen sat in front. They drove off to a nightclub in Vick Town.

As they were in the nightclub dancing, some men who knew Pamela beckoned her and even tried to dance with her, but she behaved as if she had never known nor seen them in her entire life. They danced all night, met some old friends and had great fun.

It was not until early on Sunday that they left the nightclub and drove back to Bart. They were too tired to go to church and slept all day long to Jerry's mother's annoyance. She hated it when her kids didn't go to church. Sometimes she left the house earlier than them but she had a way of knowing if they came to church or not. She would always sit in the front row and when it was time for alms, she would look out attentively to see if all her children would walk up to the altar. Failure to do so meant absenteeism. This meant punishment to go and work on a small farm she owned.

But this time around, it was an exceptional case of absenteeism and so she did not even mention their absence from church at all.

On Monday, Pamela finally picked up her visa to travel to Germany. She and Jerry travelled to Esisi to bid Pamela's family farewell. When Sone heard of the news that Pamela had come with a husband to the village, he collapsed. Pamela's entire family was very impressed and gave Pamela and Jerry their blessings. They travelled back to Bart with Pamela's mother.

Didier, who had heard it rumoured that Pamela was having what he termed an affair with a *Bush Faller,* had sent Pamela a *bushitting* letter immediately after he got the confirmation from Pamela's friend. In the letter, he wrote, "And your friend has confirmed it to me." But he did not mention the name of the friend. Pamela was angry with this unfinished information; she very much wanted to find out the name of this betrayer. This was certainly a bad friend and she needed to discard her. Didier, thinking Pamela wanted to ask for reconciliation, refused to grant her any audience when she requested to see him. Pamela simply sighed and waved the matter off while she continued to celebrate her *Bush falling*.

Mr. E was very happy for Pamela and they celebrated in their usual hotel room, in their usual special way. "You never told me you liked going abroad. Do you think that would have been more than me to do for you, my little baby?" Mr. E asked.

"No Daddy, I wasn't quite sure how you would have felt about it."

"Make sure you keep in touch with me when you get there, o.k."

"Yes, of course I will," Pamela answered.

Mr. E gave Pamela 300,000 CFA Francs as a parting gift. Pamela gave some of this money to her mother, put some in envelopes for her junior sisters and brother and then she used the rest to pay for her Rasta hairdo and buy a few things she thought she might need immediately once she got to Germany. A few days later, Pamela's mother, her uncle and Jerry's parents and his sisters saw the pair off at the Commercial International Airport.

Fifteen

Tegel to Ferdinand Thomas

Swiss Air touched down at exactly 10am on one fine spring morning at the *Flughafen* Tegel. Jerry and Pamela checked out by the Customs Officers. They pulled their baggage towards the exit.

"Put on this jacket. It's cold outside," Jerry said, offering Pamela a jacket.

"Thanks, darling," Pamela said as she moved sluggishly behind Jerry to board a taxi. Jerry and Pamela sat on the back seat of the taxi.

"Are you okay?" Jerry asked.

"Yes darling."

As the taxi drove along, Pamela stared out the window. She was visibly happy. She leaned on Jerry's shoulder as she marvelled at the infrastructure and the entire atmosphere. Presently, she kissed Jerry as a way of expressing her love for him and her appreciation of him. Jerry smiled back at her.

"Are you happy?" he asked.

"More than happy, and it's all because of you darling, thank you so much, - love you."

"I love you too, baby. I am more than happy that I can make you happy. I told you, I'll bring you over and here we are. Pamela simply smiled, closed her eyes and leaned on Jerry's shoulder.

The taxi finally stopped at the last traffic light, turned left and then turned right in front of the student hostel Ferdinand Thomas in Storkowerstrasse. *"Welche Hausnummer nochmal?"* The driver asked. *"Hier ist richtig,"* Jerry said. The taxi came slowly to a halt. Jerry and Pamela alighted from the taxi, Jerry paid the driver and they moved into the student hostel building, took the elevator on to the fourth floor and then moved down to the third floor where Jerry's apartment was. The elevator stopped only at the second, fourth, sixth, eighth and tenth floor; a kind of Two Times Table.

Before leaving for Pays, Jerry had found himself a room in the same hostel where Nji and his other friends lived. A room became available when a friend decided to save money by moving in with another friend, and Jerry took the opportunity to have his room for himself.

Jerry opened the door and Pamela immediately found herself standing in the middle of a brief corridor, which led briefly on both sides to two brief rooms facing each other. On the corridor, there was also a mini-kitchen facing the door to the toilet and bathroom. Jerry's was a one-room apartment in a two- room *Wohngemeinschaft*. At one end of the corridor was a sofa with a small table in front of it. Jerry put their luggage near this small table, opened the door to his room and then took the luggage inside. He also helped Pamela inside with the box she was pulling. In Jerry's room was a bed, a wardrobe, a sofa and a table, a mirrored dressing cupboard, a TV and a musical set in their appropriate places. The place looked well arranged and clean.

"So! At last, here we are. You are heartily welcome to Germany. Feel free here. Here is your home," Jerry said to Pamela.

Pamela looked around the tiny room critically and sneeringly. She sat down on the sofa and a feeling of disappointment swept over her, which later on turned to annoyance and finally to anger against Jerry. She stared outside through the window for a while and then, after it seemed she had made up her mind over something, she screamed rudely at Jerry, "please can I have my bath?" Jerry who did not notice her all this while because he was busy unpacking their luggage lifted up his head with a start.

"Of course dear, you can. But come let me show you around first, although there is not much to be seen."

"Eh! I do not have time for that. I am terribly tired! Please just show me the bathroom," she retorted.

"Okay, dear. Pam! Pam!" Jerry tried to smile. Pamela frowned, opened her box, picked up a few things, and Jerry led her to the bathroom door and started to move away. Pamela tried to open the door but the door would not open. She became restless as she went back into the room.

"Where is the key? I mean, . . . the bathroom door, it's locked. "

"Oh! Sorry, just hold on for a while, my flatmate is using it," Jerry said as he tried to point at the neighbour's door sheepishly. Pamela sighed long and took in a deep breath.

"You see, never mind, we will soon move out of this place to where we would not have to share the bathroom with other people. In fact, I hope to make some money as soon as possible." Pamela did not react nor say anything. She looked at Jerry indifferently. Jerry stopped and thought hard and then walked into the room to continue unpacking their luggage.

Jerry hated the feeling of inadequacy. It reminded him of how he and his family used to struggle to live comfortably with the coming of economic crisis in Pays when a new President took over power. Economic crisis or *crise économique* started like a joke in Pays, but before the people knew it, it became fashionable and embedded in their spirits. This was especially the case when the President confirmed in an official speech that there was an economic crisis. This provided husbands who did not want to provide for their families with a way out. It gave youths who did not want to work hard a way out. It also gave young girls who wanted to go after more than one man, both young and old, a way out. This was a kind of *motif* everyone took to escape being responsible. As the economy went worse, some few thinking ones started to ponder over the *crise économique* through newspapers. They came up with facts that proved that the former President had printed a lot of counterfeit money and on coming to power, the new President burnt all the fake currency and there was bound to be economic crisis. The people had wondered as they felt the pinch of the economic crisis if it were not better to have kept that President who printed out counterfeit, whether or not this led to inflation they didn't care, after all, when that President, that omnipotent papa ate, there were crumbs from his table and everyone was happy. "He was a real father," they started saying. The people, Jerry's people most especially, talked about those good old days in beer parlours. Each time the pinch of this crisis almost led them into a revolt there would be some economic development in the brewery sector of the economy that would re-enkindle their hope. However, 'the thinkers' did not bother to think out properly for how long the economy would remain *crazed;* or after having analysed its causes in newspapers, to start analysing solutions, suggesting solutions as real researchers ought to do.

It was amidst all this that teachers, including Jerry's mother, had their salaries reduced in order to replenish the military sector for internal and not for external use. It was because of all this that there was a fall in the prices of cocoa and coffee and Pamela's school fees and up-keep needed subsidization. It was because of all this that Jerry realised it was a crime for him to have read *Lettre Moderne Anglais* at the University. It was because of this that he realised he belonged to a minority in a nation he loved and would always love. He used to wonder what would have been his fate if only the Germans had stayed on, or had at least returned when they promised they would. He used to tell his friends that, as a child, he had read it somewhere that Adolf said he loved Pays. He was certain that although everything began with the institutionalization of *crise économique*, there wouldn't have been any *crise* anyway, that is, if only at least the Germans had not left untimely, at least that.

During hard times in his family, Jerry would make up

his mind to work harder in life so as never to find himself in any tight situation. He cursed himself for not thinking about a bigger place before travelling to Pays to bring Pamela. On the other hand, he thought, he would not have had enough money then to follow up on his visa and Pamela's as well. He merely sighed and told himself that it was nothing to worry about. Eventually, he would make the money and they would move into a bigger apartment.

Pamela finally had her bath. She wanted to brush her teeth and wash her mouth from the wash hand basin, but realised that their neighbour had put his dirty plates and cutlery, which he planned to wash later, in the basin. She looked very disgruntled as she came back into the room. Whilst applying lotion on her body, she hid her body from Jerry by covering herself with a loincloth.

Jerry was surprised, "You are very interesting. Why are you covering yourself with a *wrapper*? Are you feeling cold?" Pamela looked at him sneeringly and grumbled something he couldn't quite understand. He couldn't decipher what was making Pamela so agitated, but he knew there was something wrong. He planned to take his time to come to that. So, for the meantime, he planned to throw a welcome party for Pamela, hoping that she would be impressed by it.

Sixteen
A Welcome Party

It was about 9pm and there was music, dancing, drinking, and eating. People moved in and out, chatting with one another in Jerry's little apartment. Akwi helped in the serving of food and drinks; she was assisted by a friend of hers called Marie. Some minutes later, the music was turned down and Jerry moved to the centre of the room. He cleared his throat and started, "Good evening everyone and welcome. I thank you all for being here tonight to welcome my future wife to the land. Right now, I will love to introduce to you the future Mrs. Asongbang." Jerry held out his hand to Pamela who walked up to the middle of the room and stood by him.

"So this is Pamela Besem Tah. You can call her Pam or Besem and why not Mrs. Asongbang. So once more, you are welcome. Enjoy yourselves."

Everyone in the room started clapping and shouting out praises to Jerry as Pamela took her place with Jerry's close friends who conversed with her. She responded reluctantly to their numerous questions about herself and Pays for her mind was not there with them in spite of the praises they showered on her to keep her happy. She was busy stealing looks and glances at the boys who came in. Then, her eyes fell on Agwe, who looked a little bit over-dressed for the occasion. She looked at him, their eyes met and she smiled. Agwe was a Paysan entrepreneur of about thirty-two years of age. He owned a telephone kiosk and an Audi 80. Agwe quickly looked around and walked up to Pamela, shook hands with her, and while he did this, he scratched her palm with his index finger most secretly. She gave him a smile of encouragement. Agwe walked about, greeted a few friends, took a can of drink, opened it and took a sip. All along, he eyed Pamela who smiled back secretly. Then he loitered around briefly and went out to the staircase. Pamela followed him with her eyes, loitered around too and followed him. As Agwe was putting a piece of paper, with his telephone number on it into Pamela's hand, someone let out a shout.

"Pamela! Come back here," Akwi screamed as she hurried down the staircase to where Agwe and Pamela were standing.

Pamela turned around abruptly with a big grin on her face and defensively said, "He's just a family friend. I was asking after his sister, my very good friend." Akwi took Pamela back into the room while Agwe continued down the stairs and rode off in his car.

The party, however, continued in a festive mood. After some hours, people started taking their leave, most of them shaking hands with Pamela and Jerry. At last, only Pamela and Jerry were left. Jerry moved about picking up bottles and used plates here and there. And while he washed the utensils in the toilet/bathroom, Pamela sat on the sofa very relaxed with her attention focused on a late night erotic show on television. It was amazing to her to watch the naked women and listening to their voices saying all the time, "*drei, drei, eins, ruf an.*" She was puzzled at first but then figured out that the ladies were asking men to call them on those numbers. She was really fascinated and somewhat grateful for the fact that she had become a part, no matter how tiny, of a society in which all these things and a lot more she still hoped to see were taking place. Jerry finished washing the plates and tidying up the place. Immediately he stepped into the room, Pamela changed the channel.

At last, it was time to go to bed; Jerry had a shower, came back and putting on a pair of boxer shorts, he yawned.

"It has been a great day. Let's go and sleep, baby." But Pamela pretended as if she did not hear him. She focused her gaze on the screen half-absentmindedly. Jerry walked over and sat down beside her.

"Darling, aren't you coming to bed?" he asked.

"I am not feeling sleepy yet. *Ahhh!*" Pamela, who was bored by the question, retorted.

Jerry stood up slowly and then, thinking hard, he said, "in that case, I will wait for you." Pamela barely threw a glance at him. He sat down once more and waited silently for some time and then said, "You mean you are not yet tired after all this bustling?" He tried to smile, but no answer came from Pamela who simply stared at the TV screen and made faces. "Okay let me just go and lie down a bit. I am waiting for you," Jerry said and went to bed. Pretending to be half asleep, Pamela said "Oh, yes, go to bed, I am joining you shortly." Jerry went to bed.

Pamela looked around and made sure that Jerry was already asleep. She stood up, put on her pyjamas, a slumber net around her head, a pair of socks, and then tiptoed to the backside of the bed making sure not to wake Jerry up. She climbed into bed and went to the extreme edge, covering all her body including her head. It was only at dawn when he got up to prepare for church service that Jerry realised Pamela was in bed.

Seventeen
Work

It was Monday morning and Jerry had to go to work while Pamela was still asleep. He put on a suit, carried a business bag and a KaDeWe plastic bag. Then, touching Pamela gently on her back, he said, "*Darling*! I'm going to work. Darling, darling, I will see you later in the evening." Pamela stirred from her sleep and gazed at Jerry in the suit and business bag and then the plastic bag caught her attention.

"What's in that plastic bag?" she managed to ask half asleep.

"Oh! Some *eh..........eh...* con – consignments for the office," Jerry stammered.

"Oh! I see; materials you are going to use in your office."

"Oh yes," Jerry responded with a smile. He took Pamela's hand, kissed it and hurried to work.

When Jerry arrived at his work place, he stopped and quickly took a full view of his entire jobsite, which was a construction site with debris here and there, machines used for breaking down walls and so on and so forth. Then his eyes settled on his two friends who were already there. His friends on their part did not recognise him at first. When they realised it was him; they were amazed at his attire. They came forward to meet him in their work clothes, looking at him in surprise. "Jerry, good morning! Aren't you working today?"

Nji greeted.

"Of course I am," Jerry, answered. Jerry hurried off, shook hands with the other boy and headed straight to the changing room as the boys followed him with a questioning stare. When he returned in his usual work attire, Nji asked him if he slept out the previous night. "Me! No, no. Sleep out for what!?" Jerry was angry.

Chuckling, Nji asked, "Then why, why were you..., I mean why the suit?" Jerry looked around and then walked up to Nji, very close so the other boy would not hear. "You know...," Jerry explained his reason why he had the suit on. This didn't satisfy Nji who became even more curious. When he had finished explaining, Nji looked up at his stressed up countenance and was surprised.

Nji was further surprised at the content of Jerry's lunch pack during break as the trio settled down away from the others, who were mostly Mongolians and a few Germans. "Come off it, man, you are working this hard and cannot afford to get yourself even a good meal?"

The other boy was eating a chunk of roast pork and *Pommes frites* with ketchup, drinking 100% apple juice. The boy looked at Nji's home-prepared meal and exclaimed, "Wao! Nji the boy. E*i fine for people dem way dem get wife oh.*"

"I've told you to get married, what are you waiting for?" Nji teased him.

"Ah! Marriage!" the Boy exclaimed as he eyed Jerry's meagre meal. "Okay, is Jerry married or not?" he asked.

"Yes, of course. Just like him and Pam, we can say that Akwi and I are married too. Although we have not gone in for any formal marriage rites, we know in our hearts that we are married," Nji replied.

"That's quite interesting, people getting married in their hearts. What is it like, getting married –did you say by hearts or in the hearts, sorry, heart, because they are now one, *oder?*"

"What I mean is that we are living together and assisting each other where necessary and possible. I mean, you don't take a girl and start living with her when you know you cannot or are not going to marry her," Nji explained.

"Why not?" the boy asked.

"I second Nji, I don't find it proper, because after that, who would you want to marry this girl? Myself, I cannot get married to a woman who has been living with another man; it's like getting married to a divorced woman. See! We are Africans, M-a-n! Let's not forget that," Jerry said. "So what?" The boy was angry.

"Look, the white people have their way of doing things that suits them. We have ours. Let us not mingle up, lest we get lost. Let's not hurry up. There will come a time when we too will reach that stage. When we will see our women smoking and not call it a taboo. After all, these are two different worlds – the developed world and the under-developed world," Nji said.

"No, developing world, not under-developed," Jerry tried to correct him.

But the boy said, "I disagree with you, Jerry. To the best of my knowledge we are not developing in any way. We are just simply under-developed, period and that is it. You are just trying to be euphemistic."

"So you see what I was saying, this whole issue of under-development or developing, if you like, does not end just at the economic level or political, but also at the social. It's a slow process. We can copy and learn from the white people but we need to do that slowly; I mean slowly. There are some attitudes I can't still bear to see a black woman practice, but which of course I find alright with a white woman," Nji insisted.

"What *zum Beispiel?*" the boy asked.

"Let's take smoking for instance, nearly every white lady smokes. But does it mean they are not morally upright? No! It's just their style, how they grew up, their environment, their society. But tell me how many good black women, I mean African women, do you know who smoke? Not African-American. I mean born and bred in Africa. None! Let's just limit it to say Pays which we are more vest with,"

Nji continued.

"After living in Europe you still talk like this?!" the boy exclaimed

"Why not? Was I not born in Africa? Did I not grow up there? And will I not return there after my studies?"

"Which studies, boy?" the boy asked.

Nji indicated the *Baustelle* with a wave of his hand. "This, of course," he said. The three boys burst out laughing sarcastically.

Then, in a very sad tone, the boy said, "*Massa*! Europe is hard o! I won't allow anyone I know to just come here like that without any strong sense of purpose. Look at me, a graduate, doing all this."

"You! A graduate! *Na und*, so what about that? We all are graduates and you know it. So what do we do? Aren't you happy that you even have this job? Very soon the work here will get finished, then we won't have anything else to do. *Chef* is even nice to have left us here up till now," Jerry said.

Yes, this particular *Chef* was indeed one of the few very nice people who sympathised a lot with foreigners, especially Africans. Some ladies from Marzahn who came at one time to do *Baureinigung* were treated so nicely by this *Chef* that all the time that they were there, they called him *chefchen*. He used to converse with Jerry and his two friends some times, trying to cheer them up, and on one occasion told them that it would have been better for them to have stayed in Africa.

Break was finally over; Jerry yawned, stood up and stretched his body tiredly. He scratched his body roughly and sighed. "It's a snare, my brother; a snare in which all of us are caught up," said Jerry. The other workers stood up to resume work, and the trio also moved on slowly while they still conversed.

"The fact is that the people who go back to Pays don't tell the truth about this place. They make those who are back home think it's all roses, which is but a lie. Look at me, I don't even have time to go to school. Too much responsibility here and back home," Jerry was saying.

"Are you sure if you knew all this before, you wouldn't have insisted on coming to see for yourself?" Nji asked.

"In fact, if I knew it, I wouldn't have come here in the first place; stress, stress, stress all the time. What kind of place is this?" Jerry cried.

"Before I forget! On this issue of marriage once more," the boy said. "If being married is to live like J.J., I will rather remain unattached to any black girl. I will continue to manage my deutsche woman. At least I know she is white, so I won't be expecting much from her."

The boys continued working, and at the close of the day, Nji and the boy dressed up casually while Jerry donned his suit as they left for the road.

Eighteen
Something is Wrong Somewhere

Jerry continued going to work in a suit and business bag. During the week, he left his KaDeWe plastic bag with its contents in the changing room at the construction site and only took them home on Fridays to wash them for the following week. Then on one Friday, when he took the plastic bag home, he immediately changed into a casual attire and made for Nji's residence as usual.

The main door of this student hostel was often left open by students hurrying in and out of the building. In fact, someone had actually blocked the lock in such a way that the main door seemed not to close anymore. So, the students hurriedly bypassed each other up and down, flipping the great door to swing in and out. Jerry took the three times table mannered lift. Since Nji lived on the fifth floor, he took the lift to the sixth floor and then descended to the fifth floor using the stairs. He rang on Nji's bell and Nji came to open the door with a knife in his hand.

Nji, who now lived with Akwi in a two-room apartment, was about to prepare food when Jerry got there. On the kitchen table he had *Suppenhuhn* which was still frozen. He also had a packet of *Rahm spinat*, some packets of *Grieß*, and a tin of fresh tomatoes.

Looking at Jerry's KaDeWa plastic bag, Nji said, "*Massa* how?"

"Fine," Jerry responded.

Then, looking once more at the plastic bag, Nji said, "You with this your KaDeWe bag! What's up? How is Pam?"

"She is fine. Is Akwi not yet back from work?" Jerry was saying as he took out his dirty clothes from his plastic bag.

"No, not yet. But she will soon be back," replied Nji.

Jerry took out his work clothes from the plastic bag and was saying to Nji, "I . . . I just . . . you see, I just want to soak them in water. I will leave them overnight and will wash them early tomorrow morning, so I can just dry them on your balcony. You know, it's Friday; I will need them fresh on Mon..."

Nji cut in before he could finish, "Please, Jerry, no! I am sick and tired of this your nonsense. If you know that girl is your woman, then she has to know who you truly are. I mean, you and Pam are planning to get married, not so? To me, you two are already married, because to pay someone's air-ticket to this place and then live together with her in the same apartment sharing everything, except the truth about who you really are though, and..."

Jerry tried to calm Nji down to no avail. Nji continued to scold him, "No! You wait, I am not yet through. You feed Pamela, clothe her, you buy her bus ticket; you even give her money to send to her people back home. I mean all this expenditure, yet you cannot face a simple truth with her. Where do you think you are heading? Tell her you work at a construction site; she either accepts it or refuses to stay with you. You don't work in an office, Jerry, you don't. So, stop lying to the girl, and even to yourself."

Jerry shook his head slowly. Then he started to explain to Nji that he wanted to give Pamela time to realise what life in Europe really was. Jerry was quite convinced that after the period of honeymoon, Pamela was going to accept the reality of Europe and he would not have to pretend to her anymore. He was actually afraid to change the image Pamela had of him in Pays as a catch with a Mecerdez Benz and money. He knew that she was already unimpressed by their living quarters and did not want to shock her any further.

"You see, I might lose her. With time, you know, she would understand; with time," Jerry pleaded.

"You are already losing her by not making her know on time! You see, if she finds out later on, she can use it as a *motif* to abandon you, saying that you lied to her. So it's better you tell her now, if she truly loves you, she will not leave you; if she abandons you for another man, it means she never truly loved you," Nji said angrily.

Jerry remained silent for some time and then thoughtfully he said, "You are right, my man. *Huhhn*! Pam. Pam." As they were still talking, the bell rang and Nji opened the door for Akwi. He welcomed her with a kiss. "How was it today at work?"

"Fine! Not bad."

"Hi, J. J.!"

"Ah! Ma-ma, are you back?" Jerry responded.

"Oh yes I am." Then, Akwi went in to change her dress. Nji went back to Jerry who said to him almost absentmindedly, "What you were saying is quite true. True. I will think about it. Meanwhile, let me just wash the clothes at once. No need to soak them and make your bathroom look untidy."

"Whatever way you choose, Jerry. My house is your house and so too is my bathroom, brother, just want you to be more careful."

Jerry washed his dirty dusty clothes. He washed them with a lot of pitiable despair, squeezed them with a sigh. He took them to the balcony and started spreading them on a dryer. Akwi picked up Nji's work clothes, filled water in a bucket with soap and soaked them. Then she went to the kitchen, helped Nji and they later on served food and drinks together.

"J.J., food is ready," she called out to Jerry. Jerry came in from the balcony and they ate *Grieß* and *Spinat* soup. Akwi and Nji cleared the table; the two boys continued drinking BECK'S beer while Akwi drank juice. Then, Jerry stood up to go.

"It's weekend. Why are you leaving so soon?" Nji

asked.

"Let me join Pam, she is all alone. We might come back later on," Jerry replied and thanked Akwi for the meal.

"Is it just Akwi you are thanking? What about me who prepared the meal?" Nji teased.

"Get out! Can you cook?" Jerry said. All of them just burst out laughing.

"So! See you people, maybe later on or tomorrow."

"O.k! Jerry, my regards to Pam," Akwi said.

"So boy, hold tight," Nji added. They shook hands and Jerry departed.

Akwi asked Nji why Jerry preferred to launder at their place, but Nji did not answer, he merely sighed, looked at Akwi, giggled and then said playfully, "because it is his buddy's place, or what do you think?"

"You're kidding, aren't you? There is something you are hiding from me. I noticed Jerry looks …I mean he looks stressed up. I can understand there is a lot of stress in this place. All of us have stress-yes! But Jerry, he looks somewhat pale and not wholesome. On a serious note, I see a kind of loophole in him. I fear Pam might be stressing him too much."

"Pam! Is that not how you women are?" Nji said with unexpected annoyance.

Akwi was angry. "Excuse me. Since when did the noun Pamela become a synonym for women? Pamela is Pamela; women are women. There are some women like her and some who are not like her. So, stop generalising issues here."

"*Na ja,* it's true. But how would one know? How can one differentiate?" Nji was apologetic. He was carried by his concern for Jerry. "It's a snare. It's a snare in which most young men are caught up once in a while." Then, he became angry. "But this Pam of a girl, I don't know what Jerry has seen in her."

"The last time I was talking with Pam, from the way she talked, it seems as if she thinks Jerry is working in an office. I hope Jerry has not been deceiving her. That wouldn't be nice, you know," Akwi said.

"But that's what she wanted to hear *oder*?" Nji answered.

"Oh! But that doesn't make it right, does it?" Akwi asked.

"Most women like to be lied to. They believe in shadows rather than in substance. They want a ready-made husband. A husband, who owns a car, has plenty of money, investments back home and so on and so forth. I wonder if they themselves are ready-made," Nji said.

"Take it easy. I now see. It looks like Pam herself doesn't want to work," Akwi said.

Pamela was looking like a Princess when Jerry reached home, her hair was neatly done. She was yet to prepare dinner, if the tin of sardines she was trying to open was any indication. She apologised to Jerry for preparing food late. She told Jerry she had a headache and had been lying down all day. She did this therapy because she hated taking medicine all the time. Jerry felt her forehead with his palm and told her he was sorry.

"Just relax, relax your brain, your mind, everything, it will get better, okay? I have told you I am by your side. If you have any problem, just tell me; I'll take as much care as I can," Jerry consoled her. Pamela smiled and then she started, "*Em* . . . em, what about the *dough,* the money you promised to give me to send to my mother in Pays. Do you remember my junior sister needs school fees? The younger one who failed her exams, Monica? She has to repeat the G.C.E."

"Oh yes! I brought some money home today. We actually got paid. How much is it that you need? Get my bag from behind there please."

Pamela brought his bag to him. "*Em . . . em . . .* about two thousand D-Mark. I think they can manage with that for now. *Eh-en*! KFC, tomorrow Saturday; don't forget," she put in.

"You see, this is the money for this month, it is two thousand D-Mark. We can't just send all the money. Let's send one thousand D-Mark now and then we can send the remaining part later. So we can manage with one thousand until I make some other money. Then, concerning the KFC issue, let's postpone it till next time. You see, it is very expensive going to eat at the restaurant all the time. So just keep this one thousand D-Mark and manage it well," Jerry told her. "*Ja-ah*, no prob, no prob. You're really a darl-ling," Pamela said and gave Jerry a peck on the lips. She soon brought jellof rice served on a plate for him. The food was not very tasteful and he was already full, yet he pretended to be savouring every spoonful.

Ever since Nji made Akwi understand that there was something wrong going on between Jerry and Pamela, she had been thinking over the matter. She particularly felt pity for Jerry, whom she admired for trying to settle down with a black woman. She knew that most guys who were trying to make it in Germany went for white women, even old and ugly ones like Steffi. She was therefore determined to show Pamela how lucky she was to have a man who was willing to do everything to make her happy. A man who instead of looking for a *sara chap* for *docki* preferred to save money, fix his papers and bring his darkie *chap* over. Akwi found an opportunity on a Sunday when Jerry was visiting them. While Jerry and Nji were drinking beer and watching a football match on television, she dashed out to visit Pamela. Pamela was happy to welcome Akwi as she was surprised to see that she had a day off from work. Akwi complicaloonmented Pamela's beautiful hairdo and was shocked when Pamela told her about her stylist.

"I had it done in one salon in town! I hear it's an American salon. It's Jerry who knows the place better."

Akwi was bewildered. "W-h-a-t? An American salon?"

"Yes, of course I go there at least once a week. What's wrong with that anyway?" Pamela was astonished.

"No, nothing *em...em*. It's just that it's a little bit . . . a little too, too expensive, and . . ." Akwi stammered.

"Too what? Expensive, you mean?"

"Oh yes!" said Akwi.

Pamela just laughed, "*Hehn*! I must do my hair o! I like keeping my hair in order. Even when I was in Pays I did my hair every Saturday, sometimes twice a week, especially when I have some *rendezvous* to follow up, you know *nah*?"

Akwi looked at her keenly and cleared her throat before saying, "but it is far cheaper in Pays than here. I mean it costs a whole fortune here to do your hair in a salon, moreover in an American salon .Why don't you get one of our fellow sisters around here to do it for just a little compensation or better still for nothing?"

"Let me tell you something: Salon is salon; and *quartier* is *quartier*. I always like my hair to be handled by a professional. All these low-class things around the quarters, count me out!" Pamela responded rudely as she looked at her hair in the mirror and made faces.

"Anyway, when you will start working, you will hardly bother much about all that, for you are going to be very busy. You wouldn't need to do your hair weekly," Akwi said slowly.

"Start doing what? And when do you think that is going to be?" Pamela was annoyed.

"I can get you a job in the hotel where I work at the moment," said Akwi helpfully.

Pamela laughed sarcastically. "To come and do what there? *Zimmermädchen* or what? You are very interesting indeed!"

Then Akwi said, "Okay if you don't like working as a *Zimmermädchen*, we could get you a kitchen job, to wash plates, or something else."

"Like I said, you are very interesting," Pamela told Akwi. Akwi had anticipated that this was not going to be easy and so she didn't care much about what Pamela said or how she said it. "What's bad in working? If you are registered in Heinzelmännchen or TUSMA or say Effektiv, you can always have a job. Maybe you could help wash plates in a restaurant, or clean an office or something. Those are all female jobs. I mean you could always have something to do. Or maybe you can go to school since Jerry had registered you in BSI."

"The registration in the BSI language school was just to enable me to extend my visa, although Jerry said I could attend the school. But that is if I wanted to," Pamela told Akwi.

Jerry had gotten Pamela an admission letter in the language school as proof that she was a regular student in order for her three months visa to be extended to six months in accordance with the duration on the admission letter. Pamela would only get registration in a university thereafter when she had the final language certificate. Also, Jerry had borrowed money from friends to put in her bank account for a *Kontoauszug*; this bank statement of account was proof of the fact that she could sustain herself. He also signed a contract with an insurance company just to use the contract for the visa extension, and they had annulled the contract on their way back from the foreign office immediately after Pamela's visa was renewed. Then, a week later, he removed the money from Pamela's account, put it in his own account, looked for another insurance company, and a language course admission letter from another language school and then extended his own visa. Finally he took out all the money and returned it to the lenders. This was so, as he explained, because "one needs sense to survive in this place."

Pamela stared at Akwi as she kept encouraging her to find something to do and stop idling. Pamela simply made faces, and then laughed out briefly. "Akwi, the working mama! Me! Work? You can just forget it. I mean, with all the cold outside. Thanks anyway, but just know I can't work."

"Is it because it's cold? But it is not even winter yet! It is not yet cold. We are still in autumn. In any case, you'd be working indoors, not outside," Akwi tried hard to insist.

"Winter or no winter, I am not going to do any stupid dirty job. Even in summer, I will not work, *ah*! Don't you get it?" Pamela was now very angry with Akwi. She looked at her sneeringly from toe to hair and immediately started to develop a deep hatred for her. Akwi noticed this but she did not care. She was someone who believed in the saying that, "The truth is bitter, but must be spoken." She thought it her duty to direct or correct Pamela.

"Pam! I fear for you with your kind of ideas. In fact, this place is different from Pays, you know. I mean, here, it's fifty, fifty. You don't just sit and fold your arms and only rely on a man. It won't work! Life is so demanding over here."

"Demanding what? And from whom?" Pamela snapped. Akwi would not give in and simply continued, "See! You have issues like house rents to take care of, electricity bills, water bills, your bus ticket, feeding, clothing and then the people back home. Think, Pam! Suppose something happens to Jerry's work, you need to assist him. I mean, in this country where nobody has a permanent job. When one job gets finished, it takes time to get another one."

"Wait a moment! Do you mean Jerry's job isn't per...." Pamela was about to ask when Akwi realised she had said something she was not supposed to say; at least not at that moment, so she quickly cut in, "No, no, that's not what I mean. That's not what I said. O.k., what I mean is, take Pays for instance, if a woman relies so much on a man and doesn't do anything for herself and then suddenly the man loses his job or his life."

Before Akwi could even finish, Pamela cut in with a loud and long laugh. "Ha! Ha! Ha! Like I said earlier, you are very interesting, Akwi. Don't tell me that all the men in Pays or in the whole world could just lose their jobs or their lives in one go! *Auf einmal,* as the Germans would say it. I mean, just all of a sudden." She laughed again, very much amused at Akwi´s display of innocence.

"That's not exactly what I mean," Akwi struggled to explain. By this time, she was getting a little bit agitated and fed up with Pamela. Pamela was quick to notice this and she was very pleased with the situation. She, Pamela Tah, must always have an edge over everything; anything whatsoever, no matter how big, small or mean. Seeing that Akwi was beginning to feel some pain, Pamela was light-hearted and talked with much more ease and arrogance. "Look, let me tell

100

you something, men are like trains, if you lose one you catch the next. *Est-que* there are not many fishes in the water? There are many fishes in the ocean, girl. By the way, why must I assist him? Does he assist me when I make love to him?"

Akwi was shocked. "Pamela!" she called out, "See, you make love to a man, I mean to Jerry, because you love him."

Pamela laughed loud and long. "Akwi, stop teasing me. Love! See my love died years ago when that fool of a boyfriend dumped me for another girl, though I am more beautiful and more intelligent than her, simply because my parents are poor and the girl's parents are rich. I promised ever since then to teach him a lesson, not just him, but all men. My love is dead, *tot*! It had an accident on a *Fahrrad*," she laughed.

"But Pam, this is a bad way to solve the issue. You are doing yourself harm by being incapable of loving," Akwi pleaded.

"What bad! Is it me or that boyfriend of mine who is bad? Don't you listen to R. Kelly, my dear? And I quote, "Every no good woman was made by a no good man," end of quote," Pamela said as she snapped her fingers and smiled victoriously. "As for going to school, I went to school in Pays, what good did it do me when I graduated?"

As it is often said with saving drowning persons, one can end up being drowned. This can be because the drowning person is too scared and does not follow the rules of rescue. But in some cases, either because of evil or the misery-loves-company syndrome; the drowning man deliberately pulls the rescuer into the water. So it is often said that, you have to have enough stamina before attempting to rescue someone. This was what occupied the unconscious of Akwi as she remembered her mother's words clearly, when Pamela said, "Come on Akwi, you worry too much! See how pale you have become just because of too much work. When the time comes, you shall see. Just come to me, and I will teach you how to fish, I will make you fisher of men if you follow me.

As you see me like this, I have never lacked anything in my life, money, clothes, nothing..." Pamela talked on and on and then she became more friendly and coaxing, "A.K, see how your beauty is fast fading away. Let's stay at home; don't go to that work again. See, I will teach you how to fish, especially here where there is plenty of water."

Akwi was perplexed as she stared at Pamela and all she could utter was, "*Huhhn!*"

Pamela nodded and said, "*Ehen...,*" and then she continued, "*Em...em,* let me tell you something. As I was just walking past Paul-Junius Strasse today, you know, one man stopped his car and asked me out for a drink. And do you know what he told me while we were drinking?" Akwi shook her head in denial. "He said he wants to make me his secretary, in his company."

"What race is the man? A German or an African?" Akwi asked. "And what kind of company does he own?"

"He owns an insurance company and he is a German of course. A pure German! Not a *Turkei,*" Pamela replied. Akwi did not believe her. She looked into Pamela's face to see any trace of joke, but she saw none.

"What? Are you sure of what you are saying? Didn't he take note that you don't have a grasp of the German language yet?" Akwi asked in disbelief.

"I told him that for now I could be fluent only with the English language and he said no problem. You see, A.K., I can always work out something even for you too. *A swear, a fit find you bolow for dis land.*" Akwi did not know what to feel or how to react, but somehow, her unconscious got the better part of her and she decided to quit conversing with Pamela just in time for her not to get drowned.

"Pam, let me be on my way. I want to get something from the *Spätkauf.*"

Pamela smiled at her and said, "So think about it. Anytime, I am there for you." Akwi left, but on her way, she pondered on what Pamela had been telling her. "A German wants to give you a job as a secretary. I am not sure. Pam tells lies. A black secretary in his office, in this country, *nobi for dis Miango*, lie, lie," she told herself.

Nji, knowing where Akwi had gone to, made sure that he held down Jerry with conversation until Akwi was back. When Akwi got home, Jerry left for his apartment. When Nji asked Akwi how her discussion with Pamela went, Akwi did not know where to begin and so all she told Nji was that Pamela should be given some time. She would learn either way, mild or hard. But all the same, time would tell. "Anyway, she might still make it. Who knows, but I fear for her. It is not easy in this Europe. She is pretty, yes! But then, she is not the only pretty woman alive. There should be at least a little bit more than good looks over here."

Nineteen
KFC

Jerry met Pamela at home and they sat down and watched television. Suddenly, Pamela's mobile phone rang; she got up and dashed out of the apartment to the staircase to answer the call. When she returned, Jerry looked at her and swallowed hard. He took some time before speaking. "Who called you?" he asked.

"Who? Me?" asked Pamela.

"*Ehen*, yes, you," Jerry said firmly.

"*Em.... Em*, this person – one – *Firma* – yes work. *Ehen* I will go to work tomorrow in the evening, to clean – *Reinigung*."

"Is that so? Are you sure of what you are saying?"

"Why should I lie? Maybe it is Akwi who asked them to call me. So you don't trust me?"

"No, no, why should I not trust you? I was just a little bit surprised that you went out to receive the call," Jerry said.

"Oh that, *ah*! I am not used to receiving calls where there are strangers and so each time, I have to move away, it is just out of reflex."

"It is o.k. When is the job starting?"

"Tomorrow at six in the evening."

"In that case, I have to hurry home after work in order to see you off."

"No, no, that won't be necessary. I can find my way; I

104

just need to alight from the train at *S-Bahnhof* Lehrter Stadtbahnhof, which is a stop after *S-Bahnhof* Friedrichstrasse. You would be very tired. No need to bother."

The following day at six in the evening, Pamela was standing in front of the Europa Center. Agwe had told her to meet him in front of a certain Italian shoe shop, which was inside the centre. Pamela instead came and stood in front of the centre. Her reason was that she saw the name Europa Center and thought that it was meant only for Europeans and so she was afraid to get in. "Agwe must be mistaken," she thought to herself.

Meanwhile, Agwe waited for Pamela in vain and so called her on her mobile phone and directed her to go to KFC and take a particular seat inside just behind the great door. Then he joined her and they both sat down and he got them some fried chicken, French fries and some drinks. They ate and conversed and Agwe asked Pamela if Jerry knew where she was. She just laughed. "Why do you laugh? What did you tell your guy before leaving?"

"Oh! Trust me. I told him I was going to work. Work, that's what he likes to hear. Do you know he went and arranged with his friend's girlfriend to come and tell me that I should *em*... work ... this, that," Pamela told Agwe.

"Don't you want to work?" Agwe asked. And without waiting for an answer, he said, "*Em*, I can see you don't like to, o.k. Are you through, let's go."

Agwe walked fast out of the KFC restaurant, Pamela moving some few metres slowly behind him. He reached his car, looked around stealthily and then opened the door to the co-driver's seat. He held the door, still looking around, while Pamela walked up slowly and got into the car. He slammed the door, went round to the driver's seat and drove off very fast. Agwe drove through the city to Innsbruckerplatz 22, which was where he lived. He dropped Pamela off in front of Innsbruckerplatz 22 and looked out for a parking space. He finally parked the car and joined Pamela in front of the house. He opened the main door and went in with Pamela, and then he overtook her and took the stairs. Pamela ascended the staircase more slowly and tiredly. However, she finally made it to the fourth floor where Agwe was waiting for her.

Agwe opened the door and they went in. He lived in a three-room apartment, the sitting room was furnished with a set of chairs, a large cupboard, a large musical set, a large TV set, a video recorder and a DVD player. Hanging conspicuously on the walls, were pictures of Agwe and his family, a wife and three kids. The house was well arranged though on the sophisticated side. Pamela who had quickly taken stock of the contents of the house was well pleased with everything but for the conspicuous family portrait. She slumped onto a sofa breathing heavily.

"Why didn't you stay on the first floor?" She asked Agwe. "Or better still, look for an apartment with an elevator," she added before Agwe could respond.

"I just got here in a rush when all the other floors were occupied. Anyway, it's just for a short time. I am going to move over to Charlottenburg soon."

"All the same, your place is nice," she said.

"Oh! Thanks." Agwe served some wine and as they drank, Pamela's eyes were on the portrait. Agwe noticed her discomfort and before he could think of something to say Pamela asked, "How long do your wife and kids still have to be on holidays in Pays?"

"One week," Agwe answered.

Pamela looked at Agwe, and then she said, "So, then I won't be able to see you again?"

"Why not? Because of that element? No! That girl you see like that, she is very terrible. Can you imagine that the idiot left my kids at home with my mum just because she wanted to help her friend who was moving house? I have told her enough is enough. If not for my kids, I would let her stay in that Pays for as long as it takes for her to learn some sense. Even when the fool was here, she would just be troubling me each time about paper this, paper that. You know I have a German passport, don't you? In fact, I am German. Let me show you, maybe you think I am lying." Agwe went to the corridor, searched the pockets of his jacket and took out his German passport. He showed it to Pamela who was quite impressed.

"You know, you never really told me you and your wife were having problems," Pamela said, smiling at the passport.

"Forget that bitch, she wants me to go and present our marriage certificate so that this nationality would cross over to her. But I told her that she shouldn't think that German paper is chocolate. She will stay in that Pays and suffer. Even the one week can still be increased, that depends on me, you know. So you see, nothing stops me from seeing you except myself or you." As Agwe said this, he put on some *makossa* blues. He sat very close to Pamela and was soon kissing and fondling her.

Meantime, Jerry and Nji were watching a black American movie, *Baby Boy*. They were engrossed especially in the scene where Jody and Yvette were making love. When the scene was over, they laughed and the bravado ended suddenly when Nji asked where Pamela was.

"She went to work," Jerry answered passively, still evidently enjoying the movie. Nji looked at him and remained silent. Seeing that he could no longer concentrate on the film, he burst out.

"What kind of work could Pamela be doing at this hour?"

"What do you mean?"

"Big man, it's 11pm," Nji said.

"So what? What are you insinuating?"

"I mean what kind of work at…"

Jerry became very angry and cut in, "Enough of that insult, bro. I think I have taken more than enough from you. I will not have you come into my home and tell me what I have to do with my woman."

Nji was astonished. "But…"

"You better leave. I mean: Leave now! It's 11pm, so why don't you just go and meet your own woman. She should be missing you by now. Don't you think so?"

Nji did not believe his ears; he shook his head and stood up to go. "Okay, I will go, but don't say I didn't try to warn you. See you tomorrow." Nji left and Jerry closed the door.

"At first it was like Pam didn't want to work, then now, it's, at this hour? Everyone should let the poor girl be," Jerry grumbled as he dialled Pamela's number.

Pamela was dressing up while Agwe watched her languidly from the bed when her phone rang. She quickly told Jerry that she just finished work and was already on her way home. As she picked up her purse to leave, Agwe offered her 100 D-Marks.

"What is this you are offering?" Pamela asked.

"Money, of course. *Eh!* That is about 32,000 Francs, take note," Agwe laughed.

"Get out! Are we in Pays? What can 100 Marks do for me in this Europe? The value of 100 Marks to Pays standard is about 5, 000 FCFA." Pamela looked at the money in her palm annoyingly. "What can I do with this money? Don't you know I'm a woman and need to take care of my body?"

"Take it easy; don't you know times are hard? Besides, I can't go to the bank now."

"And what is stopping you from going to the bank? Aren't there any *Geld automats* around here? This is the same discussion we had last time and just so you know, I am not happy about this." She said, and turned to go; Agwe allowed himself a cynical smile for a moment and feigned seriousness when Pamela turned to look at him.

"Please drop me off, will you?" Pamela said in a very harsh tone. As Agwe's car left the curb, another driver stopped in front of Pamela and the co-driver's window descended, she leaned forward to see who was inside and was soon tucking an address card in her purse as she walked towards her building. Jerry was fast asleep when she finally let herself into their apartment.

Twenty
A *Rendezvous* at Malingo

It had been a while since Akwi saw Pamela. On a winter evening as she was returning from work, Akwi saw Pamela coming out of the building. They were both pleased to see each other and so they returned to the building together for a chance to have a conversation. They sat on an abandoned table in the building as they talked. As always, Pamela was critical of the fact that Akwi had to work in the winter. Akwi laughed as she was accustomed to Pamela's way of thinking and informed her that a woman's job made her worthy. She told Pamela that men were not used to keeping a jobless woman because sex was cheap and there were many women out there even willing to pay for it. Pamela looked at Akwi in shocked surprise.

"In this society, there are women who also need a man mainly for sex. It's unlike in Pays where mostly the men go in for a one-night stand. And see, if it's sex he wants, he will tell you straight to your face and will not pretend that he loves you," Akwi continued.

"Tell me straight to my face? It's a lie!" Pamela protested.

"It's true. After all, a man would expect you to be getting the same satisfaction or even more, if not, why would you suffer yourself to go to bed with him. He will never imagine that it's because of money. He didn't meet you in a brothel, so what will make him think you are a prostitute," Akwi laughed.

"Brothel! Prostitute!" Pamela exclaimed.

"Are you so surprised? Anybody who has sex with another because of money is a prostitute. Be you male or female.

"But I am not a prostitute. God forbid! Me! Prostitute? Oh no!" Pamela was saying. Then she thought hard and then said, "But see, let me tell you something, if you are a strong *chap* you can have some luck to catch a powerful millionaire in this Europe or even a Minister."

Akwi simply shook her head in disapproval, "Forget it. Do you think that Ministers in this country are like those Ministers in Pays? Also, how many millionaires are there in this Europe and how many beautiful strong *chaps* are already living in Europe eyeing these millionaires before you came? And lastly, how many millionaires are ready to squander their money in that direction? My sister, think."

"Not with me-o. I have my star with men," Pamela said.

"What is it you call star? Sex appeal, you mean? That won't do you much good and the peanuts you must have collected from one or two men will fetch you no solid future. Moreover, if a Whiteman loves you, more often than not, he will prefer to buy you flowers, rose flowers, every now and then, as a show of love."

"Rose flowers to do what with? Do I eat rose flowers? You're crazy," Pamela said.
"Honestly, it's only a black guy who is involved in illegal business like hard drugs or *fae* who can give you any reasonable sum of money and just for a short while, anyway." Akwi told her.

"So what? Money is money, hard drugs or mild drugs; is *egal*," Pamela said.

They talked about other issues as they walked out of the building towards the market. Akwi walked Pamela a little distance before going home, as Pamela continued to the market.

Later that evening, Jerry returned from the video shop to find Pamela provocatively dressed and definitely on her way out. Jerry enquired and got no satisfactory answer as to where she was going. Pamela told a tall story about going to meet an old friend Jane at the Malingo nightclub. Jerry was not buying the tale. He followed her in an attempt to stop her from going to the nightclub that night with a promise to take her there some other time. Although she protested, it was to no avail. Jerry followed Pamela right onto the train and she finally got off the train at Platz der Luftbrücke and walked down Mehringdamm. Jerry didn't have any money on him and so he stopped in front of the nightclub and watched helplessly as Pamela entered without a backward glance. He stood there for a while with his hands on his head before turning around sadly and moving to the train station. Back home, he could not enjoy any of the movies as he kept thinking of Pamela's defiance. He tried to force himself to sleep, but to no avail.

The ambience at the tight-spaced Malingo nightclub was huge as always. Though an Afro Discotheque, the DJ was a Paysan which gave Paysans an added advantage. Their love for clubbing made it look more like a Paysan nightclub. Mainly German women and Africans frequented this nightclub. On this particular evening, there were many German women there as usual and all of them were fat. Some were with black boyfriends, others still seriously searching. There was a particular one with a blinking light stuck on her dress, just above her left breast; she was not only very fat, but very tall as well. She paraded up and down the nightclub; glass of wine in hand, smiling encouragingly. There were some other two in African attires, they carried cane baskets and were spreading African loincloths on the seats where they were just about to sit down. These were the self-acclaimed experts. What they were experts on wasn't quite clear. The question still remained whether the *Afrikanische Experten* were experts on Africa or on Africans or African men.

Pamela entered the nightclub and immediately saw the man who gave her his card when Agwe dropped her off the last time. He was a robust Awala man and conspicuously dressed. He had on a pale yellow suit, a gold chain around his neck, assorted rings on his fingers, wrist and ear. He also had on a gold wristwatch. He looked more like a homosexual and the colour lip-gloss added to that impression. He smiled as Pamela walked in and a gold tooth glittered. In fact, Emeka was gold-plaited. He embraced her and escorted Pamela to the narrow VIP section of the club which was made separate from the rest of the club by a red thick red twine; the type used in Pays to tie goats to their posts.

Emeka served Pamela a drink from a bottle of Moet. They drank and talked. He showed Pamela his assortment of bank cards ranging from Master card, Barclay, Visa and EC Cards, among others. Pamela was completely taken by the show of wealth and was soon drinking from one glass with Emeka. They danced together all night and left for Emeka's hotel room in the small hours of the morning.

It was late in the afternoon when Pamela and Emeka got up from a tiresome sleep, both feeling worn out and hungry. They had their bath, went out for a meal and came back. They lay in bed and conversed. "So tell me, what kind of business are you into?" Pamela asked.

"Do you want to know?" Emeka asked. "Just cool down. Cool down, *abi you must know? Make you go cool down for Jesus nah.* Must you know? Calm down for Christ's sake."

Pamela feigned annoyance and in an attempt to appease her, Emeka told her he was dealing in powder. This answer puzzled Pamela as she was ignorant of what he was talking about. Emeka simply laughed and said, "*Weti come make me de tell you sef about ma business. Ina; na you go kill me oh.* Why should I be telling you all this *sef*?" Emeka looked at Pamela, shook his head in disbelief and said, "You know, when I look at you like this, I just feel like . . ." Just then, Emeka's phone started ringing. He picked it up and gave some instructions "Hallo! Y-e-s. Okay *na you*? See! *Make you go follow waka come da place wey a tell you. Make you de lukot de way you de waka ooh! Okay nah, a di wait for you.* Be careful, I am waiting for you." He hung up and turned to Pamela, "Baby, get up, I've got to go. Business calls," he said. They got up, got dressed and Emeka handed Pamela 3000 D-Mark *Bargeld*. Pamela looked at the money, 3000 D-Mark in cash. She could not believe her eyes. She gave Emeka a big hug. "I love you, darling," she said. Just then, someone knocked at the door. Emeka opened the door, and a boy walked in and placed a bag on the table. Emeka opened the bag, took out a packet of cocaine, tasted it and nodded in approval. He returned the packet into the bag and closed it up. Pamela merely stole glances at the cocaine and at the boy. Then the three of them moved out of the room and drove off in Emeka's car. "Where do you say we will meet tonight?" Emeka asked Pamela as they drove through the city.

"At my place. I told you he will not be home. He will be working at night. He has night shift at a different jobsite."

Emeka finally dropped off Pamela at the bus stop at *S-Bahnhof* Storkower Strasse and she strolled home. Jerry was not at home, he was still at work. Pamela changed into her nightdress, listened to some music, ate a light dinner, and then drifted off to sleep. Jerry came home from the day's job, entered the room quietly in order not to disturb the sleeping Pamela. He bathed, ate, sat on the sofa and also fell asleep. By the time he got up it was 8pm. He hurriedly dressed up in a pair of jeans, pullover and jacket and then put on his cap and took his bag. He sat on the side of the bed, contemplating; afraid to touch Pamela lest he disturbed her. He put his hand lightly on her and then removed it. He finally mustered the courage. He touched Pamela gently, "Pam, Pam. I am going to the night shift which I told you of." Pamela barely stirred and nodded her head. "Okay, see you later." At about 10pm, the bell rang from down stairs and Pamela went to the receiver.

"Ye-s, who is there?" "*Na me*, Emeka," was the response, which of course she was anticipating.

"Okay!" Pamela opened the door and waited there for Emeka to come in; she embraced him and they both sat down on the sofa. She poured out some wine and they drank, talked and laughed.

Twenty-One
Rape! Rape Case!

In the meantime at the jobsite, Jerry was so disturbed he couldn't work; he walked up to his employer and told him he had a headache and could not continue work. His *Chefin* granted him permission to take the evening off. Jerry let himself into the apartment with his keys and was shocked to find Pamela and Emeka on his bed having sex. They both jumped out of bed when he screamed; each trying to cover their nakedness. Emeka managed to pick up his clothes and dashed out for the toilet.

"It is not what you think. *Em*, you know I told you..." uttered Pamela in confusion.

Jerry slapped Pamela. "Who is this guy?" He asked, panting with fury.

Pamela went on her knees with just a small loincloth about her chest as she said, "Please, I beg you, don't kill me. You see, I ... told you about bad friends. He is a bad ... *em* friend. You... keep bad friends. He even tried to rape me. Let's call the police... Rape case. Rape! Rape! You see ... I mean, he came... I ..."

"Pam, Pam! Oh, Pam why? Why? What have I not done to keep you happy?" Jerry sank on the sofa and wept. Pamela snatched a *caba* and ran out of the apartment, as Jerry continued weeping. She hid on the staircase upstairs. Jerry continued to weep. "Oh! Pam, I bought you all the nice dresses and shoes you ever wanted. I gave you money and above all else I gave you love. Why do this to me now? You say your mother is sick, I send her money; I pay your junior ones' school fees. Why, why?" He lamented.

Nji was worried about Jerry especially the way he left the night shift. It was about 7am and he opted to check on him before proceeding to his apartment. He pushed the door and was surprised that it had been left opened. He went in and found Jerry on the sofa. Jerry, who had inadvertently fallen asleep, woke up and thought it was Pamela, but seeing Nji instead, he started crying. Nji was perplexed when Jerry burst into tears and on investigation learned that Pamela had left him. He took Jerry to his apartment.

Nji and Akwi were shocked at Pamela's indiscretion, they knew she was a flirt but could not believe that she could go that far. Jerry was inconsolable; he sat in Nji's apartment thinking of all the things he had gone through just to make Pamela happy. Meanwhile, Pamela sneaked into the apartment and packed up her belongings. She called Emeka and waited impatiently for him to pick her up in front of the building. Akwi came out to throw away refuse and spotted Pamela getting into Emeka's car.

She called out to her but Pamela only looked at her with annoyance without bothering to respond to the greeting. Akwi went in and reported the latest development to the guys. They headed for Jerry's apartment and by the look of things confirmed that Pamela had actually left. Jerry broke down into another burst of tears as his friends tried to console him. After a while he started singing:

> *Pa-me-la o; aye; aye*
> *Pa-me-la o; aye; aye*
> *When a remember you o o, a no go chop*
> *A remember you o o, a no go sleep*
> *You take me troway; be ni a ning me yene wa-ah!*
> *A ning me yene wa-ah! Beni you take me troway.*

Nji and Akwi were confused at what to do as they merely

stared at each other. They tried to beg Jerry, consoled him and even asked him to eat something. He merely laughed foolishly. They took him to their place once more. They talked to him and promised they would do all in their power to find Pamela, but he had to eat something. Jerry finally ate something and spent the rest of the day with Akwi and Nji. At night he slept on their sofa. Seeing that everything had returned to normal, they got up very early in the morning, when Jerry was still sleeping, and went to work. By the time they returned, Jerry was nowhere to be found. They went to his apartment but he was not there.

Twenty-Two
Total Derangement from the Case

Jerry was in the heart of the city, referred to as Zoologischer Garten or Kurfürstendamm, without the knowledge of his two friends. He was looking really shabby and dirty. He was holding a bible with Pamela's picture inside. He laughed hysterically when he read a particular passage. "He, who finds a wife, finds a good thing." He laughed and then sang:

> *Pa-me-la o ; aye, aye*
> *Pa-me-la o ; aye,aye*
> *When a remember you o o, a no go chop*
> *A remember you o o, a no go sleep*
> *You take me troway; be ni a ning me yene wa-ah!*
> *A ning me yene wa-ah! Be ni, you take me troway.*

He sat in front of Ullrich supermarket drinking one bottle of beer after the other from a plastic bag. He was the portrait of total derangement. He smashed the empty bottles on the curb without caring whether he hurt any passerby. He opened his bible, then closed it and swinging it about, he was saying, "Noah was a good man; Mary was a good woman, Noah was a good man in the house of the Lord, in the house of the Lord." Then he lifted up his hands to the heavens and brought them down again, "Hallelu...? Halleluya! Hallelu...? Halleluya!" He laughed heartily, approached some African

117

passersby "Come to our church oh ye brethren; you see, when Habakuk went to…" The Africans slowed their pace, looked at him pitiably as they also watched an ambulance and police vehicles which were approaching the scene at great speed.

The police were the first to arrive as the Africans quickly disappeared. Gossip ran wild among the Paysans. "I hear the mother of that guy and her whole family belong to an occult society. Since it is payback time, the family has offered Jerry, that is why he is mad, so he won't be able to tell what is happening to him," one of them said. "And I am sure after this, the poor boy will just die," another added.

A police officer came to Jerry and said, "*Ausweis, bitte.*" Jerry laughed.

"Passport, please," the police officer repeated, indicating with a square sign. The ambulance stopped, the rescue team came out and tried to take Jerry away but the police officers insisted that Jerry must present his identification papers before getting on the ambulance. An argument ensued between the law officers and the medical team. The doctor tried hard to explain to the adamant police officer that Jerry was ill and needed medical attention first and not identification. At least his identification as a human being was enough to get him treated. So what other identification could be more important than a man's life? In a quarrel that ensued, the police argued strongly that Jerry was not sick. He asserted that Jerry was an illegal immigrant trying to cover up and the doctor would be depriving them from doing their job if he didn't allow them to prepare Jerry for repatriation. Jerry who did not seem to understand what was going on and why he was surrounded by police men overheard the word repatriation, he laughed and muttered. "No condition is permanent in this world. Repatriation or no repatriation," he said. He looked at a particular police officer with a hard-set face and said, "You, for instance, when around the year 1919, you left Motobolombo, you said you were coming back. Where are you today? Since then, have you come back?"

The officer looked at him and asked, "*Was ist

Motobloblo?"

Jerry laughed at the man's ignorance. *"See me dis oyigbo, you no know common Motombolombo?* Pays *oboso.* When Englishmen and Frenchmen drove you out, I mean, first they beat you and then drove you out. We were not the ones who drove you out, instead, we were very fond of you; we wept as you left, while you, having compassion on us and for the rubber and banana plantations, said, "don't worry, we will come back. We must find a way to come back. We must look for another Sarajevo." You went to Poland and went round and round, you ended somewhere around Pearl Harbour, but you never came back. You see, that's why I said no condition is permanent in this world." He laughed again and then started taking off his trousers. "Oh! But if only you had come back or even stayed longer, maybe things might have been a bit better, a bit, just a bit, *bitte ein Bit!* Why did you leave us before time? And so we were broken, divided, inflicted." At this point, the police officers were convinced that Jerry was a psychiatric case.

Twenty-Three
A New Home

Meanwhile, Emeka took Pamela to an apartment he had rented for her. "So! This is the apartment I have been telling you about but you wouldn't listen to me. You made me go and disgrace myself in front of that little rat," fumed Emeka.

"I'm so, so sorry, darling," Pamela said.

Emeka hugged her, "Don't bother. All that is now in the past. Now, these are the keys for the door and the letterbox. He held Pamela on the waist and gave her a tour of the apartment. She was impressed with her new home. "I just decided to pay the guy who was living here before for everything. But if there is anything you don't like, just tell me, I will replace it immediately. I will be travelling straight away to Stuttgart. It's a long time since I was home," Emeka said. He handed Pamela two thousand D-Mark. "Take this and buy the remaining little things you need. I know you women like little, little things. You people are never tired of shopping."

"All this for me alone? Whoa! I knew I could never love anyone better," Pamela leaped up and embraced Emeka, kissing him passionately. "Oh darling, I will miss you," she said.

"Don't bother. *Abi*, I am coming back next week. I will call you when I arrive," Emeka was saying this while he put on some music and asked Pamela for a dance. He held

Pamela close and they danced slowly to a hip-hop sound, swaying slowly about the sitting room. Pamela leaned on his shoulders and made funny faces. "This one is very primitive," she thought to herself. "How can he hold me tight to dance to hip-hop, and why the dancing anyway?" She giggled a little and wished it would end and the fool would be on his way. Emeka interrupted her thoughts when he said, "I almost forgot. Give me your account number for your monthly allowance."

"That's why I love you so very much," Pamela thought as she rummaged through her handbag. She scribbled the information from her bank card on a piece of paper and gave it to Emeka. Emeka kissed her passionately and took his leave. Pamela saw him to the door, closed the door behind her and sank onto a sofa.

"Yes! This is a real jackpot!" she exclaimed.

On Friedhofstrasse in Stuttgart, Emeka sat down in his three-room apartment. His wife was sitting by his side. They were both smoking cigarettes and drinking coffee. Then, Emeka took up his mobile phone and called Pamela.

"Hi, Emeka, darling! Did you arrive safely?" Pamela asked. "Yes. Baby *a reach fine-o sheloko. Na yi a say make a call you before you start dey feel lonely.*"

"It's good you arrived safely, and of course, I'm feeling lonely, what do you think?" Pamela said to Emeka. "Anyway, how is your *whitie*?" Pamela asked.

"*Na coffee way ei gi me na yi ei tink say na better thing.*" It puzzled Emeka that each time he came back home, instead of setting food on the table, his wife would bring two cups of coffee and a packet of cigarettes for them. As he told Pamela this in Pidgin English, he looked at his wife and smiled. Then he turned and kissed her, saying, "She says I should give you this kiss on her behalf. I mean, my sister." The wife smiled. "Say hello to her for me," Emeka's wife said as she went to the kitchen to get some more coffee. Pamela laughed from the other end, *"A di hear the entire thing way you di tell yi."*

"*Baby, forgive me-o, na just for short time, just to get the kwale.*"

"But you have a permanent residence, what do you need the passport for?" Pamela asked. "Baby, you don't understand, my job, job. Wait, when I come over, we shall discuss. *Baby, make you stay fine. Call me anytime. Make you no fear nothing.* See you next week."

"Okay, bye. Love you," Pamela said.

When his wife returned from the kitchen, Emeka told her that his younger sister worried too much! She had been feeling lonely since she left home. His wife proposed that they invite her over. Emeka quickly agreed, telling his wife that his sister was looking forward to seeing her too.

Twenty-Four
From the Grill Party

One fine afternoon Pamela was feeling bored and rang up her friend Jane, who told her about a grill party organised by a Paysan. The host of this party had invited Jane's friend and so it was understood that Pamela was as well invited to the party. That, notwithstanding, even if Pamela had merely had news of the party, she, like every other Paysan had a right to be there, except she decides otherwise. Pamela and Jane both planned to go shopping for dresses early the following morning in preparation for the party. Jane checked her little notebook and asked Pamela to meet her in front of a particular shop.This little notebook contained the names of shops with beautiful things on sale. This book also consisted of lists of all the little items Jane yearned to obtain and hoped they would be on sale eventually.

Pamela and Jane met in front of the first shop on Jane's list and went inside. Jane went directly to where she had seen a nice skirt the last time she visited the shop. Unfortunately for her, it was gone. Someone else had purchased it. She lamented, especially as the other items in the shop were too expensive for her. They moved on to the next shop on the list called H&M, where she had seen a pair of nice trousers at a good discount.

Jane found the trousers all lined up with red price tags on them carrying the writing: 50% *reduziert*. She was elated;

she took her size, which was XL, and rushed to the *Anprobe* cabin. But the trousers did not fit her. It got stuck below her buttocks and refused to go any further. She pulled and pulled in vain; she finally sighed in disappointment and dropped the coveted trousers on the bench of the dressing room. Pamela, who was watching her, laughed. "I have told you to watch your weight, but you continue to eat too much, Jane," she said.

"Why should I not eat? The last time I tried these same trousers on, they fitted me well, but at that time they were not yet on sale. By the way, the problem is also with the fabric, if it were elastic, it would have fitted quite well, no matter what."

Pamela was not very impressed by the shop since she already had items like those on display. Nevertheless, she picked up a set of silver jewellery which would match her silver handbag for the occasion. Since Jane badly needed a pair of black trousers, they moved to the next shop on her list, which was C&A, in the hope of getting something that would fit her. They found a pair of black trousers that fitted Jane very well, but she did not have enough money to spend on it. So, Pamela offered Jane 20 D-Mark to cover the cost of the item which sold at 50 D-Mark. Thereafter, they parted ways after agreeing on meeting up later for the party.

As planned, Pamela joined her friend Jane, who was already waiting at the train station - *S-Bahnhof* Papestrasse, and they both strolled to Jane's friend's friend's place. This friend, Marisa, was married to a German. She was doing the *Born House* for their son who was six months old. She had really wanted to cook *Born House* plantains for this birth celebration, but she couldn't find green plantains. She checked the few Afro shops that had emerged over time in Berlin and most of their plantains were ripe already. So she settled for a grill party in the garden behind their building. She bought a carton of fresh fish commonly known as *morocco* from the Afro *Laden* and prepared some peppered sauce to eat the grilled *morocco*.

"Marisa's husband is a very good man," said the

Paysans, and even the boys acknowledged this. From this girl's relationship, it was rumoured among Paysan girls that, German men were very caring. Their son was very dark, and when the child was born, every Paysan who went to the maternity to pay Marisa a visit came out with a congratulatory message to Marisa's Paysan boyfriend. Even some people who did not go to the maternity ward, on hearing the news of how much this boy resembled the father, did not fail to congratulate Mula for a great job. As the little boy grew darker, Marisa's husband explained to his friends and relatives that, the child took after his mother in terms of colour. Marisa's friends were happy for her, but most of them were too timid to get into a love relationship with German men. "What will these *darkie* boys, especially our Pays guys say has become of us?" they thought. Even those like Marisa, who dared, did it timidly, half-heartedly, and excused themselves with the fact that it was for *docki*.

After greeting Marisa and Mula, Pamela and Jane took their seats and were later on joined by Jane's friend who had just finished handing over the child's present to the father, who was sitting with his son on a *Dreh karussell*. The three girls giggled, made faces and looked critically at every nice-looking boy who came around. Then Pamela's heart skipped as she noticed Egbe at a distance.

Egbe was a handsome Casanova, who was always fabulously dressed. Pamela stared at him and then called the attention of her friends, "Hey! Who is that guy? See. Just look over there." Egbe, who had taken note of Pamela's extremely short mini skirt, noticed them stealing glances at him but pretended not to notice. Egbe strolled to a quiet corner and lighted a cigar. Pamela followed him with her eyes, drifted slowly from her friends and finally walked up to Egbe. Then, like Princess Volupine and John Donne's Mistress rolled up into one, she said, "Hello. Good afternoon."

Egbe turned as if seeing Pamela for the first time, "Do I know you from somewhere?" he asked haughtily.

Pamela was a little startled by this response.

"*Em...Em...*I just want to. What time is it please?" she stammered. Egbe was pleased to see that he had succeeded in making the lady feel uncomfortable. This way he had an upper hand and he was on a good footing. Smiling triumphantly he said, "It is just 4pm. The day is still young, isn't it?" Egbe offered to shake Pamela's hand. Pamela took his hand gently, with casual coyness.

"I am Egbe, Egbe Bond! *Null, Null, Sieben,* if you like," Egbe said jovially.

"Zero, Zero, Seven. I see," Pamela was delighted. She liked tough guys like this one, who believed they were a blessing to women. She sure knew how to handle such guys.

"And you! What's your name?" Egbe asked.

"Pamela Besem. Egbe, Egbe. So you are a Bamsee child?" Pamela asked him.

"Oh yes, you are my sister."

"Yes, my mum is from Bamsee while my dad is from Njegwe," Pamela answered.

"Wao! You have a pretty face. For how long have you been in Germany?" Egbe asked.

"For close to a year."

"Where do you live?" he continued to ask.

"In Wedding. Usedomer Strasse 2. Around U-Banhnhof Voltastrasse."

"What line is that? Is that the U-8?"

"There you are," Pamela said.

Egbe and Pamela talked at length and exchanged telephone numbers. Egbe promised to visit her soon.

"When you come, just ring on the name Emeka. That's the name of the person who helped in signing the apartment over to me."

Egbe patted Pamela proudly on the cheek, "Okay, see you then." He said as they parted. Egbe joined two girls who attacked him with words. "Yes, Mr James Bond! So you have seen new girls; that's why you are neglecting us, not so?"

"*Eh*! No. She is my sister's friend. Judith. Don't you know Judith?" Egbe laughed and went on to tease the girls about his irresistible charm.

126

Some weeks after the grill party, Jane opened her door to a hysterical Pamela. Emeka had caught her with Egbe in the apartment he rented for her.

"Who is this Egbe too, for Christ's sake? What are you doing with him? To me, he looks like some *adoro* guy who doesn't have any pfennig of his own. He looks very deceitful," Jane said.

"Please, don't say so, I love him," Pamela said.

"Love what?" Jane laughed. "If it's a joke, just stop it. See, let's call Emeka and tell him any lie. You can say Egbe is a friend who has just come into the country and you just wanted to help him. After all, he didn't catch you on it. Did he? And then, you tell this Egbe of yours to stay far away before he pours sand into your garri."

"No way! He won't believe anything. It seems someone had already told him about Egbe. In fact, he drove all the way from Stuttgart to confirm the story. He knows we met at the garden party and he knows how many times we have seen each other. I don't know who gave him all these facts. Paysans in this Berlin gossip a lot. That notwithstanding, if he wants to go, let him go. I love Egbe," Pamela said defiantly.

"Pam, don't say that. Consider all the financial assistance he is offering you. I know, anything you tell Emeka, he will believe you no matter whatsoever anyone must have told him .The guy loves you so much," Jane said.

"Let him go away with his financial assistance. I say, I love Egbe. Emeka has told me to quit that apartment. I will quit, after all is that anything. *Ehe!* The spare room you told me of, is it still free?" While they were still talking, Emeka called Pamela and asked her to bring over the keys to the apartment immediately.

Twenty-Five
Girl Selling Eggs

Two months after he was released from the psychiatric hospital, Jerry was still heartbroken. At the slightest opportunity he drank and his best hangout was a popular bar owned by a Pays woman. Many Paysans frequented this bar while some girls, especially those who were unwilling to work, prepared small treats to sell there and sometimes even sold themselves.

Nji had done all in his power to help Jerry get over Pamela, but with little success. He finally resolved to find another girl for him. He came home with a girl one Friday and since Jerry was not at home, Nji suspected that he would be at the bar. Fearing that Jerry might embarrass himself, he kept the lady near the train station entrance and went off to pursue Jerry. When he got to the bar, he saw Jerry, but the latter did not take note of him because he was busy doing a bargain with one of the girls who was selling boiled eggs served with pepper. From Jerry's manner of speaking, it was clear that he was slightly out of his senses, which pleased the girl. Jerry touched the girl and said, "So, the girl, how much do you sell your eggs?"

The girl looked at him and smiled, "Which of them do you want?" she asked as she indicated the bowl of eggs with her head and tapped at her genitals slightly with her fingers. "That one or this one?" she chuckled. "*A get market,*" she said and smiled again. Jerry wiped his eyes with the back of his hand and smiled wryly. Looking down at her genitals, he said, "This one."

Nji who had been watching at a short distance, still unnoticed by Jerry, could not take it anymore; he stepped in and tried to convince Jerry to leave. "Let's get out of here," Nji pulled him by the arm.

Jerry pulled back his hand, "Leave me, I want my egg."

"What egg?" Nji asked. "Since when did you start eating eggs? Have you forgotten you are allergic to eggs?"

Jerry continued to eye the girl, this time in the manner of a greedy child who never gets enough of ice cream. "Yes, I am allergic, but I want this one, not that one." "What is this one, that one?" Nji asked. Then, he noticed the girl selling eggs smiling seductively at Jerry. He gave the girl an angry look and shouted at Jerry "What?! Have you become possessed? What do you want to do with that nasty girl? Look at her. She is not even pretty."

"Stop insulting me. It's your mother who is nasty, you bandit," the egg seller shouted at Nji who paid no attention to her but pulled Jerry out of the bar.

Nji tried to talk to Jerry about the necessity to move on and about the nice girl; he had brought to meet him. Jerry did not seem convinced, so Nji promised to give him the opportunity to assess the girl from a distance before making up his mind. Nji went across the road leaving Jerry leaning on the wall in front of the bar. Nji started speaking with Marie. Jerry was a little bit excited, he looked anxiously across the road and the moment he set his eyes on the girl he was reminded of Pamela. He sat down on an old abandoned stool which was beside him and watched as Nji rotated the girl for him to appreciate her curves especially her beautiful buttocks. Nji escorted the girl to board the train and came back to take Jerry home. Jerry insisted he liked the girl, and Nji promised to plan a meeting in the near future, which happened to be later that same evening.

When Marie got to Jerry's place that night, he was

sitting on the sofa watching television. Marie sat down beside him and sipped the juice he had served her. Jerry opted to take Marie out, but she said she would rather watch a movie with him at home. They settled on the sofa, conversing and enjoying the movie. Later, they started kissing and fondling, and before he knew it, Jerry was moaning Pamela's name, "I love you Pame..." Marie pulled away and left, despite the fact that Jerry tried to apologise.

Twenty-Six
A Perfect Honeymoon

Pamela finally decided to move in with Egbe rather than look for her own apartment. She did not mind that he lived in a small room in a student hostel in Coppi where her friend Jane also lived. They were very happy and this surprised many Paysans, since she was only ever happy in the presence of money. It was as if they were on honeymoon. Egbe always opted to prepare the meals. They ate together, went to bed late and woke up even later. Sometimes Egbe teased her,

"You too! How did you come about that funny *Awala* man?"

"Whom do you mean?" Pamela asked.

"I mean your love- Emeka. Have you forgotten so soon?" Egbe asked, smiling.

"Whose love? I am not joking with you," Pamela laughed and then said, "I never really loved that idiot."

"*Eh....eh*! Don't insult him now," Egbe said.

"Truly. I was merely using him to get some money. Ah! *Awala* men, of what use are they? *Ehe!* But, what of you? How about your former girlfriend?" Pamela asked.

Egbe simply laughed. "Me? Honestly, I don't have any girlfriend or former whatsoever," he said.

Pamela looked at him and smiled cunningly, "A handsome boy like you with no girlfriend. I don't believe it."

"Anyway! I used to have one or two wild bitches

131

around. But I have never had any real *darkie* chap."

"Don't try to lie to me. You even make yourself sound much more suspicious, because it's better to say you had somebody as a girlfriend but it's over now, than to say you had none. That might as well mean you had or still have all. Or maybe you have someone you are planning to retain."

"That's very clever of you. But I say, believe me, I had none, have none," Egbe said as he kissed Pamela and they both burst out laughing.

The manner in which they teased each other showed how much they were in love. They had the same hobbies like shopping and dancing, which they explored together. They visited night-clubs almost every weekend and once made an appearance at the Malingo nightclub that was marred by the snipe remarks Pamela received from the Paysans in the place. Everyone seemed aware of her treatment of Jerry and her escapade with Emeka the *Awala* drug dealer.

Pamela got to enjoy only three months of harmony with Egbe, before he started disappearing without explanations. The first day he spent the night out, Pamela was badly tormented, especially as Egbe's phone number was not going through. All she got was, *„Der gewünschte Gesprächspartner ist nicht erreichbar. Bitte versuchen Sie es später noch einmal."* She could not sleep; she pulled the window curtains open and stared into the darkness outside as it struggled to overshadow the strong beam of the security light. She focussed her gaze on the once green vegetation turning brown and the trees shedding their leaves; and she wept. She took one last look at the vegetation, wiped the tears from her cheeks and then closed the curtains. She took in a deep breath and sighed heavily. Then, her eyes wandered towards the clock and she saw it was past midnight. She sank into a sofa as her eyes kept wandering from the clock to the door. She drifted off to sleep, and by the time she got up, it was 5am. She left the building in her nightie, and standing in front of the building, she peered up and down into the glimpse of daylight to see if she could get a trace of Egbe, but all in vain. After some minutes, she saw a car drive by and Egbe alighted from it. Then a fat white lady came over and kissed him passionately before driving off. As Egbe approached the entrance to the building, Pamela attacked and hit him fiercely. "Egbe! You kiss that white woman right to my face?" Pamela shouted at him. Egbe tried to by-pass her to get into the building, but Pamela held his shirt tightly.

"Take it easy. I say calm down, this stuff is from Gucci m-e-n" Egbe said to her. But Pamela held on, struggling to hit him. Luckily enough, Jane was coming out of the building on her way to work. She quickly intervened. She held Pamela tightly and Egbe quickly dashed into the building and made his way to their apartment.

Jane took Pamela back to her apartment. She begged Pamela to be calm and reasonable as she hurried away to work. Late in the afternoon, when she returned from work, Pamela went to visit her and she asked Pamela what happened. Pamela told her that Egbe had started seeing other women.

"Yesterday evening, when we went shopping, he left me at the *Kasse* to get some cigarettes from those Vietnamese dealers in front of the supermarket. After paying for the items, I came out, but didn't find him. I came home, prepared food with the hope that he would show up any moment. But he never did."

"Did you try to reach him on his phone?"

"Yes. I did later on, when it was taking too long. But his phone was switched off. But see, Egbe was not like this before. I mean, for the last three months he's been so wonderful to me, as you can well remember. But for just three months?! Three months, and then he changed overnight!" lamented Pamela.

Jane laughed. It surprised her that someone as experienced as Pamela in life could become so naive to think like a novice, simply because she is in love. "Pam, come on, you and I know very well that there is nothing like 'he changed overnight.' It's just that you seem to have forgotten all about men so soon. Or is it because no one had ever dared treat you like this? I am sure it's because you have never been in love before. This thing called love is a snare; it is a snare into which most young women get caught. Some say it is when you fall in love with the wrong person. I say there is more to that, for there is no such thing as a wrong or right person. How long you've got to wait for the so called Mr. Right is undefined."

Pamela merely stared at Jane.

"See, what I am saying, Pam, is this; that's what Egbe has always been. Those three months you are talking of, happened just because you were new to him. Men like variety; they like a change of women. He was just excited because you were new. Maybe now he has had enough of you."

"But I know he loves me. He even told me at one time that he would marry me," Pamela insisted.

"Forget those things, my dear! Have you suddenly become so naive because of love?" Jane asked her. Pamela's countenance darkened. She was annoyed and didn't want to continue the conversation.

"Besides, the way you carry on with your life, in my own opinion no man would want to settle with you for life. In fact, the young men of nowadays are very vigilant. They don't like women who are not hard-working," said Jane, who was intent on making a point.

Pamela looked at her questionably with a sigh. "You know I am someone who likes show biz as well, but now I struggle to work so that someone can pick me. Let me tell you something, if you want Egbe to really marry you...," Jane got Pamela's attention one more time.

"Do something, Pam, go to school."

"What school? I went to school in Pays, what good did it bring to me?"

"But at least change your style; start behaving like a family person. I mean, look for a job and try to take care of the house. So, where is Egbe at the moment?" asked Jane.

"He is at home sleeping," Pamela answered.

"What did he say about the white lady he was kissing? And why did he disappear from the supermarket just to meet another woman?"

"He said he was sorry. That he doesn't know what came over him." Pamela stood up, stretched her body and told Jane she was going home.

"Okay! Take care. Think over those things we've discussed," Jane told her.

"Yes, I will. Next week I will go and look for a job."

When Pamela got home, Egbe had just finished eating the *eru* she had prepared for him the previous day. He thanked Pamela and went on his kneels to ask for her forgiveness. Then he took Pamela in his arms and asked her to kiss him. "Or are you still angry with me?" he asked. Pamela frowned, trying to get the best out of the situation. She sternly asked him about a female singer who called Egbe on his mobile phone the previous week.

"I've told you, it's you I love, baby. I mean, it is you I'm living with. You think I can bring down myself to live with a woman if I don't love her? Who is that girl even? She is merely running after me for nothing. Last week I had to go to her to put an end to whatever might have been between us. Okay, do me one favour, if she rings my phone, I will give it to you. You tell her I'm your man, and she should not disturb us," he said seriously.

"Are you afraid of someone who is a woman like yourself?" he asked when Pamela insisted that such a drastic move was not necessary. They kissed and made up, especially as Egbe professed his love in many words.

Twenty-Seven
Studentenjobvermittlung

It was almost 8am when Pamela came out of the train station and started running because she was almost late for the student job centre, Heinzelmännchen. There were already many students, mostly foreign, who had already dropped their membership cards in a bucket. They sat down quietly, waiting for the numbers to be announced. Some of them muttered brief prayers. Pamela was among the last students to drop their cards.

Immediately the woman in charge announced over the microphone, "Now will be the reading of the numbers." Pamela looked around and saw a few black students made the sign of the cross. She had a weird feeling about this since it made them look desperate and miserable. Pamela hated this.

As Pamela watched the sullen faces of her fellow *darkies*, the woman read out the numbers into the microphone. It was like a lottery. She took out the cards randomly and announced: number one, number two, number three, and then number four was Pamela Besem Tah. A few Paysans who knew Pamela looked around for her. She felt uneasy; she knew they were wondering about her current low position in life. Yet, when she looked round she rather read admiration in their glances. She heard a Bulgarian boy saying to his friend, *"Die mit der Nummer vier ist die erste Studentin. Sie hat Glück. Sie bekommt heute den besten Job."*

"Okay, I get it," Pamela smiled to herself. "The number four thing means I am getting the best job today. Let's see how it goes," she thought to herself. All Pamela wanted was for her man to stick to her.

The name reading finally ended and those who had very huge numbers ranging from fifty, sixty and above, took their cards and left looking discouraged. The numbers determined the kind of job one got. The first usually got the best jobs and it got progressively tedious to get a job as the numbers advanced.

During the reading of the jobs, which took place thrice a day, there was always a pre-reading. During each reading, the students always listened attentively and places were often very still, so much so that, a few heartbeats could be heard; either from the stillness of the atmosphere or from panic over the fact that one might not pick up a job. Students feared especially the fact that some other person with a better number might be planning to have the same job as they had ear-marked during the first reading. More often than not, the students imagined themselves already having a particular job they were aiming at. So in their minds they quickly do a rough calculation of how much money this could fetch them. They see with their mind's eye, either their house rents or telephone bills being settled, or whatever bill they were owing. This often brought an unconscious smile to their lips and a sense of satisfaction on their sullen faces. The students were afraid to lose any opportunity to pick up a job, this would mean that they would have to come back the following day and try their luck again. So, there was always an air of anxiety around them. Some of them had families back home who were depending on them.

It was not unusual to find Pays students in Deutschland take up projects at home, such as building a house for their parents or for themselves after building one for their parents or at least buying them a car. They also lived in dread of frantic phone calls from home which often went like this: "*Heylo! Na me, a beg, call me back.*" When someone had such a call they were obliged to call back, and those who could not afford the call would become disturbed and seek out their friends to complain. The friends would ask, "*Massa* how?" And the reply would be: "*na stress, na only stress massa. A just get call from Pays, dem say make a call back,*" the worried Paysans would respond with a sigh. Family ties were very important to keep, even when this reliance was unreliable. Most times the friends will opt to pay for the call. The problems usually ranged from school fees and hospital bills to many other expenses.

This day at Heinzelmännchen began as a lucky day for Pamela. The boy who had number one "A" as a privilege because he was handicapped on his arm chose a job called *Umzug*, helping someone moving to a new flat to transfer. The lady handing the jobs out was surprised that someone with such a disability would chose this job which involved carrying and transporting of loads.

The lady continued with, "*Zwei Leute gesucht als Bürohilfe für drei Tage in Lichtenberg, achtzehn Mark pro Stunde.*"

A boy said, "*Nummer eins.*" Another said, "*Nummer zwei.*"

The lady asked, "*Gibt es eine Frau mit einer Nummer zwischen eins und fünf?*"

"*Nummer vier,*" Pamela shouted, and all eyes were on her with admiration.

"Okay," the lady said. "*Erstmal die Frau. Noch jemand?*"

"*Nummer eins,*" the boy shouted out again. "*Gut! Nummer vier und Nummer eins.*" But there were a few black students who shook their heads in disapproval, and a girl murmured *Bürohilfe* with disapproval.

"*Gibt es eine Frau mit einer besseren Nummer?*" the lady asked, but there was silence. "*Vermittelt!*" she said. Pamela and the boy, who was also black, had won the job.

Twenty-Eight
Wann Kehrst Du Zurück?

Pamela and the other *Afrikaner* got to the jobsite that morning. Their job was to cross-check stocks taken from supermarkets. They could see many files on stocks on the shelves the moment they got into the office. The office also possessed two desks facing each other. Their supervisor, a German was sitting at a third desk. When Pamela and the boy entered the office and greeted him, he responded reluctantly.

Then he asked rather slowly, *"Haben Sie ihre Papiere dabei?"*

Pamela said, *"Ja,"* and handed over her *Schein to* him. The boy handed over his *Schein* as well. The man showed them to the two empty desks facing each other as their workspace and showed them what they were supposed to do. They got to work but were soon interrupted by their supervisor, *"Woher Kommen sie?"* he asked as though he could not hold back the question.

The two students looked up at him and said almost simultaneously, *"Aus* Land." Then the man continued,*"Wie lange sind sie schon in* Deutschland?" They each told him in German how long they had been in Germany. The man finally hit home after setting the scene; his utmost aim had been to know how soon they would leave his fatherland. He did not mince words when he asked, *"Wann gehen sie wieder zurück?"* The students were lost for words; they simply looked at each other, then at the man, then at the files. They continued their work quietly. The man's countenance darkened as the minutes and hours went by. He tried to concentrate on his own work but failed. Suddenly, he became very, very restless. He started fidgeting and fuming. He went out of the office and returned with a cup of coffee. He tried drinking it, but realised that he could not enjoy it. Then he looked angrily at Pamela and her partner, who were both, oblivious of his mood as they concentrated on their work. "You can now take a break." He barked the order in German. Pamela and the boy raised their heads. They looked at the clock; it was not even noon yet, and they had only arrived when it was already past 10am.

However, they left the office and went to a nearby café to buy some bread and sausage. They ate hurriedly, although they were not hungry. They did not know the duration of their break and were too scared to enquire. Pamela and the boy finally returned from break. On their way they made sure they emptied their bottles of drinks and dropped the empty containers in a dustbin by the roadside before hurrying to the office.

On reaching the office, the man was not there, so they looked for new files and resumed work. After some time a lady came in smilingly; speaking in German, she said, "Hello, I am Mrs. Burkhardt, the manager. Why are you people not drinking anything?" Pamela and the boy looked up from their work, very much surprised. "What would you like?" she asked, still smiling broadly. The two were surprised but grateful.

Almost at once, they answered, *"Wasser, vielen Dank."*

The lady smiled again and said, "Okay, I will get some for you." This pleased the two *Aushilfen.* The lady returned with two bottles of water and two glasses, placing each by the side of the two office assistants, they thanked her and felt easy for the first time in that office.

They continued their work. A few minutes later, the supervisor returned to find Pamela and the boy each with a bottle of water. Pamela was about to pour out some water in her glass when the man said in a sharp tone, "You can now close down for the day." They stopped abruptly and Pamela put down her glass. Pamela looked at the time, it was 1pm. She looked up at the man and said, "But why? It's not yet time. And we are supposed to work for three days." The man did not say anything but handed each of them their *Schein* and payment for two hours of work. "You don't need to come again, I am done with your documents already, here is your money," he said.

Pamela and the boy were very disappointed and angry. They took the documents and the money to the manager's office. "This is unfair, where did we go wrong?" Pamela grumbled. When they reached the office, Pamela allowed the boy to speak all along. She did not like speaking German when she was very angry because she made many mistakes. She therefore aired her grievances in English while the boy acted as interpreter. The manager soon summoned their supervisor who categorically stated that they were not fit for the job. Amidst their protests, the manager resolved that the man should at least give a whole day's pay to the two. The two grumbled about racism on their way home.

Egbe was surprised to find Pamela at home in the middle of the day.

He consoled her while lamenting on the cankerworm called racism that was marginalising some groups of people. "Even in Pays, do Francophones and Anglophones not discriminate against each other? South-Westerners discriminate against North-Westerners and vice versa. Will a Mungaka person not discriminate against a Ta'ah and vice versa, even though all of them are from the North-West Province? Even a Bamsee might discriminate against a Nko'si when it comes to marriage especially. I mean there is discrimination everywhere, although it might be a little bit too much for us as strangers here to bear," Egbe continued while he puffed out smoke light-heartedly.

"Anyway, take it easy; at least, some of these people are also very nice and kind-hearted. I can remember the first day I came to this country, a man helped me to carry my luggage. It was very cold, my fingers were quite numb and almost half-frozen, I couldn't lift up my box. This gentleman, responsibly dressed, a Professor, carried my luggage for me and took me to the bus station, waited for the bus to come and put me inside and bade me farewell. As we walked to the bus station, there was something he told me, he said to me, 'It is better to stay in Africa.' It was a sincere statement." Egbe puffed out more smoke from his cigarette.

Then, Jane came to visit them. As soon as she slumped on the sofa next to Pamela, she sighed. Pamela and Egbe were surprised that she was not at work. She explained to them that her employer told her yesterday to stay away and to call after three days to enquire if there was a possibility for her to come and continue work. Jane complained that she had spent all the money she had and even sent some to Pays a few days back immediately she got this job, but now things had turned out differently. Jane told them how Herr Land had deliberately not put her name on the list although he needed workers. Instead he had called the Student Job Center and asked them for workers. "Racism." Jane sighed. "How can one concentrate on one's studies when one cannot have a stable part time job?" She continued.

The doorbell interrupted them; Egbe opened the door to welcome his friend Desmond, who walked in drowsily. "Good morning, or is it afternoon or what? It's now I am getting up from sleep," Desmond said this as he too slumped down into a seat looking very much stressed up. Egbe shook hands with Desmond saying, "*Massa*, its evening. So, just know you've missed breakfast and lunch."

Both of them laughed half-heartedly, ending with sighs.

"The better; the better, m-a-n," Desmond sighed one last time.

Egbe offered him a cigarette and they smoked silently for a while. Pamela poured out some juice for the four of them and walked to the kitchen section to prepare *Blattspinat* and *Grieß*.

"No job?" Egbe asked Desmond.

Desmond scratched his head and asked, "What job? An *Adoro* like me, an asylum seeker, even if there is a job, where will I get the papers. The papers I often use are unavailable; the student himself has been working a lot and so has already worked the amount of money allowed for this *quartal.* I don't know how I will pay my rent this month. The student who helped me to rent my apartment in his name warned me the last time about paying the rents late each time. It is not good for his records. These people keep a record of everything, paying the rents late might affect his stay and other opportunities here, if not now, maybe in the near future, who knows. The only option I have is getting a white woman and work myself out."

"Whatever! For, what else can one do?" The two boys laughed more heartily and shook hands once more. "I wonder what these German ladies have seen in us." Egbe continued.

"Sex, sex, my brother. What else apart from good sex, my brother? That's what they say we are good for; I wonder who told them we don't have other qualities," Egbe said. Pamela and Jane stopped conversing abruptly, looked briefly at the two boys and then looked away and continued their conversation. The boys lowered their voices and spoke in whispers.

"They are draining us, I know, some of them are so old, old enough to be one's mother. But what can one do?" Desmond said rather sadly. He sighed and puffed out smoke.

"This is what we used to criticise our girls for back home; going out with very old men for money, but here we are."

Pamela served some food and the four ate while they conversed.

"Pam, you prepared this sauce well, it is delicious." Desmond said.

"What sauce are you referring to?"

Desmond indicated the vegetable with his hand as he continued to pound the *Grieß* in it. "This *Soße*," he said.

"This is not sauce or *Soße* or whatever you have been

stupefied to call it for Christ's sake, Desmond. Is this tomato sauce or tomato stew? This is vegetable, or better still, say *njamajama*." Pamela hated the fact that the illiterate Desmond, who was in fact a *Garage Boy*, a local mechanic back home would struggle each time to reassert himself by foolishly and wrongly imbibing words. She hated especially his translating German words into English *mot à mot*. Pamela didn't find any fun in Desmond's word-for-word translations. At times instead of saying testis or testicles, Desmond would say eggs. It irritated her. It reminded her of their neighbour Julius in Pays, who would deliberately use French words each time he spoke as a mark of superiority. Julius would say for instance, "Yesterday we drove at high speed on the *gudron,* and so, we took a very short time to arrive Bart." Or, "I have to *voyager* tomorrow once more to Commercial." Each time, Julius had paid a visit to Commercial, which is in the French-speaking part of the country, his manner of speaking changed totally. Instead of saying, "Come, let's go." Or *"Viens on pas,"* he would choose to say, *"Viens on go."* At one time he told Pamela, *"Viens on go pour aller manger les poison braiser."*

"Please, if you really want to speak to me, it will be better to stick to one language," Pamela had told him. Julius told her that this is how the guys in Commercial spoke. "You see, I am a Commercial boy," he added. Desmond always reminded Pamela of Julius.

Twenty-Nine
A More Befitting Job

Weeks passed and Pamela found a more befitting job in a hotel this time. At 8am she was already in *Zimmermädchen* attire; a white gown, white socks and white sandals. She pushed a trolley up and down as she moved from room to room, laying beds, cleaning toilets and entire rooms. She had learned the trick of not spending so much time in one room and still be efficient in her work. She would go into a room, look around, lay the bed very fast, and clean the bathroom and then the mirror. She used a used towel to wipe the mirrors of the toilet, the toilet seat, the bath and the drinking glass or glasses on the table in the room and finally the table itself. This enabled her to work faster, since she did not have to constantly rush to her trolley for a new rag or sponge. She just used one rag for every purpose. Nevertheless, the work was still tedious. During work, Pamela would stand up several times to stretch her waist, which ached. At times, when she would be in the twentieth room, the *Hausdame* would call her back to the first.

"Pamela!" she would shout out, "*Komme her!*" Pamela would follow her and she would take Pamela back to the first room and show her an imaginary, invisible spot of dirt on the mirror. Pamela would clean the mirror repeatedly. The lady would stand at a distance, observe it and then will show Pamela more invisible spots that she had missed.

One day, Pamela, returned home from work with her bag full of bed sheets, pillow cases, towels, pens, napkins, all carrying the mark of the hotel. She took off what she had on her bed and dressed up the bed, and it looked exactly as the ones in the hotel.

"These are good quality sheets. Where did you get them from?" Egbe asked.

"From the hotel. I mean, this is the only compensation one gets from the low pay one receives. Can you imagine that they pay us only 4 D-Mark per room? I was lucky today, I did about 20 rooms. That is about 80 D-Mark, but my back aches," Pamela said as she stretched her body.

Egbe, who had been listening keenly, asked, "Then, what magic did you use to lay beds and clean twenty rooms within seven hours or maybe just six hours because you probably went on break?"

Pamela just gave a brief laugh, "Ah! You don't know! There is a trick in all this. They trick us with the money; we trick them with their work. Look, you don't go into a room and start trying to be perfect; you just do what you can to get the place to look neat without wasting too much energy and time." As Pamela said this, she went to the mirror and checked her complexion; she noticed that she had grown a little pale in the face. The hard work was taking its toll on her. She sighed and spoke with a kind of regret and resolution in her voice, "But this *Zimmermädchen* job, I hear, after doing it for quite some time you find it difficult to conceive."

Egbe gave one of his mischievous smiles, "Conceive! *Huhn*! And now you want to conceive or something?"

Pamela looked at him and smiled.

"But not now, you know. That should be after our marriage. By the way, when did you say we were going to go down to Pays to get married?" she asked as she served some *eru* which she had been warming up with *Grieß*. As they ate, Egbe was silent for some time and then he said, "*Huhn*! Get married! You girls of nowadays like getting married. But tell me, why is it that you girls are so courageous about getting married, more than us boys?" Pamela refused to allow Egbe to joke his way out of the discussion this time around. She was firm and he finally complained about the lack of money to organise a wedding befitting for Pamela. Yet Pamela countered the argument by announcing that money was not the issue. She estimated the total wedding cost to be 18,000D-Mark, an amount that will be easy to attain since she had already saved up some money even before meeting Egbe. Egbe had no choice but to give in and start on wedding plans.

Pamela was very pleased, and as she moved about the tiny room arranging things, she said, "Those Pays girls, I hope they will not take advantage of the bach's eve and start seeking notice from you or try to steal you away from me."

"Are you jealous?" Egbe teased.

"Jealous of what? Those Pays girls?" Pamela clapped her hands.

"Just take a look at me," she said, "Which of those girls can stand up to me? Besides, I am coming all the way from *Bundes. You wan try ma how far?* I beg, let all of them go to sleep – Third World girls, I am a *Bush-Faller.*"

Egbe laughed, "Pays *chaps,* not so?" he asked.

"*Massa o!*" answered Pamela. She looked at the list she had made with great satisfaction.

Pamela decided to do her wedding shopping at a new mall called Ring Center. She invited her friend Jane to escort her and blatantly lied that Egbe had provided the money for the wedding preparation. This surprised Jane and she actually thought she had misread the man. He looked too mischievous and Jane had found it very difficult to trust him. But now she was truly happy for Pamela and wished her all the luck. She helped her friend and they bought Pamela a very pretty dress, a crown, white gloves, a pair of white shoes, a little white handbag, a bouquet of flowers, and a small laced umbrella. Pamela looked very happy and prettier than ever as she tried on everything.

When Pamela got home that day, she was nothing but smiles. She grinned as she set eyes on her future husband and then she walked straight to the wardrobe.

"Did you find a dress?" Egbe asked.

"A very wonderful one. But you are not going to see it until that day. You know, if you see it before then, it will bring ill luck. Besides, it will be sweeter for you to get a surprise."

"Is that so? Okay, how much does it cost? Or am I not supposed to know that too?"

"No! I never said so! The dress cost 700 D-Mark and the marching shoes cost 100 D-Mark. You know everything has to be white. The dress and shoes were originally more expensive, but I was fortunate to get them on sale. So, you can just imagine the type of dress I am talking about."

"Yes ma! You say all together 800 D-Mark right? I will take care of that. I'm going to give you the money back." Pamela was surprised to hear Egbe say that. Pamela knew he had no money, but the fact that he could even think in this light pleased her. Egbe was a man who never let himself down, not when it concerned the opposite sex. He knew them like *book*, as one would say in Pidgin English. His motto was, making the ladies happy, even if it is for the moment. He was a very pleasant fellow, coupled with his good looks.

After placating her, he demanded 3,000 D-Mark for the car that they were going to use in Pays. They went to the bank, where Pamela took out money for the car and their flight tickets.

A week before they had to travel to Pays, Pamela stopped working in the hotel in order to refresh herself, lest she looked unhealthy when she got home. She also needed time to do her shopping and buy presents for her family, friends, relatives, neighbours, well-wishers and above all else members from Egbe's immediate family and a few extended relations whom she conjectured might have an influence on her marriage to Egbe. She bought dresses, shoes, handbags, perfumes, body lotions, hand creams, roll-ons. That done, she realised that she had more than the required number of kilograms they were allowed in spite of the fact that she had already sent some things by freight. Other items such as wine, paper napkins, cutlery, and souvenirs for the wedding were put in the car that was already awaiting clearance at the seaport. On their day of travel, they put on many clothes before boarding the flight because they didn't want to leave anything behind. While on board, they took off the extra clothes and put them in plastic bags.

When they came out into the airport premises at Commercial, Egbe's mother, Pamela's parents and some of their uncles and aunts and a friend to one of Egbe's uncles in police uniform were there to receive the couple. They were all very happy as they rode all the way to Bart late that evening. They went first to Pamela's uncle's compound, where many people were awaiting their arrival and a huge party commenced immediately.

Pamela and Egbe left with Egbe's family through the back door while the party was still going on. As soon as they reached the Egbe's residence, they went straight to bed since they were completely exhausted.

Thirty
December Marriages

For the sake of propriety Pamela had to move to her uncle's house for the duration of the wedding preparations. Egbe visited Pamela every now and then. They spent long hours together mostly visiting old friends and family members, with whom they would sit, either at home or at a drinking spot.

Like every other person who returned to Pays from abroad, Pamela and Egbe spoke with a slightly different accent, often with the interference of German words or phrases like *Ach so!* Also, from their complexion and sophisticated dressing, the people around could tell Pamela and Egbe were from *Bush*. The manner in which they looked strangely at everything showed they had not only been away from home for too long but were from some place which the people at home had never been to; been through things they had never been through and seen things they had never seen.

Pamela and Egbe moved hand in hand, stopping on the way at times to kiss one another, to the embarrassment of the town people. They didn't care much but even took pleasure in the sensation they were creating. They carried on in their best of spirits, conversing and laughing happily. Many passersby threw admiring glances at them.They met some friends and told them about their wedding and the forthcoming bach's eve. They handed them the invitations and had a drink with them.

On the fourth day of their stay, they decided to go to the sea port to clear their car since the date for the bach's eve was already at hand. It was not easy for them to clear this car. They went on the first day, but they were told by the Customs Officer who was responsible for this that they needed a Clearing Agent. He even recommended one for them. They met the agent and they were very happy because the agent told them that without his services, it would have been more costly for them to clear the car.

But then the agent started telling them of a series of taxes they had to pay. He moved from one tax to another. When they paid one tax, the next day he came up with another one, seaport tax, road-worthy tax and so on. It continued like that for three days and by the fourth day, they decided to go straight to the customs office and pay the clearance fee even without the help of the agent who was delaying them unnecessarily. On arriving at this office, the Customs Officer was not in but the secretary was there. She looked at the receipts they brought and was shocked at the fake receipts of all sort of taxes which she saw. She told them their file was complete even without most of the taxes they said they've paid. They were happy that although they had been duped, at least it was clear that they had a complete file which meant they would have their car out of the port in time. They were also surprised because it was the Customs Officer who recommended the agent. They told this to the secretary, but she told them that her boss merely helped them to look for an agent and did not ask the agent to dupe them. Moreover, how could she even be sure if they were not the ones who had faked the receipts.

"Okay, no problem, we want to pay the charges and get the car out," Egbe said. But the secretary told them that her boss, the Customs Officer, was not yet around. She gave them the bill they had to pay. For the car alone to be cleared, it cost a million Francs CFA and for the items in the car, an additional half a million. Pamela and Egbe had the money with them but the Officer was not there, although it was already 10:30am and he was supposed to start work at 8am.

Pamela and Egbe were surprised. They questioned the secretary, trying to find out if she was certain that the Officer would actually come to work on that day. Maybe he was ill or maybe he had travelled and so she should just tell them and give them an appointment when she knew he would be on seat. They were tired of wandering about under the scorching sun for almost a week just to compile documents and clear a single car.

The secretary was very annoyed with them. She told them that, first and foremost, they couldn't expect a big and responsible man like that to hurry to work. "He is a big man, he can come at any time he wishes to." She, on the other hand, was a mere secretary, and so if she was hurrying to work, this didn't mean that her boss too should hurry to work. Secondly, even if her boss had travelled or was sick, how could they expect her to reveal it to them and maybe tell them when he was to come back. She could not release such information. "He is a big man," she told them again. She told them that if they couldn't wait, they should go to hell. Pamela and Egbe were very surprised because they had the money to pay for a simple service and all what they got were insults. They did not know what to think. They decided to go back home and struggled to see if a relative of theirs who was familiar with the system could clear the car. Just as they were about to leave at about 11:00am, the boss strolled in. So they decided to wait.

When the Customs Officer started work, instead of the secretary collecting their file first because they were the first on the queue, the secratary took a different person's file. When they complained to her, she merely laughed and looked at them with disgust. They had no choice but to wait. Then, it was noon, the man who was inside came out, the Customs Officer was behind him also moving out for his mid-day break. At first, Pamela and Egbe thought he was merely going away for a few minutes, but someone on the queue told them that he might only return at 2pm if they were lucky, and if not, he would come back at 3pm or would not come back at all until the following day. Pamela and Egbe knew that they would seem mad if they still stayed there.

They went back to Bart and told Egbe's parents about their ordeal. One of his young uncles laughed at their ignorance. "You people should have bribed the secretary," he told them. "I don't know why you people, after living in Europe, you come back home thinking that here is Europe. See, we are not in Europe here, this is Africa," he laughed. "You have to follow the African tradition and culture." Then he told them a story about a boy who came home from the United States of America. This young man was clearing his car, and he had some boxes in the boot of his car. He was about putting the boxes into the boot after the control when a bandit who pretended to be a security guard took one of the boxes and started running away with it in broad daylight. The young man shouted and ran after the guy, while the police officers who were there on duty instead burst out laughing. "*Mais lui aussi veut manger*," they said as they laughed. The young man continued to run after the bandit, and then he shouted out to the bandit, "See, I am an American m-e-n, and as you know I too got a gun. I'm gonna shoot you, M-e-n." Believing what the young man said about having a gun, the bandit stopped and the young man was able to retrieve his box. Pamela and Egbe simply sighed at the story. "Never mind, just give me the money, and then we will do a transfer of the name of the car owner from your name to my name, and then I will see what I can do," the uncle said as he laughed at the two.

Due to the delay in clearing the car, Egbe had to change the date of his bach's eve and that of their wedding as well. Egbe's uncle opted to help and took a week off from work to pay the clearing fees and get the car out of the seaport. Everyone praised him for managing to clear such an expensive car from the seaport in such a short time.

Thirty-One
Bach's Eve

At last, it was bach's eve day. Egbe's friends had organised the party to take place in a popular nightclub in town. They had also arranged for him a girl with whom he would go to bed that night after the celebration. The street on which this nightclub was situated was very busy with so many young people waiting to get in. One of Egbe's friends was at the gate collecting gate fees from the boys, meanwhile the girls entered free of charge. Egbe and Pamela were the talk of the town that night.

"I hear the guy of the bach's eve is from Germany. His name is Egbe," a girl was telling her friend.

"And who is his lucky bride-to-be?" the friend had asked.

"I hear her name is Pamela. I hear she is very beautiful, she too is from Germany."

"Some people are really born lucky. Egbe is also very handsome, a woman killer I hear."

While the Bach's eve fever was in the air, Pamela was at her uncle's residence in Prisso. Her old friends Beri and Immaculate had come to visit her. They discussed about the wedding among other things. Pamela told them about life in Germany and the many exotic adventures a girl could find there. She promised to take photographs of her friends to help them get partners on her return.

Beri embraced and hugged her. "Thanks very much...*oo*! You are really a friend indeed."

"Ah so-o? What are friends for? As my best friend and chief bridesmaid, I am supposed to arrange such things for you. If I don't, who else will do that? By the way, the dresses I last sent you did you like them?" she asked.

"What a question? I love them so very much," Beri said.

"Ah so-o? And the jewelleries? Did you like them?"

"Oh Pam, what will I do without you?" Beri answered as she moved to sit closer to her friend.

"You girls shouldn't worry, I'm going to fix openings for all of you. Even with Germans, if you want me to. I have a few male German friends. I will talk them into liking black ladies and I will just present your photographs to them." The two girls were pleased as they watched Pamela with admiration.

"We are so fortunate to have you as a friend, Pam," Immaculate said.

"Ah so-o? Ehen . . . before I forget, lady chief bridesmaid, come, come, come," Pamela called out to Beri. Pamela took out a very beautiful and expensive white gown from her wardrobe. "You've got to try on your Saturday dress. I bought this for you, you know as my chief bridesmaid, you and I have to look almost the same at the wedding," Pamela said to her. Beri tried on the dress.

"Wao! This dress must be so costly! It fits you so well, Beri," Immaculate said.

"Oh Pam, thank you so much," Beri was very happy.

"For nothing. Still very little for one's best friend, you know. So, when are you girls leaving for the bach's eve? It is already 10pm. Don't forget to take good care of my man, especially during the dance. Don't allow him to rub shoulders with those girls too much." Her friends simply laughed and teased her. "Are you jealous?" Immaculate asked. "You should have taken up to do a Spinster's Night instead."

"No, I trust my man, he won't mess around," Pamela said.

"Yes, he is such a good guy to have lavished you with

all this, Pam. It means the guy is really caring. Very few young men are this caring nowadays, especially a handsome guy like Egbe," Beri said. Pamela smiled happily. Then Immaculate got up to go, but Beri told her to go ahead since she wanted to spend a little more time with Pamela. Beri took her leave soon after.

Meanwhile, Egbe was already dressed in shorts, a T-shirt, a casual pair of shoes and a baseball cap for the bach's eve celebration. But, instead of going to his bach's eve, he drove to a nearby place. The place had sheds because the town's open-air market was held there. He parked his car at a dark corner and sat on its bonnet puffing out smoke from his cigarette; it was evident he was waiting for somebody. After a while he made to leave but stopped when he saw Beri alighting from a taxi at a distance. He opened the back door of his car and sat down inside. Beri walked stealthily to the parked car and sneaked in. "I thought you were no longer going to come!" Egbe said as Beri quietly closed the car door. "No, I told you we were to visit Pam, and so I had to wait for Imma to take her leave first." He stared at Beri, and then Beri turned to look at him and he quickly said, "You look very sweet tonight." He started kissing her and was soon fondling her. After their love-making, Egbe watched her leave before following her in his car to his bach's eve.

Egbe's friends had been looking for him in vain since 10pm. The show was supposed to start then. All the ladies had gathered on the dance floor. They had already formed a big circle. A pot of punch stood in the middle of the circle. The friend who had Egbe's Bachelor's coat stood in front of the nightclub looking left and right. He sighed when he finally saw Egbe's car approaching. "Big man, where have you been all this while? People have been waiting for you." Egbe smiled and took the coat from him. He wore the coat and as he moved into the night club, the Master of Ceremony announced his arrival and all the ladies clapped. "The man of this night's occasion is around. Right now, I want all the unmarried women to get up and give him a farewell dance. Mr. Egbe Eyong Arrey Ako Agbor Takang Obi Ayuk . . ., once more you are heartily welcome. Please, come right here to the floor and have a last dance with all the ladies. Once more accept our congratulations for declaring that you want to be having sex with just one woman over and over and again," the MC shouted out into the microphone. Then, the DJ immediately turned on the music "*Femme il faut supporté, c'est le marriage.*" Everyone had a hilarious time as the women dragged him around in the circle. When he had danced with all of them, the guys poured the bowl of punch on him.

Then it was time for the taking off of the bachelor's coat and so all the men gathered. Egbe took off the coat dripping with punch and flung it into the crowd of young men. Some of them scrambled over it and some avoided it; one of them finally caught it. This guy was cocksure because his own wedding was coming up in a few weeks time. Then, Egbe's friends took him out to present him with their special gift for that night. They took him to the car, bypassing Beri who had come to the bach's eve but had stayed outside. The gift was waiting at a nearby hotel; Egbe was not one to bypass a great opportunity, so he had a great time.

Thirty-Two
Wedding in the Air

It was Friday, a day before the wedding day. The atmosphere was a happy one and the air filled with wedding preparations. There was the frying of chin-chin, cooking, and choir practice and so on and so forth. Pamela lay down in her room in very low spirits; she sighed and muttered to herself, "I wonder why I am feeling this low." She got up, walked briefly about, looked out the window and hoped Egbe would come soon. She was just sitting down on her bed absent-mindedly at about 11 am when Egbe drove in, greeted everyone in the compound, aunts, uncles and well-wishers of him and Pamela.

Then, he went to Pamela's room and gave her a peck on the lips. Pamela was very excited to see him. "How are you?" she asked as she hugged him.

"Fine and you?" Egbe asked.

"So so. I was thinking of you just now."

"*Ehe*?" Egbe said.

"How was it yesterday?" Pamela continued.

"Fine. Fine. Where is my suit?"

"Your suit? Please check for it in that bag over there." Egbe looked for his suit in the bag as Pamela went out to get him something to eat. He took it with him and was going away when he met with Pamela at the doorway. "Where are you going to?" Pamela was surprised.

"Just to see some friends and to clear one or two things. *Em* . . . to arrange for the drinks, you know, I will see you later. See you!" Egbe said rather hastily.

"When are you coming back? You know, according to the tradition, we are not supposed to sleep in the same house today; I am supposed to stay with my people while you stay with yours," Pamela said looking very worried.

"I will come again at about 7 pm," Egbe said and gave Pamela a peck.

"Love you!" Pamela said and Egbe murmured something incoherent and left quite hastily.

At 8pm Egbe had not yet shown up and Pamela was beginning to worry again. Pamela thought hard as she kept looking from the clock to the window. At about 8:30pm she decided to take a bath and retire early. This was when Egbe drove in. He did not come out of the car but called out to Pamela's younger brother who was assisting with the slaughtering of the wedding pig. He ran to the car and Egbe enquired about Pamela, Tatah told him that she was having a bath. Egbe stayed in his car for a few minutes and then drove off.

When Pamela finished bathing, she put on her nightie and called for Tatah. "I heard the sound of a car when I was bathing; who was it?" she asked.

"It was Brother. Brother Egbe," Tatah told her.

"Ah-so-o! And where is he?"

"He drove out of the compound," Tatah said.

"What did he say before leaving?"

"He asked after you and I told him that you were bathing and he said okay."

Pamela frowned, "Okay? Didn't he tell you if he was going to come back or. . ."

Just then an aunt who had been eavesdropping cut in trying to console Pamela, "Ah! Ah! Besem! Why should he come back eh? Don't worry, you will see him in church tomorrow. Normally, according to tradition you people were not even supposed to see each other today." She moved over and took Pamela by the hand and Tatah left. "Look, you

159

worry too much. I have been watching you the whole day, you don't look very happy. Anyway, it is normal when one is getting married. Come over to your room and sleep, my dear, you have a long day tomorrow."

Pamela looked at her and smiled. "Thank you, Auntie Arrah," she said and retired into her bedroom.

The next day, the preparation team continued their work. They decorated the church hall with balloons and other conspicuous decorations. Slogans like 'Pam and Egbe forever' and 'happy married life' were strewn among the decorations.

The wedding was scheduled to commence at 1pm, and, there was singing going on inside the church hall in anticipation of the arrival of the couple. It was now 3pm as more and more people kept streaming into the church premises, dancing happily. Everyone was richly dressed while some beautiful cars littered the church compound.

Meanwhile, at her uncle's compound, Pamela had been dressed up by her aunts and she looked very pretty in her wedding gown. Her six Bridesmaids, two of whom were her sisters, two small flower girls, two small kids who would bear the rings; a boy and a girl, a little bride and little groom, all sat down around her. A decorated Mercedes Benz convertible was in the middle of the compound. But her chief bridesmaid had not shown up. "Where is Beri?" she asked Immaculate who was sitting with the other girls. "She knows she is the chief bridesmaid, yet up to this hour she is not around," Pamela was restless.

"Calm down Pam, she is going to come. There is still time," Immaculate said.

"Yes, I know she will come but why this lateness? She knows this is my special day. *Na ja,* maybe something serious might have delayed her, who knows. Let's just wait a bit more. We still have about an hour to leave. I am sure Egbe and the groom's men have already taken off for the church since he has to be there first and wait for me." A faint smile caught Pamela's lips as she said these last words.

Meanwhile at the church premises, some two

hooligans attracted the attention of the people when they stepped out of a taxi and shouted to the crowd of people that the wedding was annulled. They announced that Egbe had left the country with Beri. Everyone was stupefied, yet others started confessing how they had seen Egbe and Beri one time too many. They had always seen them coming out of hotel rooms.

The tricky thing was how to break the news to Pamela. She was about to step into the beautifully decorated car with her bridal train when Auntie Arrah burst into the compound, rolling in tears. She could not contain herself, "My dear Pam, you have to take heart o!"

"What is it Auntie?" Pamela asked.

"Your best friend o! Your best friend, Beri has eloped with your to be husband!"

Pamela collapsed instantly, as did her mother. The father paced up and down muttering to himself and shaking his head. Pamela regained consciousness and wept bitterly, "Oh! Beri what wrong did I do to you? You take my man? Oh! Beri, Beri, Beri... Egbe has killed me o...!" She sank down gradually and became unconscious. This time she was rushed to the hospital along with her mother. This was great news in the gossip grapevine. Some insisted that Jerry had paid Beri to deal with her. Nobody thought Egbe had done an evil thing, most people after hearing the story simply said "serves her right."

Thirty-Three
Back to the Scene

Pamela and her mother spent three days at the hospital. On the third day, they were discharged and they went home to her uncle's place. In the evening, the family gathered in the sitting room. Pamela's aunt, uncle and a few other relatives were all present. Then, Pamela's father stood up and addressed everyone, "I thank you all for coming around. Like I told you before, I was in Commercial yesterday and have paid 50,000 Francs for the date on Pamela's return ticket to be changed to today. Pamela says she wants to go back to Germany immediately. In fact, she has to travel tonight. She even wanted to leave the hospital yesterday but for the doctor's restrictions. So, I thought it wise to call you all here."

He sat down while an uncle of Pamela stood up, "Pamela, I want to say that you are a very strong and courageous child. But I want to also ask you if you think you are strong enough to travel right now."

"Yes, Uncle Mbah, I can travel. I need to go back and sort out things for myself as soon as possible," Pamela replied.

"Let her go. I think it will be better for her. Let her go back to her station, the earlier the better. Pam, don't mind, everything will be fine. You are a beautiful girl. Don't try to kill yourself because of that good-for-nothing boy. Our people say that, the disease, which attacks cocoa pods in the farm, will certainly attack the coffee beans. When you go back, Pam, don't try to attack neither Beri nor Egbe. Just leave them, God will judge them," her mother said in a very low tone.

An elderly paternal uncle of Pamela who was next of kin called Pamela out to the middle of the room. He poured out palm wine in their great great grandfather's cup made out of the horn of a cow. This *contri fashion* cup is handed down from generation to generation. The uncle handed the wine to the relatives who passed it round for everyone to hold and speak words of blessings for Pamela into the wine. Some spoke and spat in the wine as well. They prayed to their ancestors to guide and protect Pamela from wherever they are; to arise and manifest. Uncle Mbah stood up holding five slices of kola nuts in his hand, he went down on his knees, lifted his hands up and down three times and then holding the kola nuts in his left palm, he dropped them down using his right hand one after the other; calling the names of their ancestors as he made the offering; "Baba Ticha, this is for you, wherever you are, receive it, Baba Fon, the great hunter; this is your own, Baba Tawum, remember us, Baba Abang, the wise one; *afor zie*, Baba Foncham the great drummer, may we dance well." When he finished, he gathered the kola nuts, took them out and flung them in the compound.

Then, the cup went back to the elderly uncle who chewed some grains of alligator pepper mixed with *contri kola* and spat it in the wine. Then he added a drop of spittle in the cup and insisted that Pamela drink at least half the content. He poured libation and as the drops of wine touched the floor, he chanted:

"Our daughter Besem, you are the apple of our eyes, whosoever touches you, touches us.

As you go, May you go well; when you hit your foot on a stone, let the stone break and not your foot.

May you be content with any little thing you have.

When your enemies look for you, they will not find you.

Your face will shine brightly and your star will no longer be darkened; any darkness unto your star which has brought you this misfortune be cleansed."

He went outside and poured out the rest of the wine saying: "Our ancestors, this is for you."

When he returned, he asked Auntie Arrah to give a song of praise. Auntie Arrah started off,

"Only Jesus can save; halleluya
Only Jesus can save; Amen, Amen.

All the others, including Pamela sang along with her and in the end Auntie Arrah made a prayer to the Almighty God, thanking Him and asking Him to take control. Then she said, "*Psalms 91,*" and everyone recited *Psalms 91:*

He that dwelleth in the secret place of the Most High shall abide under the shadow of the Almighty

. . .

A thousand shall fall at thy side, and ten thousand at thy right hand; *but* it shall not come nigh thee

. . .

With Long life, will I satisfy him and show him my salvation.

Auntie Arrah: Glory be to the Father, and to the Son, and to the Holy Spirit.

And the rest of the family members answered:

As it was in the beginning, is now and ever shall be, world without end, Amen.

Everyone was happy that the ancestors had been appeased and nothing bad was going to happen to Pamela in the future. A meal was served and soon after, a few relatives accompanied Pamela to the airport to catch the 11pm flight out of the country.

Pamela's flight touched down in Germany at about 10am. She had not called any of her friends to pick her up. She boarded a taxi home. When she was on the way she called Jane and told her to wait for her in front of the building. Fortunately for her, Jane did not have to work on that day.

When Pamela alighted from the taxi, she handed the driver 35 D-Mark. The driver looked at the money and was surprised. *"Nein, ich nehme keine D-Mark mehr,"* he said. Pamela looked at him and said nothing and then she looked up and saw Jane coming. Jane hugged her and started collecting one of her bags from the trunk, but Pamela explained to her that the driver would not accept her money. Pointing at the counter in the taxi, the driver said, *"Kuck mal, das sind fünfunddreißig Euro und keine D-Mark."* Jane laughed at Pamela. *"Pays chap,"* she said as she took out her purse and paid the driver 35 Euro. She helped Pamela with her luggage.

Pamela was at a loss and Jane explained that things had changed; they were now using the Euro, which was engendered by the Maastricht Treaty and finalised by that of Lisbon. They both commented on how policies were adopted and voted into law in Europe through the EU. This was unlike in Pays where it was all talk and no action. *"Ma sister, whiteman, na whiteman,"* said Jane as she helped Pamela with the luggage. These people are different. Have you ever taken time to observe how the trains come and go at the train stations? It's amazing how the trains keep to time."

The two girls came out of the lift and went to the room which Pamela once shared with Egbe, Pamela looked around. "So, he has moved out all his things from this room?" she asked Jane.

"Yes. I hear he now lives with her in Stuttgart." Pamela sat down and sighed while Jane tried to console her and helped to unpack her bags.

"Things have changed," Pamela sighed heavily.

"Yes, things have really changed," Jane said as she looked around the room at those places where Egbe's things used to be chauvinistically displayed. She was waiting for the right moment to ask Pamela what actually happened in Pays, because she had heard so many controversial stories in Berlin. Paysans who happened to have phoned their people on that day when the incident happened came back with many contrasting stories. Some said, Egbe had caught Pamela with another man and others said Beri had used a charm on Egbe.

Jane was hoping that Pamela would speak about this to her, but Pamela instead asked, "When did they start using the Euro and have you tried to find out why Britain refused using it?"

Her friend was perplexed. "Have you gone mad, of what use is that to you?" Jane was certain Pamela was avoiding the obvious discussion.

"Anyway, all I heard was some nonsense about the queen's image on the British pound and its significance. But I don't know about the validity of this, of course I don't care to know. What is that to you anyway?" Jane asked.

"*Huhn*! Things have changed," Pamela sighed again sadly.

Then, Jane finally gathered the courage to ask Pamela about the allegations concerning her breakup with Egbe, but she denied everything, "He just left me, just like that. I did not hurt him, I did not cheat on him and we did not even quarrel, not even once since we got to Pays. The last time he came to see me, he just asked for his suit and left, just like that. I could not imagine that Beri could do that to me." Pamela burst out crying while Jane tried to comfort her. She took Pamela to live with her at least for some time.

Thirty-Four
Celebrating

A few months after returning home, Pamela was still shy of going out, she was scared of people's reaction. "Have you considered going for the excursion?" Jane asked.

"Do you mean the one at the *Reichstag?*"

"Yes," said Jane.

"I don't think so."

"But, I thought you had a question for the Minister."

"Yes, I do, but they are specific on what they want us to ask. We are limited just to ask questions concerning development, science and technology transfer in relation to what the Germans are doing in our various countries. Besides, why would they tell us what is important to us? This is neo-colonialism, the globalisation agenda is nothing but a new medium of exploitation."

"What question did you prepare?"

Pamela merely smiled. "Honestly, it's of no use, *Hauptsache*, I am not going there."

"Okay, what about the Carnival?"

It was a Sunday and the *Karnival der Kultur*en promised to be very interesting. Pamela had bought a new wig for her head that was skinned during the *contri fashion* in Pays. She looked critically once more at the wig on her head in the mirror before venturing out with Jane. They boarded the train to Hermannplatz where they got off and strolled in the streets. Standing at a corner, they watched the various groups dancing through the city following a particular route. All the dance groups were beautifully dressed and displayed a great sense of the various cultures they represented.

Carnival day in Berlin was a day of the celebration of multiculturalism. Talking about multiculturalism in Berlin people often had Prenzlauer Berg or Kreuzberg in mind. But there was more than these two mountains could contain. Berlin consisted of so many cultures. And it was very interesting how these cultures could come together and celebrate culture without minding their differences. Countless groups danced in vibrancy and verve as Pamela and Jane watched; the Brazilians, the Mexicans, the Turkish, and the Ghanaians among others.

Pamela was not just thinking about the many cultural groups, but about the changes that she suddenly noticed. It occurred to her as something too rapid. Some years back, when she first came to Berlin, very few Africans could be identified during the carnival, but today things were different. So many African dance groups could be identified so much so that a country like Pays, which had so many tribes, came up with four dance groups: the MECUDA dance group, the GRASSLAND, the BACDA and the MANYU. Apart from the Likis, who were bilingual, the English-speaking parts of this country had culture as their fort. As the GRASSLAND group dance passed, Pamela wondered about all the recent changes. She remembered how the previous Sunday, she had watched a group of women in uniformed *wrapper* and blouse hurry to a nearby church. For a split second, she had thought she was either in Britain, France, or the United States, if not in Pays. Pamela had looked intently at her environment to ensure she was not dreaming. "It was time to start thinking of going back to Pays, she thought to herself." This place was fast becoming a black man's country, not the Whiteman's country she used to know. She was sure this was not a good sign. So many *darkies* have travelled abroad with the notion of collecting "colonial debt". Certainly, the colonials would not be able to distinguish her from them. Her main aim of travelling was just to enjoy life abroad to its fullest, and be contented.

Change was something Pamela particularly dreaded. It showed that time was passing and she was getting old. She was yet to find a man who would marry her and by the look of things, her options were becoming very limited.

Pamela tried to take off her mind from her present predicament but everything around her reminded her of her plight. She looked over across the road, and saw African children of about fifteen years moving and chatting happily. It was a pleasant sight to see in a country like this, but it brought pain to Pamela because it confirmed that things had changed, times had changed. She too needed to change and change was one thing Pamela could not easily take in. She contemplated the present state and started thinking about what steps to take to fit in her changed life within all these changes. Even the names of the train stations had changed, *S-Bahnhof* Papestrasse had become Südkreuz, Eichkamp had been renamed Messe Süd and Hauptbanhof was now Ostbahnhof, and there were plans underway to change Lehrter Stadtbahnof to Hauptbahnhof, tram 23 had become M13. She thought about all these changes and sighed, and Jane gave her a questioning look. "It's nothing, I just wonder sometimes about the many changes," she told her friend.

"Yes Pam, a lot has changed; you have to reconsider certain things before your beauty finally fades away," Jane quickly put in.

"Yes, I have reconsidered what you told me and I have settled on *oyigbo*. I don't want any *darkie* boy again. Next Love Parade, I am going to look for an *oyigbo* man. I have to look for *doki*. I just want to have *Mutterschaft* like many girls do, but then, I don't want to have a mulatto, what do I do?"

"But you must not have a child with a German before getting that paper. You can have a child with a *darkie* guy and then you pay any German to go to the foreign office and lie that it is his child, and you will be given the paper," Jane told Pamela. "You know these people, they are very dull, they are colour blind, to see a pure black child and accept that it is a mixed breed," she added.

"I don't know what you mean by dull, these people are more than us, that's all I know, I don't know how to relate that to dullness. It's dull to think them dull," Pamela told Jane.

When the two girls got home that evening, they were quite exhausted and Pamela slept very soundly for the first time in weeks. In the morning, as she lay in bed, she thought once more over all what Jane had told her about the advantages of having a white man; money, and even papers too, since their student visas would soon be expiring. She thought especially about the money and told herself, she might give it a try. She finally made her mind firm for a Whiteman.

A week later, Pamela moved out of the room she had shared with Egbe and got herself another room in the same student hostel but in another block. Most of the time she was either paying Jane a visit in her room or Jane was visiting her. They talked about the forthcoming Love Parade and German men. Their discussions usually surrounded issues of survival in Europe and marriage. As they contemplated on trying white men, they thought that the Love Parade will be a good avenue to find single Germans. They talked about how in the past, it was unusual for a *darkie chap* to have a white boyfriend, but very alright for the *darkie* guys to have white women. They laughed and were happy that things had changed as a few heartbroken black girls like Marisa took up the challenge a few years back and it worked out without any stigmatization. "Is it true that a certain Ginain man sent his wife to marry for real, not on contract basis to a German man?" Jane asked.

"I don't know," Pamela said.
"I also heard that this man became very angry with his wife because the German demanded too much sex from her." Jane continued.

"I now remember; I heard that story too. But, of course the man didn't know the girl had another husband waiting at the side, who even lived with them some of the time. Papers, that's all they want. The girl actually told the man openly after three years in marriage, when she already had her papers and finally succeeded to get a divorce from the man, she told him that she had a black husband and had wanted a German husband just for papers. She went along and married her black man again, so he too got the papers. It was then that the German realised why she had been postponing having a child with him. The German however, acknowledged that, while the marriage lasted she had been a good wife. Surprisingly, he longed for another black woman."

Pamela and Jane shared their ideas about white men, again and again as they looked forward to that year's Love Parade. The day finally arrived, but Pamela and Jane realised they were too shy to put on their pants and brassieres at home to attend the Love Parade. They carried them in their bags, and when they were around Kurfürstendamm which was one of the high points of the parade, they hid behind some bushes and changed into their spectacular undergaments. They carried their dresses in backpacks, bought a can of BECK'S beer each, joined a gang of crazy dancers and started marching to the sound of *Techno.* They nodded and hopped around town, each time replenishing their drinks from the roadside vendors. More often than not, a few hooligans came around them, danced into them, bought them drinks, offered them cigarettes, hashish, marijuana and even cocaine. Pamela and Jane accepted just cigarettes and the drinks. They danced around, cigarette in one hand and a drink in the other. Then, two females approached them and clothed their heads with colourful feathers. They tried to kiss and fondle their breasts, but Pamela and Jane quickly moved away. After a few more minutes of dancing, a boy came to Pamela and suggested that they should go to the bushes at the side to celebrate love in a most special way. *"Keine Angst, ich habe Kondome mit,"* he encouraged her. He continued to tell Pamela about his strong potency. Pamela was perplexed and suggested to Jane that it was time they get something to eat.

While they sat under a tree in a nearby park to eat,

they saw that people were having sex in the open, some were injecting themselves with hard drugs and a crew was shooting a pornographic movie in the open where all could witness. Pamela took in a deep breath as she looked around her. "I can see the devil has one day each year to have dominion over this city," she murmured. Then, she turned to Jane and asked, "What are they, I mean, we, really celebrating?"

"Sometimes one just needs to celebrate Pam. Anything, culture, multiculture, anything, love, or maybe sex I don't know," Jane said vehemently. Pamela simply looked at her.

"Is it true that the authorities are planning to put a ban on this Love Parade thing?" she continued to ask Jane.

"I don't know, they said so, some time ago but it still goes on," Jane answered her.

After eating, the two girls stood up and walked about, conversing and just looking at places, the people and the dance going on. They noticed some German men whom they wished would ask them into a relationship. These men looked responsible, they merely stood by and watched the dancing, and they were dressed normally and not a part of the dance. Some of these men moved slowly behind the dancing train, some simply leaned on their cars. Once or twice, the girls made themselves noticeable to such men and all the men did was look at them, their breasts and buttocks and merely smiled.

They joined the dancing party once more, but after a short while, they became fed-up with the depraved celebration and the unsolicited young men who were bent on cajoling them into having sex and they decided to head home.

Thirty-Five
More Celebrations

A week after the Love Parade, Pamela and Jane were invited to a friend's child's birthday anniversary. They knew and understood that as usual, the party will not commence until it was close to midnight, in spite of the information that had accompanied the invitation stating that, it was a kid's party and has to commence as early as 8pm. When Pamela saw the invitation, she found it ridiculous, because, at 8pm kids should be in bed.

Pamela and Jane got to the party hall at midnight. The place was full and some people and kids were dancing while others were just sitting and talking. So they thought that the party had already started. They saw Jane's friend Marilyn who had invited them to the grill party of a friend - Marisa. She was dancing alone in front of a big wall mirror. They went to greet her. "Hey, Monroe, *long time no see*," Jane said.

"Oh! Since Marisa's party," Marilyn answered as she hugged both girls. Pamela asked about her son, for Marilyn now had a two-year-old son with her black boyfriend and they had paid a German some money to sign that he was the father of the boy. Marilyn now had papers to live in Germany for at least 18 years. She, her boyfriend, and her son lived in a government paid apartment and she received social benefits as well as allowance for her child. "I hear the birth rate in Germany is very low. Germany needs kids, I hear," she told her friends as she explained to them her good fortune with her son, while continuing to dance at the mirror. Jane and Pamela asked her when the party started, but she told them the party had not yet started at all, it was still to start, for the hosts, the little girl's parents and the little girl herself had not yet shown up. She took Pamela and Jane to where her son was sleeping in a perambulator behind the bar counter near a huge loudspeaker out of which a blast of *mapouka* flowed. There, the two year old boy was sleeping soundly. "He just fell asleep a short while ago. All the time he had been on the floor, jumping and dancing with those other kids you see dancing there," the mother informed her friends. Pamela and Jane had not seen the boy yet since he was born. They looked at the sleeping boy and congratulated their friend.

Marilyn went back to the dance floor and continued dancing at the mirror while Pamela and Jane looked for a place to sit; bypassing little kids on the dance floor and a table full of assorted food laid open and looking provocatively appetising. There was especially a dish of *koki* beans and half-ripe plantains. The smoothness of the well-sliced pieces of *koki* spread on a tray looked very tempting.

Pamela and Jane sat down and made themselves familiar with a girl and a boy who were already sitting at the table. After exchanging greetings, they joined in eating the popcorn served on the table as aperitif and listened to the conversation of their tablemates. The boy was telling the girl that, it was better for her to have brought her three year old daughter to the party than to have locked her all alone in the apartment. But the girl said, the child was sleeping soundly and nothing would happen to her. "With all the cold outside, I couldn't bear to push the perambulator all by myself. Nothing will happen to her, I always leave her like that when I go to the nightclub," she added.

Just then, the hosts of the party, a young couple, arrived with the little birthday girl beautifully dressed. Everyone was happy as the family proudly marched in and took the floor. It was 1am. They made a speech each, first the young man and then the lady. Both of them said the same things in their speeches, the only difference was their voices.

There was a lot of clapping after that, but Pamela was turned off by the theme of the conversation that had taken place between her table mates. She pondered over the reasons why her mates were having children and this disturbed her somehow.

There was eating, drinking and dancing after the birthday song was sung and the cake dispensed off. Pamela noticed a German who had been sitting very quietly with some two black guys. Pamela noticed he was paying her a lot of attention and she almost walked up to talk to him. She was not surprised when the man finally mustered courage and walked up to their table, but then, to her surprise, he instead asked permission to speak to Jane and merely greeted her.

After speaking with Helmut outside the hall, Jane returned smiling. "Pam, that guy loves you."

"Which one?" Pamela asked.

"The one I was speaking with, Helmut, that's his name."

"How come he asked to speak to you instead?" Pamela was taken aback. The truth was that some of Helmut's Pays friends had advised him that an easier way to get to their girls was through the girl's best friend. So Helmut had followed this advice.

"See, Pam," Jane said. "He wants you to have coffee with him sometime next week."

"I don't even drink coffee. I hate coffee, and you know that," Pamela said.

"No, Pam, it's not just coffee. The guy means that he wants you people to go out, anywhere, to eat or drink something so he can get to know you better. He just wants to do a kind of courtship. He promised he will take care of the bills. See Pam, I have told him that to date a girl like you, he really has to prove that he loves you very much," Jane continued whispering to Pamela.

"And what did he say about that?" Pamela asked.

"He said of course he would."

"Okay, I hope he is loaded," Pamela smiled.

"I am sure he is," Jane said.

Thirty-Six
Love

Pamela finally met Helmut at a Chinese restaurant. They ate, drank wine and exchanged some information about themselves. Helmut told Pamela that he would like to go to an African restaurant next time. He dropped Pamela off late in the evening and promised to give her a call. A week later, Helmut asked to visit Pamela, and Jane advised him that this was the time for him to express his love to Pamela. Jane informed Pamela and told her that, from every indication, Helmut was ready to "spoil" Pamela.

"I hope his 'listening and encouragement fee' will be encouraging," Pamela smiled.

"I told you Helmut has a good job and you know these people do not have extended families like us and so they have no responsibilities. Pam, just think about it, he is going to indeed spoil you with cash." Jane was excited and Pamela was pleased.

It was Saturday morning when Helmut showed up at Pamela's apartment with a big bunch of very beautiful roses. He walked in gentlemanly and presented the flowers to Pamela. When Pamela saw the flowers, she remembered something which Akwi had told her about white people and flowers. She was half-shocked but told herself that it couldn't be. She quickly pushed the thought to the back of her mind. Helmut had only just arrived, most people showed their love

176

when they were leaving. She put up a broad smile, gave Helmut a big hug and asked him to make himself comfortable. She looked at the flowers several times, sniffed and kissed them just as she could remember from a scene in a certain Western movie, before putting them carefully to the side, as she didn't own any flower vases. She made Helmut coffee that she had bought purposely for this visit and he was most thankful. After they had talked for some time, they agreed on a date to meet at an African restaurant. He took Pamela's hand and kissed it in a gentlemanly fashion before taking his leave.

Pamela watched him from her balcony as he drove away. Then, she turned around to face the flowers with anger. She uttered a string of curses as she tossed the flowers on to the balcony. Then, she broke down and started weeping; asking herself what she had done wrong to deserve this ill-luck. Why? "Was she not beautiful enough?" She asked herself. When will ill luck stop to haunt her life? She needed more cleansing. She would send word back home and some money for a *medicine-man* to cleanse her properly. As these thoughts crossed her mind amidst tears, her doorbell rang and she went to open the door.

As soon as she saw her two friends, Pamela broke down and cried even more. Jane and Marilyn were shocked to find Pamela in tears. Pamela narrated to them how it all went. "Not even a cent, my friend," she concluded. She took both girls to the balcony and showed them the flowers scattered on the floor. The girls were more shocked when they came face to face with the truth. They tried to console their friend as best as they could. They sobbed softly. "God giveth and He taketh. You will overcome the grief Pam," said Marilyn.

"No, no, I don't want to ever see that man again. What an insult!"

"Pam, don't talk like that. Take it easy."

"He could have even bought me a pair of shoes, even just one, since he must buy something and doesn't want to let out raw cash. He said we will be going to an African restaurant. But I don't think..."

"Good!" Jane cut in. "You see, he is very interested in you, I am sure of that, we just have to work hard. Every relationship needs some hard work. Let's give him some time. Maybe he has not received his salary."

"Do you think he will ever change? The man is too stingy!" Pamela sobbed.

"Of course. You've barely just met him." Jane encouraged Pamela until Pamela conceded and planned to take her two friends along during her next meeting with Helmut. She would see how on dropping them off, Helmut would not give her some money.

The weekend came and the girls went with Helmut to the restaurant. Helmut insisted on eating something really African. He shouted his order from his seat to the bleached lady behind the counter. He asked for *okro* soup and pounded yam. He actually insisted that he wanted the hooves of a cow, the part with the marrow inside and some bony meat with some intestines and pepper too.

Helmut was excited as he ate his African meal the African way - with his fingers. He struggled with the slippery soup and the girls giggled all the time. As he ate the huge bony meat, some of the soup spilled on his clothes. But he wouldn't give up. Even the pepper was taking a toll on him. "Are you okay?" asked Pamela.

"I am fine," Helmut responded as he struggled with his bone.

They finally finished eating and the girls ordered for a second bottle of red wine. After they were done, Helmut went up to the woman to pay his bill and said, *"Getrennt bitte."* The girls were shocked. "How could Helmut ask for separate bills? Is this how to date a girl?" Pamela wondered as she looked angrily at Jane, who was so ashamed of herself. The girls struggled to conceal their disappointment and annoyance. They whispered amongst themselves as they contributed money to make up for their own part of the bill. Then, Helmut's stomach made a grumbling sound, *gururu, grewg* and the girls all looked up at him. Helmut himself could no longer conceal the turmoil in his stomach caused by the pepper and rushed off to the toilet. The girls watched after him and burst out laughing. "*Oyigbo, wan turn darkie*," Jane said and the girls laughed even more. "Just be patient, Pam. Remember, he still has to drop us off. Let's see what happens then. Remember, the patient dog eats the fattest bone," Jane said.

"It's a lie, the patient dog has no bone," Pamela said sarcastically. Just then, Helmut came back. The girls stopped talking abruptly, looked up and smiled broadly at him. He looked troubled.

After having settled their bills, they all rose and went out to the parking lot. When they reached his car, Helmut still showed signs of discomfort. He was beginning to regret his decision to date an African woman. Then, suddenly he glided slowly from his car on which he was leaning, and landed on the pavement of the parking lot. The girls were confused but managed to make him lie down. His face was red and he was sweating profusely and breathing heavily with his mouth half-opened. The girls quickly called an ambulance that took him off to the hospital.

The girls had to go home by train. Pamela cursed and blamed Jane for deceiving her and raising her hopes of getting money out of Helmut. Jane brought up several arguments and finally succeeded in convincing Pamela that Helmut would have given her some money if he had dropped them off. "Just give it a try, Pam, go to bed with him once or twice; you will lose nothing. Things will change. He certainly has money, Pam, he has a nice car, a Skoda, he is rich, and he has little or no responsibilities, no extended family, in fact no family. You know this is how these people are. After making yourself his, then, you can openly ask him for money. After all, doesn't he know you have a mother and younger ones?" Jane insisted.

"As for me, I am tired of doing all these odd jobs such as cleaning and working in the factory. All of these jobs are too strenuous. Meanwhile, the little money I get can barely cover necessities. I need to drive my own car in this Europe, not when I will go back to Pays which I am not yet certain of.

This is the better part of our lives we are living, there is no duplicate to it, no *Ersatzleben*. I think I will go back to Lady Beate," Jane said firmly.

Pamela slowly made up her mind too and went to spend some time with Helmut after he left the hospital. Helmut was so overwhelmed with joy. He asked Pamela to move in with him in his three-room apartment, a proposal which she promptly accepted. Pamela was soon frustrated with their sex life, she had expected regular sex but he could go for weeks without showing any interest. This caused Pamela to fear that Helmut might be cheating on her. This suspicion was quickly erased when she realised that he showed her a lot of attention and was not prune to doing anything fishy. Helmut went to work and came back on time. Almost all his co-workers at BSR knew and liked Pamela very much. "But what could be wrong with him?" Pamela asked herself. "He is good, a good man, so nice, but then all he does is cuddling me and scratching the vein of my hand every now and then, kissing me passionately. But when it comes to having sex, zero. Maybe he belongs to a secret society. These occult people used to have very terrible rules." All these thoughts disturbed Pamela's mind one fine afternoon as she stared blankly at the TV screen.

Pamela visited her friend Jane and related her problem. Jane informed her that it was normal, and that if she desired more sex, then she would have to look for an African guy.

Pamela went back home and as she pondered over this new thought, she lingered around the bathroom door when Helmut went to have his shower. As soon as Helmut turned on the shower, Pamela started to spy on him to see if he was masturbating. But she saw nothing of that sort. The following day when she went to visit Jane, the latter laughed at her ignorance, "This is how most of these people are. Didn't you know? You need to look for a *darkie* guy, I told you. Not necessarily a Paysan, you know. Paysans are too proud. An Awala man or a Ginain is better. *Sowieso*, Paysans talk too much."

"What do you mean by asking me to look for *darkie* guys? Did I tell you I wanted to join you at Lady Beate AG? I told you, I can't do that job. I need to be first of all dead to myself before sleeping with any Tom, Dick and Harry who can afford 50 Euros or so." Jane simply laughed at Pamela for she had no such problem. When she just started her job as an entertainer of the opposite sex, her only problem had been to have *darkies*, most especially Paysans, come to her room. She had resolved this issue with her boss as soon as she was made a permanent worker. She forbade her boss from sending any black man to her room with the excuse that it might turn out to be a relative, and that she wanted to avoid committing incest. "Because one never knows, the black man could turn out to be a Paysan and Paysans talk too much, they gossip a lot," she had told her friend Pamela. Jane had little problems in that area. Lady Beate was very kind to her and most of the times sent her good clients and allowed no *darkies* to her room.

That notwithstanding, Jane did not mean that Pamela should get into this profession. "Although the job I'm doing is not all that bad. Sometimes, the men who come there are very old, they do not have enough energy to do anything with you, instead they only want you to fondle them and let them feel your presence. Some come there just to get a few strokes of the leather strip on their bare buttocks and to be dominated and nothing more. Others just want you to piss in their mouths. You don't have to belabour yourself all the time," Jane told Pamela.

"What do you mean by piss in their mouths? Occultism! I knew it!" shouted Pamela.

"Point of correction, eroticism; not occultism. Bush girl!" Jane said.

"Whatever. That's nasty though," Pamela sighed.

"Besides, you know I started working in that place because Lady B.U. promised to look for me a resident permit to make my stay permanent," Jane continued. Most of Lady Beate's workers referred to her by the initials of her full names as a sign that they are very fond of their boss whom most of them hoped to be famous like one day.

"But before then, you had started hawking the streets, Jane, she was just making you a better offer," Pamela said. Actually, Lady Beate was of great help to Jane. She even promised to send Jane to work abroad if she preferred. Since Jane was too shy to work here, where she could be easily noticed, by her own *contri* people, she could work in Italy, France, and Switzerland or even in Holland, and just come to Berlin on visits whenever she wanted to. She could tell her friends in Berlin that she owned a restaurant or an African shop in any of these countries. This would not only account for the huge amounts of money she would be entitled to, but would also account for her regular absence from around town. This would satisfy her nosy *contri* people who might spoil her name and make her never to get married again. Jane had started practicing to work abroad by going to spend some time working in a city which was not too far from Berlin called Reeperbahn.

She did not understand why Pamela was always complaining; at least Helmut was learning, though slowly, that the material needs of an African woman were different from those of a white one, which is what was important.

"I mean, you should get yourself a black boyfriend or boyfriends if you care. Apart from sleeping with them, you will also be gaining at least 20 or 50 Euros from time to time, double gain", Jane continued to tell Pamela.

"But how can I do that, Jane, the man is so nice, he is a very, very good man. I really want to start minding my ways. He is so caring and so much in love. He wouldn't think of cheating. I don't think it is proper for me either, not now that I have promised myself to change for the better," Pamela was confused.

"I don't know what is wrong with you, Pam?" Jane barked. "Ever since Egbe jilted you, instead of becoming wiser, you decided to become more stupid. Most of the men from here are like that. They are not chauvinistic like our men. They are caring and loving, I know, but what is there to have a *darkie* at the side for fun. Didn't you notice that

Marisa's child was a pure black child and the man still accepted her? Okay, you must not stick to one particular darkie. Just go out from time to time and pick on them as your need arises. After all, is that not what these women are doing to them?" Pamela simply looked at Jane and smiled and decided to change the topic.

"Do you know what? This man needs to be schooled more. How can I tell him that my mum is sick and I need to send her money to enable her get treatment and Helmut asks if she doesn't have a health insurance. Each time I ask for money to send home, he will ask one stupid question or the other."

"But does he end up giving you the money or not?" Jane asked.

"Yes, he does, he is picking up gradually. But those questions discourage me from asking him the next time. Moreover, he gives it reluctantly and as if he doubts whether he is doing the right thing."

"*Hauptsache*, he is giving the money, Pam. That is what is important. We just have to continue schooling him through his friend Nguea."

Pamela re-adjusted her relationship with Helmut. She made all sorts of excuses to go out alone. She went and came as she pleased. Helmut had to negotiate for weeks before getting an outing with her. Helmut tried giving her whatever money she asked for, but it didn't change much. He just had to be contented with what he got. "She needs some time with just her own people," Helmut thought to himself. His only problem was the fact that Pamela sometimes came home very drunk, especially on the days she went out with a certain group of Nairobi girls whom she had become friends with.

As time went on, Pamela soon discovered that she wanted more from life, she needed to settle down, yet none of the many Paysans she had slept with would commit to her. She was also having problems renewing her student visa, since the foreign office demanded a report of her progress in the university until date. Of course, Pamela had no *Schein to* prove her progress, since she hardly attended classes and had validated no courses. Pamela rejected the advice of her friends to marry Helmut or another white guy for papers. Her fervent wish was to marry a Paysan, and she was hopeful that it would come to pass.

Once Pamela was walking to the train station from Jane's place, when she heard a familiar voice calling her name. She turned and saw Akwi pushing a perambulator. "*Eh!* Long time!" Pamela shouted as she went to embrace Akwi. "My goodness! I can't believe that we live in the same town and yet we rarely see each other. In fact, this city is very big. So, you have a baby now? I didn't know that. How is Nji and the rest?"

"Everyone is doing fine," Akwi answered and updated Pamela on their friends as they walked towards the train station.

"All of us are fine. Everyone has just been struggling to have a resident permit since we haven't been regular at the university," said Akwi. Even those who took school seriously and finished in record time were still sent packing out of the country, only a few managed to get good jobs. Most of these were those in the medical field and those who studied Computer Sciences. "Andrew had been repatriated while Fonjock got a child with his girlfriend and he had *Vaterschaft*, and eventually married the girl because he was targeting the German P.," Akwi continued.

Pamela enquired about Oguchuku and was told that he finally got his permanent residence permit after being with Steffi for three years. Then, one fine day, as they were having a walk, Oguchuku excused himself, entered an internet café and disappeared, to Steffi's dismay. He claimed he was paying back for slave trade and colonialism.

"Nji and I saw Ogochuku once with one very old white woman, a little older than Steffi, and we were surprised. We thought he would look for a young girl to settle with. But he told us the woman has money that was why he was dating her. Nji explained to me later on that it was a lie. The fact is, Ogochuku has become very used to old women and so, young women no longer appeal to him. He can't cope with a younger woman anymore. But, we later on learnt that, he found a man he wanted to marry, a very wealthy TV star. He has come to explore, exploit and export and the sky is his limit; that's what he said. But presently no one knows where he is. Steffi is even looking for him; she wants him to sign the divorce papers, for she found another *darkie* she wants to get married to."

"How is Jerry?" Pamela finally asked.

"I thought you'd never ask. Jerry is doing fine. He now has his permanent residence permit as well. At one time, it was bad for him, and the foreign office stopped extending his visa. He went to Eisenhüttenstadt and demanded asylum using a fake name. Then, he was doing some little, little black jobs. Finally, he paid one German woman to do a contract marriage with him. He was fortunate, it all worked out well. He now has his permanent residence permit."

"I am happy for him," Pamela said. "Do you people still live in the student hostel?"

"No, we live in Wedding, in a slightly bigger apartment. And Jerry lives in the apartment just next to ours. Our apartment was given to me by the state because a German signed for our child. I still need to renew my visa in some months to come, and then register somewhere for the Integration Course in order to be fully integrated into the system. I hope I will be fortunate enough not to be asked to bring a DNA test when I go to extend my visa. I hear they have started demanding that from certain people before issuing a visa."

"So, Nji doesn't have papers yet?" Pamela asked.

"Nji actually went back to school and got a Magister Artium now. He was given a year to look for a job, but the time is expiring so fast. He has no work permit in his passport, and so when he goes to look for a job, he is rejected. Meanwhile, the foreign office will give him a work permit only when he has a full-time contracted job within his field of study. The system is so controversial. When he complained to the foreign office at one time, he was told, all the employers have been told to employ foreign graduates with no work permit, and wait to see it later, but some employers do not yield to this."

"So when you people get a second child, that's when he can obtain *Vaterschaft* from you."

"Exactly. Pam, I must hurry, I want to get to Western Union before they close."

"Give me your address, I might visit you people." Akwi gave Pamela her address and hurried off to catch the underground train. Pamela looked at it and smiled. "Everyone now has papers except me, me of all," she told herself sarcastically, and smiled bitterly as she moved in the opposite direction to catch the *S-bahn*.

Thirty-Seven
Other Zones

When Pamela got home that evening, she looked at herself in the mirror, pondering over what Jane had said concerning her age. She was a beautiful woman, that was all she knew and that was all that mattered, she told herself. She still had high hopes of finding a nice Paysan to marry. Pamela planned to make trips to Britain, America, France, Canada, and even to Holland and Ireland in order to make her dream come true.

She applied for a U. S visa and luckily for her, she got it. She packed her boxes and made for Maryland to visit some of her old friends. It was rumoured that the Paysans in America did not get married to the girls there but preferred girls from other areas. So she saw that she could have a chance there. She was there for a week and had many Pays suitors. She started dating one of them, only to realise that the boy was not only dating another lady, but was living in this lady's house and had no house of his own. Although, the boy, like every other Pays boy, had promised her all sorts of things including marriage within this one week, Pamela knew it had all been a waste of time. All of a sudden, the place, which had seemed to be a kind of replacement paradise, started to bore Pamela. Besides this fact, every Paysan in Maryland was a workaholic, they were always very busy. Some of them had about three jobs, and all others had at least two. People were hardly at home. Everyone was so anxious about making huge sums of money. The people there could manage to meet just once a week in a bar, where they talked and gossiped about whose house had been seized because he or she could not pay the mortgage. They talked about who had recently taken what car on loan.

More and more Paysans took note of Pamela as the days went by. At first, they were all so nice to her and wanted to be her friend. Then news of her escapades in Germany reached them, and she became their object of gossip. It was even rumoured that Egbe had left her because she was HIV positive. Pamela was shocked by the level to which her *contri* people in Maryland gossiped. She had thought before, like most Paysans in the diaspora that Paysans in Berlin gossiped the most, but living in Maryland just for two weeks told her something else. All these things, coupled with the boredom she started feeling, made Maryland not only unpleasurable to live in but unbearable as well. Moreover, the friend she had come to visit was hardly ever there, she was always busy rushing from one nursing job to another.

Pamela became fed up with Maryland; she looked for a Canadian visa and travelled across to Canada to visit a man from her father's tribe who had been dying to have her. From the day this man set eyes on Pamela, he had always loved her. Without her knowledge, he had always kept track of what was happening in Pamela's life. When he learnt that Egbe did not marry Pamela, he was overtly happy.

When Pamela arrived at the airport that evening, this man was there with some friends of his to welcome her. He had brought a video camera with him to cover the whole event. Pamela was taken aback and did not know how to feel. It was a long time since she last had such a befitting welcome. At the man's home, a welcome party awaited her. Although the party was not very populated, it was a great one. But during the party, she was introduced as the man's fiancé. This made her bitter and amused at the same time. "How can a man of that age be so naughty?" she asked herself. She didn't remember ever getting engaged to the man. Besides, the man had grown really old since the last time she saw him.

Pamela felt nothing for him at all. As the party went on, Pamela grew bitterer about the man. If only she had enough money left, she would have left immediately and checked into a hotel.

The party became boring for Pamela, and so she excused herself and went to lie down. She woke up at midnight to realise that the party was over; she heard her fake fiancé putting things away in the kitchen. Pamela got up slowly and moved to the kitchen. She scolded the man until the man asked for forgiveness several times. "How could you be so full of yourself? How could you announce an engagement to the public without even first proposing to the woman in question?" Pamela shouted. The man pleaded again and again. "I am leaving first thing tomorrow morning!" Pamela told him. The man begged her to stay a bit longer but to no avail. He confessed his love for Pamela and told her that although she was going away, she should always keep in mind that he loved her.

Pamela went back to bed, but soon realised she could not sleep. Or maybe it was useless to try to sleep because it was almost dawn. She got up, took a shower and on coming out of the bathroom, heard herself addressing somebody; in the background, she heard the sound of a party. Slowly she followed the voice. Then, she heard other voices answering hers. Just then she reached the sitting room and discovered her host watching the video from last night's party. "You guys are so very *schnell* in doing things over here." As she said this, she picked up the remote control from the table, pressed on the stop button, and then ejected the video tape, and left without saying a word. The man simply watched after her, a little mesmerized. After Pamela had dressed up, the man saw her off to the airport and paid for her flight.

On arriving in Berlin, Helmut was not at home. Pamela dropped off her luggage and went to see her friend Jane. She recounted all that she had gone through in her search for a Paysan husband to Jane and both of them laughed heartily over the matter.

On returning home that evening Helmut, who had

found Pamela's box opened with half of its content on the bed, found the video and decided to watch it.

Helmut's face was red when Pamela returned home and saw him sitting in front of the TV. Pamela sat down beside him, and he immediately switched on the video. Pamela gasped. "*Em*, oh the video!" she exclaimed. Then she burst out laughing. "I actually brought it to show you. It is a very interesting story. I know you will love listening to it. You see, that man there." She pointed at her supposed fiancé on the video, "He is engaged to be married to my sister who is back home. He had to do an engagement party. So, since my sister was not around and I was there, he had to use me. This is how we do it according to our tradition and culture." Pamela smiled and nodded in affirmation. "Oh, I see...," Helmut was saying.

"Yes, you see, in some cases, a whole wedding ceremony has to be conducted just with the picture frame of either party, if he or she is not around," Pamela continued. "At least my image was better than a picture frame."

"I see, I see. So, when will she be joining him in Maryland?"

"That will depend on the visa procedure, which is why up till now, she could not join him there for the engagement."

"Why didn't he go home then to do the engagement?"

"He is very busy and he could not postpone the engagement for fear of losing the woman." Helmut nodded his head and smiled. "No one will want to lose a beautiful girl like your sister." In this way, Pamela had managed Helmut's fears and calmed him down.

A few weeks later, Pamela phoned her cousin in England and confided that she was looking for a husband. He encouraged some of his friends who showed some interest and then he invited Pamela for a visit. Pamela was angry that she had to wait for a month before getting a visa to go to England. She had thought that it would be easier since it was within Europe. But, most importantly, she got the visa. On arriving at her cousin's place, only one of the suitors showed up while she was there. This Paysan, who had also been in search of a wife complained that Pamela looked different from her photograph, "a little too old for my liking," the boy had said. Pamela went back to Berlin very disappointed and disgruntled. Many thoughts crossed her mind throughout her flight. Is she no longer beautiful? She asked herself. In those days in Pays, men of all calibre; Captains, Customs Officers, Professors, Company Managers, Medical Doctors, Directors of companies, Chief Accountants, Pilots and even Tourists from Europe, America and Japan used to melt before her. She couldn't decipher where the problem was, but, she realised that things would never be the same.

A day after she came back to Berlin, she made for Jane's place. "I am tired of moving up and down, I have to find Jerry," Pamela told Jane.

"What?" Exclaimed her friend. "For what Pam, *für was*? Besides, isn't this too late? And what the hell do you take Jerry for? A fool or what? The guy loves or rather loved you, yes, but come on, after all what you put him through, he can never make the mistake of taking you back." But, Pamela pretended not to hear her friend.

Jane tried to put Pamela off this by telling her that she had come to the realisation that, marriage was old-fashioned and that a woman doesn't really need a man in order to be happy. She told her that their mothers needed to get married in those days because they could not fend for themselves. "But come on, you can do everything a man can do, especially in this country, where we have more advantages than them. All you need a man for is just to get you pregnant. Decide on the number of kids you think you will love to have or will be able to take care of. I think two is ideal, look for a guy, have the children with him and shake him off to the side. See, you will get child allowance, *Kindergeld,* from the state and the guy will still pay you *Unterhalt."* Pamela knew that what Jane was saying could be right, but there was something in her that made her want to get married, especially to a Paysan, nothing less. She did not want to accept failure. Moreover, she needed to prove to the world, especially to Egbe and Beri, that she could still find a husband, a Paysan.

One evening, at Jerry's apartment, he was sitting on the floor, leaning against the sofa, drinking beer and smoking a cigarette while listening to some melancholic music. Nji was sitting on the other end of the sofa with a remote control in his hand changing from one TV channel to another. "Like I was saying, I didn't kill anyone in Pays before coming here. I want to go back," Jerry said.

"With what *nah boh*? Empty-handed? Abomination! No money, no certificate, I mean, nothing. You are going to meet your old classmates, who by now might have finished their education and are earning their living somewhere," Nji said. "The first mistake one made was coming here in the first place," he added.

"What you are saying is true, for I have also been thinking over the fact that, if I go back, where would I start from? My small business is no longer there," Jerry said, and they both sighed almost simultaneously.

"I know with all the discrimination and racism in this place, it is difficult for one to succeed easily. Especially when we used to live in Lichtenberg. Moreover, right now, there are no jobs. Yesterday, I was in Heinzelmännchen to collect my *Verdienstbescheinigung* for the past years to enable me to escape to the U.S. if things become worse any moment from now. I overheard one German girl fighting over a cleaning job with a *darkie* girl. Although the *darkie* girl had a better number, the German girl got the job under the pretext of *gute Deutschkenntnisse*. I wonder why one has to be excellent in the German language before being qualified to clean the floor. That was only a pretext for the German to have the job. Even cleaning jobs are hard to find these days," Nji said as he grabbed a bottle of Krombacher for himself.

"But at least you have papers now, Jerry, you can make your life here and see what you can make out of it," Nji continued. "We are discriminated everywhere. Even the Turkish, they consider us far below them just because of our skin colour."

"Those Turkish are the ones destroying this place," Jerry said. "In this place, we are nothing. Consider it in order of ranking: first the Germans, then the Turkish, then Eastern Europeans, then the Vietnamese, then dogs and cats, and finally the black man." Jerry laughed sadly as he stood up and danced a little bit to the tune from his cd player.

"But this government has a Christian's heart. The system provides for the needy, the widows, and the orphans, and even for us strangers, you cannot deny that, one just needs to work a little bit harder. Even back home, there is discrimination, although that is different from racism," Nji said.

"Ja, I know. In Pays, hard work doesn't really count because of corruption," Jerry said.

"Yes. Corruption, Covetousness or Greed? Gluttony, Sloth, Pride, Envy, Wrath, Lechery or Lust?"

"Hey! Stop Marloweing, my friend," Jerry burst out laughing.

Jerry and Nji were particularly disappointed with their relatives back home who had squandered their investments. Jerry had tried sending cars to be sold at home, yet he stopped after no one could account for the money of the sale of three cars.

Fonjock had suffered a worst fate of all since his brother had not only embezzled his money but also sold all the fifteen cars he had sent home with plans to permanently return home and establish a car rental business. On realising that he could not cope with life back home, he quickly rushed back to Germany in frustration. His father had sided with the brother and insisted that it would be against their tradition to imprison his own brother.

When Fonjock's wife heard that his family had squandered the money which they had taken as loan together, coupled with the fact that Fonjock started having affairs with other women openly, after he had his German P., she drove him out of their apartment.

Fonjock was depressed for some time when his wife abandoned him for another *darkie*. He found an old abandoned house in the back of a street, and he renovated some parts of it somehow and lived in it. He rented out part of the place to some two Paysan girls, who used it to roast and sell *morocco* fish with *puff puff* and beans. But a week later, all of them, were chased out of the place by the *Polizei*. Fonjock started sleeping from one friend's house to the other, and sometimes he would sleep under a bridge. Slowly, he became a chain smoker, smoking at least two packets of cigarettes a day. Beer being among the cheapest things one could ever purchase in Germany, Fonjock increased his drinking rate and smoked at least two packets of cigarettes a day. One day he was found lying motionless around the train station. He was rushed to the hospital and diagnosed of a certain lung disease with a very difficult name.

Slowly, Fonjock came back to almost normal, by taking medication against his lung disease. He received strict instructions not to smoke and not to drink alcohol. But due to his loneliness, he could not stop these things. Fonjock seemed to be realising for the first time how much he had been fond of this girl.

One day, Fonjock remembered that he used to have a *darkie* girlfriend whom he went out with in hiding for fear of his wife. He started nursing an interest to settle with this girl. For her part, this girl had even forgotten about Fonjock. They had broken up because Fonjock was trying to force the girl to get married to a very rich German in order to have papers and money. Fonjock asked for her hand in marriage and she was startled. "How could you have asked me to marry a German, if you loved me to the extent of wanting to marry me?" she had asked Fonjock as she laughed sarcasticly. Later on, she realised he was serious. She eventually asked him to move in and live with her. Fonjock who was used to neglecting her could not change his habits. He stayed out late and sometimes refused to pick up the girl's call when he was out drinking with his friends under the pretext that the girl was nagging. The girl was not happy with this attitude; moreover, Fonjock did not care about the paying of bills, which the girl expected him to take responsibility over and even send presents to her family members back home. Instead, when they went out to eat, Fonjock would expect this lady to pay the bills and kept on insinuating all the time that, if it were his ex-wife, she could have done it. Fonjock's ex-wife used to even send presents to Fonjock's family back home even though Fonjock never gave her own family any presents. This Pays girl made a present to Fonjock's mother, junior brother and sisters once. But later on, she realised that, Fonjock didn't care much about her own family, so she made up her mind and stopped sending presents to Fonjock's family members. Slowly, she became fed up with Fonjock and sent him away from her apartment. He stayed for a short time at a friend's place and then he looked for a job.

Fonjock moved from one job to another, a courier driver, a *Tellerwäscher, a Reinigungsaushilfe* and all the little money he earned went for the repayment of his own part of the loan he took with his ex-wife, and the rest went for drinking and smoking. He was always in a bar drinking with his Pays friends, or visiting his Jamaican friends to listen to some reggae music.

In spite of the fact that his friends kept him company, the loss of this *darkie* woman made him feel lonelier than ever and he slowly lost the motivation to work, to eat on time and even to comb his hair. He resigned from his last job as *Lagerarbeiter*, allowed his hair to grow into dreadlocks, drank more and started adding a little bit of marijuana to his cigarettes before smoking them, while enjoying his reggae sounds, a taste he had acquired from the company of his Jamaican friends. Many people thought him mad and avoided him but this was not the case, he was just disillusioned with life.

Then Fonjock decided on single mums. Soon he had three of them as girlfriends, one *darkie*, one Brazilian and one German, each of them with two children. At the end of each month, each of these ladies made a present of 150 Euro to him. This gave him an additional 450 Euro on top of his *Arbeitslosengeld*. This worked out well for Fonjock for some time. About a year later, the *Arbeitsamt* started causing him problems. He was asked to get a job or they would no longer pay him any money. He didn't get any job, and each time he had an appointment with *Arbeitsamt*, he would turn it down with one forged excuse or the other. Then, *Arbeitsamt* stopped paying him any money. As if enough was not enough, he started having problems with his girlfriends, the single mums. They seemed to complain over the slightest things he did wrong. When they started to complain over nothing all the time, Fonjock knew they were losing interest in him. Soon they limited his privileges. The *darkie* no longer prepared him pounded *Yam* and *egusi* soup. The Brazilian lady started keeping her packet of cigarette out of his reach. While she smoked, Fonjock would watch her anxiously. Having smoked about three quarters of the cigarette, getting to the butt, she would throw it at Fonjock who would smile anxiously at the butt. Finally, they all stopped giving him any 150 Euro at the end of the month, offering no explanation but a frown whenever he asked for it. They didn't want to be touched by him anymore, and they would openly stare at other young men in his presence. The German lady told him plainly, "*Ich habe kein Interesse mehr, Ich liebe dich nicht mehr und bin nicht mehr dein Baby.*" This was honest.

What puzzled Fonjock was the fact that these three ladies didn't know each other, yet they all behaved the same. He couldn't decipher what had suddenly gone wrong with his relationships. But the reason was not far-fetched. His *Leistung* had dropped. Instead of an increase in *Leistung,* which these ladies expected, Fonjock instead got *schlimmer und schlimmer*. Whatever the cause might have been, the ladies did not care to know. Their motto was: "no honey, no money."

Fonjock finally developed a habit of moving aimlessly about, boarding one train after another, most often without a valid ticket. His eyes always looked drowsy as he peered into the eyes of every *darkie* he met and said "bro--ther" with a slightly Western accent. To the ladies, he would simply say, "My sister!" The *darkies* would just laugh at him and nod their heads in greeting. Sometimes, in crossing the road, he would jump into the air and laugh. At other times he would start a quarrel with drivers who had stopped for him to pass.

196

But Fonjock was not mad. He had papers.

Jerry and Nji talked about this, and they also talked about the situation of a Paysan who was a *Fae* man, a money doubler. This boy had sent huge sums of money back home to his family members for the construction of a house for him. They sent him a photograph of a house under construction. As he sent more and more money, they continued to send him photographs of every stage of the house. Finally, they sent him a photograph of the complete house, which was undergoing painting, and with some gardeners planting flowers around it. This boy was overwhelmed with joy as he moved around with this photograph, showing it to girls whenever he wanted to court them. But on arriving in Pays, there was no house for him there. They had simply been sending him photographs of someone else's house. News of his madness was later on discussed in adjoining rooms to Afro shops, where those he left behind had continued and still continue to go to; to eat pounded yam, goat meat pepper soup, and to drink beer and smoke cigarettes even right up till now.

"I wonder if those people think we pick money from the streets here in Europe," Nji said as he shook his head in disapproval.

"I can't even go back even if I wanted to. I will look for a woman and settle down here. After living in this place for this long, I admit that it is like a second home to me. I have a kind of fondness for the place. When we were travelling back from Pays the last time, we were looking for the connecting flight to Berlin and finally saw it. We were elated not just because we didn't miss our flight, but because there was some joy when we recognised other Germans on the queue? It was like "Oh! Here we are, here are our people." These are our people, whether we like it or not. It is beginning to dawn unto me now that I cannot go back to Pays. Maybe, when I am retired but not now. After all, the people there don't have you anymore at heart. They no longer have any feelings for you; one has been out of their local system for too long. Apart from those you assist financially, all your friends and relatives are even further removed from you. I will stay here and plan my life before it becomes too late."

Jerry and Nji were conversing on this predicament of the Paysans in Europe when the doorbell rang. Nji opened the door, revealing a well-dressed Pamela who walked in confidently. Jerry sprang up from his seat and attacked her.

"What do you want in my house? I say, who invited you here? Do you want to come and show me your wedding ring, or what?" he shouted.

Nji stopped Jerry. "Calm down J.J. This is what I was just telling you earlier on. You can say anything you want to say to anybody in a calm manner. Don't waste your nerves on worthless things like this one."

Pamela warned Nji to watch his tongue, "Who is a worthless thing?" she asked him. Nji stood up, faced her, and looked straight into her eyes asking, "What do you want, for Christ's sake? Haven't you done enough?"

Pamela frowned hard at Nji, "It is Jerry I came for, not you. You better mind your business and please excuse us. I have something important to say to Jerry. It is up to him to listen and then, I will be on my way. So please just behave yourself and excuse us," she said chewing gum and blowing little balloons out of it.

"I will leave, but let me tell you one thing, your good looks won't do you any good this time around. I know you very well, you will never change."

Jerry was angry with Nji for wanting to leave. "Why are you leaving?" he asked. "Stay here and let her say whatever she wants to say. Better still, she should be the one to leave," Jerry said as he got up and shouted at Pamela, *"Comot for ma haus, witch girl."*

Nji restrained him and insisted that he heard what Pamela had to say. When Nji had left, Pamela moved forward with caution. She touched Jerry on the shoulder gently. He pushed her hand away violently. "Say whatever you want to say very fast and leave," he told her.

"See, J.J., I have come to ask for your forgiveness,"

Pamela said.

"Okay, you are forgiven. Sin no more. Now leave! I say, leave my house!"

"No. J.J., take it easy, I will make it up to you. Please, I really still love you."

"So, you don't love your husband Egbe. Or do you think I don't know that you went to Pays to get married, I even heard you have a German now. I don't know what to believe. In any case, leave."

Pamela had noticed from talking with Akwi the last time that Jerry and his friends did not seem to have an accurate knowledge of what had been happening to her. This was due to the various versions that gossip usually turns a story into. They heard so much and did not know what to believe. Moreover, many sympathised with Jerry and avoided talking about Pamela around him. Pamela thought this could play to her advantage since Jerry was not aware of her level of frustration.

"No. I don't have any husband. Look at my fingers; do you see a ring? See, when we reached Pays, I refused Egbe; although I hear some people think that he is the one who rejected me. No. I turned him down on the eve of our wedding. I just discovered he was not the man for me. You see, that is why he got angry and made away with my best friend. See, J.J. It's you I love." Jerry looked at her as if he just got up from sleep. He did not know what to think or how to feel. Pamela tried to force a kiss on him. He pushed her away as he asked, "Are you sure you are not married?" Pamela insisted that she was not married and was never going to be married to Egbe. Pamela explained to him that Paysans gossip too much as they all knew. She refuted the fact that she was living with a German and lied that she was actually living with her friend Jane. Pamela pulled Jerry up and took him to the bathroom. "See, you must have a shower, I don't like my man looking like this." Jerry accepted and like a man under some spell, quietly took off his clothes. Pamela did the same and they took a shower together.

They came out of the shower and dressed up. Pamela

combed Jerry's hair for him. She lay on the bed and Jerry joined her, after pretending to watch television. Jerry took her in his arms and tried to kiss her, but in a flash saw a picture of her and Emeka. He tried hard to wave it off, tried to continue undressing her, but in his mind's eye he kept on seeing the hoarse face of a naked Emeka half leaning on a naked Pamela. Jerry shuddered and got up. He screamed and moved slowly away from Pamela. "What is wrong?" Pamela asked him. Then, Jerry gave another loud scream, "Oh! No! Pam, why? Why, Pam? I can't, I can't anymore." Pamela was shocked. She had never heard anyone shout this loud and in such a bitter tone. She stood up and seemed to face reality and shame for the first time. This rejection was too bitter; the tears pouring out of her eyes only indicated in a small way what she was actually feeling inside.

Thirty-Eight
Shame Goes Raw

Pamela's shame did not last long before being transformed into something more dangerous. This happened one day after she paid Jane a visit and was struck with what her friend told her. Jerry threw a party on his birthday. He was not just celebrating his birthday but was also celebrating his achievements in the land such as his permanent residence permit and his successes in life, for his fiancé would be joining him in a few months' time. In fact, his wife, because Jerry's parents had already gone and made the *Knock Door,* that is, the marriage engagement to this very hard-working girl whose mother was Jerry's mother's childhood friend and classmate. Jerry showed the *Knock Door* photographs to those who were present at his party, telling them that the girl used to be his *Small* in secondary school.

Pamela had found it hard to believe this, but the evidence was overwhelming. She contemplated all the advantages she could have reaped by having a Paysan man by going back to Jerry. This would have proven to Egbe that she can still get herself any man. At least she owed herself that, she thought. Also, Jerry was a handsome and hard-working man who was well respected among his pals, especially now that he had a permanent residence permit. Then, Pamela also realised that, there was more to what she thought of Jerry. She realised for the first time that she had never let go of

Jerry. She could only be comfortable if Jerry was alone and unhappy, or with a bad woman. But a young graduate from the University of Dischange who intended to further her studies in agriculture at the University of Humboldt in Berlin was too much for her to bear. She envisioned how this new girl would get her resident permit so easily and was filled with envy and bitter jealousy. Without any further considerations, Pamela started thinking of ways to hurt Jerry, or the girl he intended to marry.

The following day, Pamela remembered that she still had photocopies of Jerry's real documents. She took these documents and went to visit Jane, telling her that she intended to report Jerry to the police on account of using a false name and his contract marriage to a white woman.

"Abomination!" Jane shouted. "Pamela! This sounds to me as if you want to go on a murder expedition. Why don't you just look for a gun and shoot the young man dead? By the way, how can you even prove that these are his real documents? Pam, that is evil! You would do no such thing!"

"Do you know how much pain he has caused me as well?" Pamela asked.

"Pam, that was entirely your fault. You wanted Egbe! Or should I say Emeka?"

"I know, but didn't I go back and apologise to him?"

"Pam, you can't blame him for your misfortune with Egbe. See, you are all alone, I won't support you to do such evil."

"Yes, I know I am on my own." Pamela was determined to act, for the jealousy and envy was deeply rooted. "I don't need anyone to show me where the office of the *Bundeskriminalpolizei* is in this Berlin," she reminded Jane as she left.

Pamela was so bitter and frustrated that she went ahead with her crazy plan. A week later, Jerry received a letter from the *Kriminalpolizei* with photocopies of his real documents. He was requested to report in court in two weeks' time. The police stated the source of their information to be Pamela.

The implications of Jerry's case were severe; Jerry would surrender his passport and face repatriation along with the young lady who was to join him to start a new life. He showed the letter to Nji and Akwi, who were shocked that Pamela could do such an evil thing.

For three days, Jerry went missing. Nji and Akwi did not know of his whereabouts. The news that he was wanted was all over the place. A day after Jerry received that letter, he had found out where Jane lived and waited there until he saw Pamela entering the building. He monitored her movements and one day saw her alone on her way to the train station. He quickly ran and hid in a tunnel, which was on the way to this station. Unfortunately for Pamela, no one was using this road at the time and as she moved into the tunnel, Jerry dashed out from nowhere, held her by the neck and said to her, "You think you have killed me, but you will die first." He stabbed Pamela several times on her lap as she screamed helplessly. He dashed off when he saw some people approaching. They quickly called the ambulance and Pamela was taken to hospital.

Nji and Akwi were very disturbed about Jerry's whereabouts and his safety. Jerry knew that, his dear and caring friends would be unsettled and so he called Nji just to tell him he was safe and fine where he was, but he refused to tell him where he was hiding.

"Jerry, why? Why should you do that?" Nji cried on the phone. "There was no legal proof to the fact that those were your real names. You might as well have won the case with the help of a good lawyer."

"I don't know what came over me," Jerry was sad. "How is she? Did she survive the wound?"

"She is fine." Nji told him. "We went to see her yesterday. She is responding to treatment."

"I have to go now," Jerry said and hung up the phone, before Nji could insist on him saying where he was.

Jerry was hiding in an old friend's apartment. His name was Fripong. He was a man above middle age and he was from Ginain. He had lived in the Western part of Berlin back when the Berlin Wall still existed. This man had a little apparatus which he carried around. It was connected to his body to keep his blood pressure in constant check. Jerry ran to him that night and honestly explained everything to him.

He took Jerry in and told him that he would keep him for some time in order for him to calm down and then go to report himself personally to the police.

"I know, *Körperverletzung* is a terrible crime in this place, it's as bad as a murder case. But there is no way you can run forever from the *Deutsche Polizei*. Settle down, we will look for a good lawyer and struggle to see to it that even if it is a prison term, your lawyer will fight for you to serve it in your country. He can use the argument that your marriage was based on a false identity and so is invalid. As a non-citizen, you can be allowed to serve your term in your country. There, it is easier because your family can just bribe and you will be released. Then, you can still look for a way to come back to Europe. Maybe Ireland, Holland or even England. Better still, you can go to the States. Although, to me, all that is not necessary. But, you being a young man, I know what you feel. You see, it is all not worth the trouble. This permanent residence permit, or say Europe, is not worth the trouble. To even harm someone and distress yourself because of it is out of the question, I tell you." Fripong told Jerry all these.

"But, Uncle, you see, where do I start from? Starting all over again? After all that I have laboured for. I have spent my hard-earned savings to pay for that paper. Sometimes, I even had to sleep with that woman against my will, just to make things go easy." Jerry lamented.

"I know, I understand. But see, you might go to your country and realise it would have been better to stay there. Look at me; I came here when I was young, younger than you are now, and full of life. I saw these white women; I knew I had met all I ever wanted. They were rushing after me. I settled for one and we were so much in love, so much in love - that is what I knew. By then, there were very few black people in this place. Time passed so fast. Then, this lady, at that time she was my wife, told me on one fine day that she didn't love me anymore. *"Ich habe keine Gefühle mehr für dich."* Those were her exact words.

"What did you do wrong?" Jerry asked.

"Do wrong? Just listen, a few weeks later, I discovered that this woman had been sleeping with my nephew, a young man I just brought from Ginain. A very young man who was young enough to be my son."

"So what did you do?" Jerry asked anxiously.

"I left, I told my nephew just one thing; that, he too would become old one day and I hoped he would not be a fool like I was. I left them to themselves; and took this two room apartment." Fripong explained. "That was when I started looking for a life for myself. But since then, I have never been healthy; I just came out of one illness to another and then ended up having to carry this *Gerät* around."

Jerry shook his head and remarked that he had rarely seen any elderly mixed couples on the streets of Berlin. He looked at Fripong and at the little *Apparat* and felt pity for him. He shook his head again; a little fear gripped him as he walked to the window.

Jerry was deep in thoughts as he stood looking at the tall beautiful buildings and the neon lights outside. All the beauty had gradually lost initial value and admiration for Jerry over the years as he came across one difficulty after the other in the land. Presently, they seem like nothing in his eyes, because they could not and had never provided that peace which Jerry had always longed for and presently needed so badly. Then Mr. Fripong called him from behind and continued,

"Like I told you, when we met in Leipzig as Extras for Till Schweiger's *Joe and Max,* I can't go back to my country anymore. Look at me, all grey-haired. The only thing I need here now is a nice black woman. In fact, from my own village."

Jerry chuckled. "So, they are meant for the leftovers."

"I am no leftover, young man," he said.

"Don't mind these grey hairs you see. Once a strong

205

man, always a strong man. Don't mind what you see now. When I was your age, I was hot cake. Moreover, once you are living in Europe with a European nationality, no woman down there will refuse you. As I was saying, I won't have a place again in that society. I was a mere fisherman at home. You are better off, you went to school. Moreover, I realized it too late, when I was already too old. I am fortunate even to have had the kitchen job I had been doing before I fell ill. I used to wash pots in the *Mensa* - the university kitchen. In fact, this place is not paradise like one thought. This place ridicules us in one way or the other. Do you know about the Woermann family in Hamburg who used to trade in those days during slave trade and colonialism? Have you been to their business venture? Do you know the statue at their gate is that of a great African warrior? Now, what do they use it for? They use the statue to represent a mere security guard to them. How ridiculous? It's time we started searching for our roots, my young man."

Mr. Fripong took out a paper from a shelf on which there were some drawings of winged figures of a young girl's statue.

"Look at this," he told Jerry. "We also had our gods before these people came to deceive us with Christianity and Islamism. You see, this winged figure is an African angel. These four are other angels, angel Oye, Afo, Nkwo and Eke. It was the god Eri who revealed these names to the people. His messenger sent rats to enter the basket of fish of these angels. The rat entered the first basket and Afo said, "Oye! A rat has entered your basket." It left and entered Afo's basket and Oye said, "Afo! A rat has entered your basket," and then it entered Nkwo's basket and Eke said, "Nkwo! A rat has entered your basket," and when it entered Eke's basket, Nkwo said, "Eke! A rat has entered your basket," This is how their names were revealed. These angels are meant to protect and guide us, but now we have abandoned them. You see, we have our deities and gods. The people of Benin have Idu; the ancestral worship deity of the royal family. The Yoruba people have Ogun - the god of iron and of war. There is also

Nyame of the Ashanti and Akan - the creator god associated with the sun and the moon."

Mr. Fripong went on and on, explaining the various gods of his tribe and other parts of Africa to Jerry, who found his talk about African gods and a certain Woermann family, whom Jerry knew nothing about and was prepared to know nothing about, a little insane. However, he did not say so, instead, he nodded slowly and allowed the old man to air out his frustration. Mr. Fripong talked about the angels: Oye, Afo, Nkwo, and Eke. He explained that these spirits formed the main support of Negro laws. They were capable of passing fair judgements.

"I know you people also have your own gods in your land," he told Jerry. "These African gods are better because one could feel their presence, unlike the Western God whom one does not even see any symbol of. In our belief in African gods, if someone commits a crime, the god of vengeance strikes him down immediately. Therefore, this made people cautious about the way they treated others. But the Whiteman's God, with the issue of church-going and forgiveness is very intriguing. Our gods are the only ones we understand, who can keep us upright."

Finding it hard to get any solace from Mr. Fripong's talk, Jerry simply said to him, "What you say makes a lot of sense, Uncle." This was just to console his friend.

"Yes, so going back home is not a total loss, you will realize many, many nice things you did not notice before in comparison or contrast to this place." Mr. Fripong conversed with Jerry at length while they drank beer. Then, he got up, stretched his body, and told Jerry goodnight as he went into his room. Jerry slept on the sofa. In spite of Mr. Fripong's talk on African gods and although Jerry was very tired and drunk, before he went to sleep, he said his prayers, starting with the recitation of *Psalm 23*:

The Lord is my shepherd; I shall not want.
He maketh me to lie down in green pastures:
He leadeth me beside the still waters.

He restoreth my soul: He leadeth me in the paths of righteousness for His name's sake.

Yea, though I walk through the valley of the shadow of death, I will fear no evil: for thou art with me; thy rod and thy staff they comfort me.

Thou preparest a table before me in the presence of mine enemies: thou anointest my head with oil; my cup runneth over.

Surely, goodness and mercy shall follow me all the days of my life: and I will dwell in the house of the Lord for ever. Amen.

That night he slept most soundly, as he had not done for days.

Meanwhile, Pamela's lap was operated upon. She had to wait for some time before the stitches would be taken off. She could hardly sleep because of too much pain in spite of the medication against pain which she received. Helmut had visited her twice on this particular day and left very late, hoping that when he was gone, Pamela would fall asleep at least from fatigue. However, Pamela had too much on her mind. She had the weird feeling that she might never be able to walk again. As if enough was not enough, she shared the hospital room with an old lady who snored all through the night.

Pamela became homesick and thought of the joy she used to derive from her family. All she wanted was to go home and be with people who actually cared about her.

Finally she fell asleep; but to her, it was as if she was half sleeping and half awake. She had a kind of fragmented dream in which she had gone back home. Her flight had landed in Esisi Village. Her mother, father and siblings had received her with great joy in their warm embraces. When Pamela got up in the morning, she felt pleased with this dream. She thought of her family once more and she smiled to herself and then she remembered something; in her dream, her parents were Chinese people; it was as if they had all been transformed into Chinese people. Most of the people she saw in Pays in this dream looked like or actually were Chinese; it was as if she was in China. Not just her parents but some of their neighbours too were all transformed into Chinese. Mami Afor, Mami Aggi and Papa Njame whom she used to know, were all Chinese now. "How could her parents and all her siblings have turned into Chinese?" she pondered. What surprised her was the fact that in the dream, it was alright for her, she didn't find anything wrong with them being Chinese. She thought to herself, since it was okay in her dream, then it shouldn't bother her now. Nothing could rob her of her yearning for Pays at this point in time.

Days went by. Many Paysans came to visit Pamela. Some brought her yoghurt or fruits and others brought get well soon cards. Only Helmut brought her flowers several times. The Paysans were very concerned and sympathetic; they talked nicely to Pamela to the admiration of the nurses. Yet, as soon as they stepped out of the hospital premises, they continued their gossip from where they had interrupted it when they stepped onto the premises. Some said, they heard that Jerry stabbed Pamela because Pamela reported to the police that he was involved in money doubling. According to them, Jerry had turned into a *Fae* man. "But it was bad to report someone to the police in this country o-oh!" exclaimed one girl as she clapped her hands. Some said Jerry had already been repatriated.

Jane, who suspected that some Paysans might not be coming there out of love and concern but to get information on what to gossip about, was very angry. She discussed this with Pamela and they both told the doctor and nurses that they wanted a restriction on Pamela's visitors.

Thirty-Nine
Still At Large

Jerry was still at large when Pamela was discharged after spending ten days in Königin-Elizabeth-Krankenhaus Herzberg. Jane took her home and kept her company while waiting for Helmut to return from work. They sat on the sofa with Pamela's crutches at the side. "Pam, stop crying, it is not the end of the world. Moreover, the doctor said you could still walk properly one day without the use of these crutches. What you need for now, is to master your steps as the wounds heal." The tears kept streaming down from Pamela's eyes. She had lost everything, she kept thinking. "I want to go back home," she managed to say in-between sobs.

"Home?" exclaimed Jane.

"Yes, home."

"In this condition? Pam, you must be joking. Do you want to die? I mean, which hospital in Pays will handle your situation better than what the doctors are doing here? You better think well, Pam. I know you always want to have your way in everything, but I bet you on this one, I am not going to let go. I can't watch you run into your own grave."

"I want to go home," Pamela sobbed.

"See, with your situation, you will be given a permanent stay in this place. There are special privileges and opportunities for the disabled," Jane told her.

"Disabled? So, that is what I have become. I, Pamela

Besem Tah?" She screamed in agony. "You see, that is why I said, I want to go home."

Jane was confused. She went on her knees and begged Pamela. "Pam, I assure you, not just I, the doctors also said it in the hospital and I was there, two of them. They said you have a chance of walking again. Pam, please, don't lose this chance, please. See, I have a plan. I will take you to the foreign office tomorrow with all your hospital papers. We will apply for a residence permit, for you and even when you are fit to walk again, you will still retain your residence permit. I am certain it will not be withdrawn."

Pamela stared at her with dried-up tears on her face and said, "What about that man who made a contract marriage and it was discovered after eighteen years and the German passport he had was seized from him, so he had to face repatriation?"

"That's a different thing, Pam, that was a case of fraud. Yours is different. These people are very sympathetic when it comes to things like this. If you care, we can ask Helmut when he comes back."

"Of what good is that? I don't need the paper, I don't even deserve it after depriving someone else from having it and sending him to jail," Pamela said with resignation.

"Do you mean Jerry? I also think there is something that could be done. Since you are the one raising a case against him, the judgement will depend greatly on what you present as a case file. Left to me, you should drop the lawsuit. Unfortunately, the police are already involved. The case cannot be totally wiped out, but its contents will depend on you." Pamela nodded slowly and thoughtfully.

"Jerry simply needs a good lawyer on his side too." Jane was very happy that Pamela could feel some remorse, she had been thinking of how to tell her to withdraw the case against Jerry.

The following morning, Jane left Coppistrasse very early, went to Walther-Schreiber-Platz to pick up Pamela. They took the subway, U9 from there directly to Amrumer strasse. They walked past the three African shops which

211

competed with each other. The owners of these shops moved to the front and looked intently into the eyes of the girls as they went by, in an attempt to persuade them into patronizing their business. None of them were in luck as they watched the girls pass the last shop.

As they approached a crossing before a bridge, Pamela and Jane noticed a black lady pushing a perambulator ahead of them. This aroused their interest most naturally and they both strained their eyes simultaneously to see who it was. "Akwi" They called. Akwi turned, and stopped to wait for them. "I saw someone walking, and I told myself, I should know this person," Pamela said.

"Hi! Pam, hi! Jane," Akwi was pleased to see them.

"Pam, I am happy you are out of the hospital. Thank God. Jerry almost destroyed you. How sad," Akwi was saying.

"But all will be fine. Everything will be okay," Jane cut in quickly, knowing that Pamela hated to be pitied. "The doctors said so. Nothing to worry about, Akwi. So where are you going to?"

"I am sure she has a *Termin* at the *Ausländerbehörde,*" Pamela said as they moved on. They finally went across the road and decided to sit down on a garden bench by the side of a nearby bush which was close to the stream of life and death, the deciding bridge of living in Germany and going back home very close by. The three ladies discussed at length.

Akwi finally summoned the courage to plead with Pamela to withdraw the case against Jerry. "It is unfair, Pam; that is like killing someone. Remember all the good things he did for you." Pamela looked to the ground and was silent. All the three were silent for a while and when Pamela lifted her head up she asked Akwi, "So what should I do?"

Akwi tried to conceal her joy as she spoke. "Nji and I have already contacted a lawyer on Jerry's behalf. He has explained to us what could be done to make things better for Jerry. Please, you just need to come with us to the lawyer, so he can explain things to you and outline his strategy, which of course will not affect you in any way negative at all. Jerry told us he will be coming home to his apartment today." There was another moment of silence again. No one stirred, but for Akwi who looked at her mobile phone from minute to minute to check the time. Her baby seemed to be observing the silence as well.

Finally, Pamela took a deep breath and said, "I will come with you people to see the lawyer." Akwi leaped up and embraced her, "Pam, you are an angel, God will bless you! We already made an appointment with the lawyer today at 5pm, since Jerry's initial court appointment is in three days time. We don't want him to miss it and we want him to go prepared. Thank you very much, Pam. Nji and I will call you on your mobile phone and we will meet somewhere to go to the lawyer. Let's continue to the foreign office, I am almost late for my appointment."

"In that case, go ahead, we will walk more slowly," Jane told Akwi. Akwi took leave of the two girls and hurried off. On the way she called and informed Nji about her conversation with Pamela concerning Jerry. Nji was elated too. He told Akwi, he would go home and wait for Jerry.

After a short while, Jane told Pamela that, they should continue slowly to the foreign office. But Pamela would not move an inch.

Meanwhile, Jerry thanked Mr. Fripong and told him that he was going to his apartment and would turn himself in to the police later on in the evening that same day. "If you need any help, just call me or better still, try to get in touch with me after seeing them, whatever the outcome."

"So, Jerry left. On his way home, he went to a market and bought some beer. He put it in a plastic bag and then went to a *Baumarkt* and bought himself a thick strong rope. All that crossed his mind as he walked was that, he could not start life all over again after all what he had been through. Even if what Mr. Fripong suggested about the lawyer pleading for him to go home and serve the term there was true, was he ready for home? This was not how he had planned his life. All he had wanted was to be happy and make things better for his family. All he had wanted was to be with Pamela. He walked on, using mostly the back streets, walking without noticing any of the scenery. Then he decided to get onto a bus.

Nordufer was a less crowded street in Wedding. Jerry decided to get off the bus from Sprengelstrasse, walked from behind to Kiautschoustrasse and through it to Nordufer. From there, he walked to his apartment on Fehmarnerstrasse 23. This way, he approached the building from the rear end of the street and not the usual start of the street when coming directly from the train station.

Pamela remembered Akwi, how she pushed her baby in the pram and said, "I am worried about all these kids. Don't you think that the same thing which made us flee our land might befall them here?"

"Pam, don't even start again, the future will take care of itself," Jane cried out as she stood up. "Please, let's go to where we are going to. Don't forget, I have an appointment with the *Frauenarzt* later today."

"Okay," Pamela said as she struggled to stand up with her crutches, but just then, she saw someone across the road, walking past, from a short distance, walking solemnly with his head down. Her heart sank as it dawned unto her who that was. She put her crutches aside and landed on the bench. Jane was surprised as she looked around abruptly. By this time, Jerry was close by. He moved slowly as he noticed them, very slowly, almost stopping, he focused his gaze on Pamela; Pamela in turn looked him in the eyes. She saw on Jerry's face a mixture of pain and regret, and then she noticed something else that almost broke her heart. There was that childlike innocence, which she had seen in him, on the first day she set eyes on him, that now still lingered on that face, that handsomeness, which its owner had really never cared much about or was not even conscious of, was all there. Jerry stared at Pamela as he moved away and Pamela at him. Neither of them said anything. Jane noticed the intense emotions passing between them without any words being spoken. She was helpless at the pain and regret that she saw.

They both watched as Jerry took a turn on to the road swinging the plastic bag in his hand aimlessly. Jane sat down next to Pamela, at a loss of what to say. Instead, she took out her mobile phone and checked the time.

"It's alright," Jane managed to say. "Let's go, before we run late." Pamela shook her head in disapproval.

"Go, Jane; go to your appointment with your doctor. I will be fine. I will rest a bit and then will go to the foreign office. It is no longer far from here." Jane refused to leave her alone. But Pamela assured her. "Rest a bit and make sure you go there, all will be fine. Here are the documents." Jane handed Pamela the documents from the hospital and told her to call her on her mobile phone immediately after she was through at the foreign office. Then, Jane hurried off.

Pamela watched Jane leave, and all of a sudden all she could see was Kromba Park. The feeling of nostalgia swept over her stronger and stronger as she listened to the music blasting from the motor park discotheque speakers here and there. She caught the sound of *Yomba, Yomba, Yomba, Yomba-ah; Mama-yeh*, and then that of *Elimbi*. She smiled as the taxi jerked through the puddles to Miango Park. The sun was high, the people were merry. She looked out the taxi window and watched the truck pushers, the *motor boys* and the hawkers all moving happily under the blazing heat. She smiled again as the taxi jolted to a stop. She was so happy, she was returning to school after the first term holidays. She was especially happy because she had spent the holidays at her uncle's place in Bart and did not have to trek on the re-opening day with other local students from Esisi Village to school in Njase. She too would come out of the Japanese four-wheeled drive, specially designed for the road to Njase, in front of the Administrative block on the school campus, and all would see her. Then, she immediately saw her friend, another Form Four girl, buying Kromba bread from a Hawker. She came out from the taxi and stood outside filled with excitement and was about to embrace her friend when she fell. Pamela fell on her face just by the side of the bench. Her head was heavy. She managed to lift it up and peeped around. Fortunately for her, there was no one around who saw her. Although, it would have been fortunate for someone to see her and help her to her seat, but Pamela hated to be pitied.

Jerry closed the door of his apartment, went to his bathroom, tied the rope to a water pipe, which was on one side of the wall in his bathroom, and fixed the other end into a round knot. He left it dangling there with a stool under it. Then, he went into his sitting room, took out his bible, read it and put it by his side. He looked at the enlargement of his photograph on the wall. Jerry has never been happy in his entire life as the smile on this enlarged photograph portrayed. The photograph had been taken at the international airport in Commercial on the day he was leaving Pays for Germany. He looked at the smile on the photograph and just gave a wry smile. He slipped down to sit on the floor against the sofa, took out his cans of beer and started to drink one after the other.

With Jane gone, Pamela sat all alone with her thoughts, which were in turmoil. She was happy to be alone. She used the time to do some thinking. After a while, she took her bag, struggled, stood up on her crutches and moved towards the bridge. When she reached the bridge, she found it hard to step on it. She looked at the water beneath and thought, this *Heiligenseer Weg* at its 5th stage going from Westhafen through to *S-Bahnhof* Friedrichstrasse, loses its holy power of sanctification upon *darkies* who use this bridge as soon as it passes under the *Torfstrassensteg* of 1979/80 on going through Nordufer. The bridge reminded her of all the struggles the black people went through just to be acknowledged whenever they went to the *Ausländerbehörde*; some even tore up their passports there because they had been refused a permanent stay.

She stood there for a few minutes, and then walked back to the bench as a kind of defunctive music under sea played in her unconscious. Pamela was deep in thoughts. She thought of how careful she had been not to be deceived in her life again, for she believed that, the world owed her too much for having taken so much advantage of her in the past, as she claimed. Then, in her mind's eye, she saw many happy grey-haired, old couples made of a black and a white person. They moved happily hand in hand, caring about nothing but themselves and their small talk. Pamela waved this vision off and struggled once more to get a foothold on her thoughts. She thought of her time as a university student, and how each time she went to look for a holiday job, her employers wanted to have her before employing her. Pamela continued in her thoughts, trying hard to think, to reflect, to think of something reasonable. Then her primary school days came to her mind. She remembered how she had been beaten by her class five teacher and referred to as a Bush Girl for speaking Pidgin English. Even in church, at the Children's Ministry, she was told to always speak good perfect English as a sister of Christ Jesus. Later on in life, she read that Jesus never spoke English but Aramaic. She was bitter and planned since then that she would speak Pidgin English and will never part from it.

Sitting on the bench, Pamela took out a sheet of paper and wrote from her unconscious.

Ei di cry - a don die oh!
Die for weti, weti you di cry? Ssh--ssh no cry
Why a no go cry? Leave me, make a cry,
Ma heart di vex me, a get to cry
Vex? Which kind vex way ei go makam you cry so?
Weti you di make like say you no know.
Why a get for toukam again and again?

O.k. a see. A understand now weti you mean
But a no say nobi ma fault
Da people dem?
Da people dem don equally make me a vex
Huhn! A no fit helep you, a no fit do anything
Na lie, you fit do sontin

Dem nack me, beat me and just disgrace me like say
Dem just cursh ma papa, wey na even their papa too sef
Time way a leave ma man, because of over suffer
A thing say, a go be happy

217

Nayi a kam for dem, way na ma real brother dem
And den, dem no only cursh me, dem even cursh ma
mami sef way na their mami too
Wasteland, Wasteland,
Ei pikin dem na Hollow men, Hollow men, Stuffed men!

You wey na you for even helep me sef, you instead run
You leave me, ma suffer, die; nobi so?
Now! You know weti di vex me
Although a look like say a small for outside,
But, a big for inside
A no go die, a no go die, a no go die
A go only wait make you kam back for me
A di cry because ma neck di kam broke
No man ni di siyam? No man ni di hear me?
Even for da place way you day?[1]

She looked one more time at the piece, folded the paper and
threw it into the water, the *Heiligensee*; maybe, it might heal
her and her likes, all of whom were still at large.

---

[1] *She is crying - I am dead! /Why should you die? Why are you crying?
Ssh—Ssh don't cry! /Why shouldn't I cry? Allow me to cry, I am very
angry, I will cry! / What sort of anger will make you cry like that?
/Why do you behave as if you don't understand? / Why should I say it
again and again? / O.k. I see. I now understand what you mean/ But I
know, I am not to be blamed/ The perpetrators, those perpetrators
have equally caused me pain/You see, Can't help your pain/Oh yes
you can, you have, you are, you should, you should/ They battered me,
beat me up, and humiliated me/ Insulted my father who is also their
father/When I left my husband, due to torments /I thought I will be
happy ./That's why I came to them who are my real brothers/But they
did not only insult me but insulted my mother who is also their mother/
Wasteland, Wasteland, your children are Hollow men, Hollow men,
Stuffed men!/And you my only source of solace, you fled./Leaving me
behind to suffer and die; now you know my pain./Though small
outside, I am big inside./I shall not die, I shall not die, and I shall not
die./But I will wait to see you come back to me./I cry, because my
neck is almost broken, can't someone see? Can't someone hear me?
Not even from there?*

Epilogue

If some man be tell Pam say nah so e life go end, e no for believe, but seyam nah. See weti don happen. You tisay man fit blame nah who for dis kind ting? A no say some people dem go start talk say, no, nah because say e no bi do so, so and so. Any man get rite for tink ting way e wan tink, but weti a di still talk na say, if som man be tell Pamela say, ehh whole yi, e life go turn so, e no for believe; na Pam e greatest problem dat na. Nobi say ei no fine - o, no bi say e no get sense, but e depen too som time dem how man di use sense. La Piro say, over done nah mbut! And den weti Jerry too do? A no say, som pipo dem go talk say, Jerry e own nah say, ei no use sense. Man no even know sef weti happen for di two pipo dem at the end. And den, how for di Paysan dem and other darkie dem wey dem di cry say stress, stress over dey for di land; weti di happen hier or rather weti happen?

Even though, som darkie dem di make like say noting no di happen, but dem know; dem di fillam. For dis place wey we day, all man wan makam by all means. No man no wan remain for back. Som dem don join church and dem di pray true true and God di answer dem, som dem di depen nah on pastor dem; kind by kind pastor dem. Dem di pay som pastor dem some time dem make dem pray and fast for dem. Som dem di follow nah prophecy and miracle. Som dem don even join society, yes, occultic society, nobi just only medicine-house again; di wan now, nah somting higher. Nah different level. From going to medicine house, small, small, dem don end up join society. Som dem, their mami and papa dem bi don put dem for dey since.

Som of da pastor dem sef, nah lie, lie; som dem wan nah dough, some dem wan nah docki, and de worse ting nah say som dem wan nah som different ting, som ting way pipo dem go reap der repercussions nah only in the future. Huh! Nah wao![2]

---

[2] *If someone had told Pamela that this is how her life would end up, she wouldn't have believed. But see. See what has happened. Whom do you think is to blame in such a situation? I know some people are of the opinion that Pamela did well, but just that she should have still done one or two things differently or better. But, if someone had told Pamala that, she of all, would end up like this, she wouldn't have believed it. This is Pamela's greatest worry. Pamela is neither an ugly girl nor someone who is not intelligent; but at times, it depends on how one uses his or her intelligence. The singer, La Piro says, "It is primitive, trying to be too intelligent." Where did Jerry go wrong? I know many will say he wasn't intelligent enough. One cannot tell what happened to these two in the end.*

Meanwhile, what about the multitude of people from Pays and other black people over here who complain every now and then of stress in Germany? What is happening, or rather, what happened? Even though, most of the black people might behave as if nothing is wrong, they feel it. In this place, everyone wants to be successful, to make it to the top; no one wants to be left behind. Some people have chosen to turn to God, they pray earnestly and their prayers are being answered. Some go to church and depend on pastors, so many different types of pastors. They pay these pastors sometimes to fast and pray for them. Some move from church to church and from place to place in search of prophecies and miracles. Some have ended up joining occult societies; not just simply going to consult soothsayers anymore. The habit of consulting soothsayers has made it easier for them to be initiated into secret, obscure societies. Some had been initiated into it by their own parents. Some of the pastors are false. Some simply want to make money out of opening a church, some want to have a visa to reside in Germany and some want something different, something of which their followers will only reap the repercussions hereafter. Incredible!

www.ingramcontent.com/pod-product-compliance
Lightning Source LLC
Chambersburg PA
CBHW070224030726
47505CB00006B/1810